FOUND GUILTY
AT FIVE

Titles by Ann Purser

Lois Meade Mysteries
MURDER ON MONDAY
TERROR ON TUESDAY
WEEPING ON WEDNESDAY
THEFT ON THURSDAY
FEAR ON FRIDAY
SECRETS ON SATURDAY
SORROW ON SUNDAY
WARNING AT ONE
TRAGEDY AT TWO
THREATS AT THREE
FOUL PLAY AT FOUR
FOUND GUILTY AT FIVE

Ivy Beasley Mysteries
THE HANGMAN'S ROW ENQUIRY
THE MEASBY MURDER ENQUIRY
THE WILD WOOD ENQUIRY

FOUND GUILTY AT FIVE

ANN PURSER

BERKLEY PRIME CRIME, NEW YORK

THE BERKLEY PUBLISHING GROUP
Published by the Penguin Group
Penguin Group (USA) Inc.
375 Hudson Street, New York, New York 10014, USA
Penguin Group (Canada), 90 Eglinton Avenue East, Suite 700, Toronto, Ontario M4P 2Y3, Canada
(a division of Pearson Penguin Canada Inc.) • Penguin Books Ltd., 80 Strand, London WC2R 0RL,
England • Penguin Group Ireland, 25 St. Stephen's Green, Dublin 2, Ireland (a division of Penguin
Books Ltd.) • Penguin Group (Australia), 250 Camberwell Road, Camberwell, Victoria 3124, Australia
(a division of Pearson Australia Group Pty. Ltd.) • Penguin Books India Pvt. Ltd., 11 Community
Centre, Panchsheel Park, New Delhi—110 017, India • Penguin Group (NZ), 67 Apollo Drive,
Rosedale, Auckland 0632, New Zealand (a division of Pearson New Zealand Ltd.) • Penguin Books
(South Africa) (Pty.) Ltd., 24 Sturdee Avenue, Rosebank, Johannesburg 2196, South Africa

Penguin Books Ltd., Registered Offices: 80 Strand, London WC2R 0RL, England

This book is an original publication of The Berkley Publishing Group.

This is a work of fiction. Names, characters, places, and incidents either are the product of the author's
imagination or are used fictitiously, and any resemblance to actual persons, living or dead, business
establishments, events, or locales is entirely coincidental. The publisher does not have any control over
and does not assume any responsibility for author or third-party websites or their content.

FIRST EDITION: December 2012

Library of Congress Cataloging-in-Publication Data

Purser, Ann.
Found guilty at five / Ann Purser.—1st ed.
p. cm.
ISBN 978-0-425-25282-6
1. Meade, Lois (Fictitious character)—Fiction.   2. Burglary investigation—Fiction.
3. England—Fiction.   I. Title.
PR6066.U758F73 2012
823'.914—dc23
2012026985

PRINTED IN THE UNITED STATES OF AMERICA

10 9 8 7 6 5 4 3 2 1

ALWAYS LEARNING   PEARSON

For Jane and her mother,
my most loyal readers.

FOUND GUILTY
AT FIVE

ONE

❧

Josie's wedding day dawned with ominous grey skies and puddles on the road outside Meade House, the result of a rainstorm in the night. Lois had heard pattering on the bedroom windowpane and comforted herself with the unreliable old saw—"Rain before seven, fine before eleven."

Now it was time to get up, and she turned over to nudge Derek awake, only to find nobody there. Then she heard footsteps on the stairs, and the bedroom door opened to reveal Derek, bearing a tray loaded with breakfast.

"You sneaky devil! I was going to do that for you."

Derek grinned. "A warm thank-you wouldn't come amiss," he said and, putting down the tray, he leapt athletically into bed beside her, only to land groaning with what he declared was a twisted ankle, certain to ruin his day as father of the bride. Lois did her best to comfort him.

*   *   *

THE MEADES HAD LIVED IN THE VILLAGE OF LONG FARNDEN FOR a good few years, having moved from a small semi on a council estate in the nearby town of Tresham to a solid family house previously belonging to a doctor who had been one of Lois's first clients in her house-cleaning activities. One of the few remaining English villages with shop, school, church, and pub, Farnden's houses came on the market at high prices. But in Meade House, the dark shadow of the murderous doctor had put off prospective buyers, and Lois, Derek and family had felt no qualms about moving in.

Lois contributed to their bread and butter by running a very successful house-cleaning service, New Brooms, and with husband Derek's one-man electrician business, they jogged along reasonably happily. Safely in the bank, earning a good rate of interest, was a comforting sum won on the lottery a few years ago.

Over a period of time, Lois had developed a special skill in amateur detecting, and this had been a very useful service for Inspector Hunter Cowgill of Tresham police. Lois's independent spirit had been maintained by her refusal to take payment for what Derek, who disapproved, grumpily called "ferretin'." Inspector Cowgill, a handsome widower with a high reputation in the county, kept his decided fondness for Lois more or less successfully to himself.

Lois was proud of her family of two sons and a daughter, and Gran, Lois's mother, underpinned them all by housekeeping at Meade House. Overworked and underpaid, she reminded them frequently.

And so now, thought Lois, as she and Derek finally downed cold tea and congealed scrambled egg, we will have another family member, young Matthew Vickers. Matthew was Cowgill's nephew and also a policeman, doing well in the force, and about to wait in the village church for Lois's only daughter to walk up the aisle to join him.

"I THOUGHT YOU TWO HAD DECIDED ON AN EARLY START?" accused Gran, as Lois and Derek brought their empty breakfast dishes into the warm kitchen.

"I twisted my ankle," said Derek, remembering to limp a little. In fact, it had been a very small twist, and he felt only a slight twinge. But in truth he was feeling nervous about giving his beloved daughter away to a young man in an increasingly dangerous profession. Derek's bid for general reassurance was shattered by Gran saying that she had never heard such nonsense, and a good run round the village green would soon fix his ankle.

"Plenty of time before you need to dress up in your finery," she added. "In fact, I think you might have a quick sprint right now."

Derek sniffed. "I don't think so," he said. "Unless you feel like coming, too, Gran. You can carry me crutches."

Gran ignored this with straight-backed dignity, and began to stack the dishwasher with such force that Lois feared for her best china.

"Speaking of finery," she said soothingly, "Josie will be here shortly to dress. I'm really glad she decided to set off from here. That crinoline skirt needs a wide staircase to accommodate it."

"It's not a real crinoline, Lois, as you know," Gran said.

"Oh, for God's sake, Mother, cheer up!" Lois was fast losing patience, and decided that Gran was best left alone. She went upstairs to check Josie's room, where the virginal white bridal dress and silk veil were waiting, surrounded by much-loved dolls and teddy bears of childhood.

Much to her annoyance, Lois felt her eyes prickling with tears. It wasn't as if Josie would be going miles away. She would continue to run the village shop, and be just as much a daughter as a wife. What was that stupid saying? It's not losing a daughter, but gaining a son? Rubbish! Josie's first allegiance will be to her husband, as it should be.

Lois dabbed at her eyes with a tissue. She heard the door open, and Josie's excited voice in the kitchen. Time to be the mother of the bride, she told herself, and walked slowly down the stairs to the kitchen.

Two

❧

THE CHURCH WAS FULL BOTH SIDES OF THE AISLE, AND ALL heads turned as the organist broke off the umpteenth repeat of Pachelbel's Canon and launched into a spirited rendering of Handel's "Arrival of the Queen of Sheba."

Lois felt the dreaded tears welling up as she watched her daughter, who was so like herself, with long dark hair and greenish gold eyes, pace slowly as rehearsed, up to the chancel steps, held steady by Derek's strong, reliable arm. Then Matthew took her symbolically from her father, and Derek stepped back.

"All well?" whispered Lois.

Derek nodded. "Fine," he replied, "in spite of dog Jeems deciding to jump into the limo with me and Josie."

"So what did you do?"

"Brought her with us," said Derek. "Gran tied her up outside the church."

"Hush!" said Gran in a stage whisper from the pew behind them.

The service proceeded, with the occasional yelp from Lois's dog Jemima outside the church, and then it was time for signing the register, whilst the choir sang an anthem. Jamie had volunteered to practise this with the choir and to play the tricky accompaniment. As they reached the triumphant final notes, light footsteps were heard at the open door, and a small, slim girl with short black hair slipped quietly into the back pew.

Lois watched as Jamie stood up from the organ seat. As he looked towards the back of the church, she saw a big smile cross his face and knew that it was directed towards the latecomer. Then there was a scuffle and low growling, and she looked round in alarm. Jeems had slipped her collar, and was struggling in the arms of the unfamiliar girl. With minimum fuss and holding on tightly to the small white dog, she left the church and a peaceful quiet was restored.

The ceremony carried on in good order, with loud applause for the magical words "I now pronounce you man and wife," and soon it was time for endless photographs outside the church door. Lois had noted that it was exactly five minutes to eleven when the sun finally shone from behind retreating clouds. Relations, friends and villagers, stationed beside the low churchyard wall, joined in the general hubbub of congratulations and jollity.

At last Lois was able to corner Jamie and ask him about the girl who had so courageously thwarted Jeems's break for freedom. He smiled. "It's Akiko, my friend who plays marvellous music on the cello. I asked her to come, and she was sad that she had a concert last evening. But she made it! Early train from London, and a taxi all the way here from Tresham.

But as usual there was a holdup on the ring road, and that's why she was late."

"Nice of her to make the effort," said Lois. "Must be a good friend, eh?"

A voice from behind them reminded them that Gran, who had just finished making sure she appeared in every family group photograph, had also had a hand in the Jeems debacle.

"I told you that collar was too loose, but you never listen to me, Lois," she said. "And now, Jamie, who is this nice girl? Says she's a friend of yours."

"This is Akiko," said Jamie, putting out his hand to introduce the girl, who nodded to Gran with a shy smile. "Akiko is from Japan," he added, "and I thought she might like to see an English wedding. This is my mum, and this is Mrs. Weedon, my gran." He grinned at his mother, and said, "Mum, this is Akiko Nakamasa, my colleague. She's a whiz on the cello."

As neither Lois nor Gran knew anything about the cello, there was a short pause. Then Gran, seldom lost for words, said she was sure it made a really nice noise, and had Akiko ever had a number one in the charts?

Lois surreptitiously stood lightly on Gran's toe and said, "Oh look, here's Mrs. Tollervey-Jones. Bless her heart, she's walking well now. Hi, Mrs. T-J!" she called, and the dignified figure, soberly dressed in navy blue, relieved by a frilly white shirt, smiled broadly.

"Morning, Lois, and Mrs. Weedon—how are you?"

So the introductions were made all round, and Lois explained to Akiko that Mrs. T-J's family had lived at the hall for generations, but she was now settled in a charming stone house with thatched roof, five hundred years old, in the centre of the village.

"I used to play the violin, my dear," the old lady said to Akiko. "Not much good, I'm afraid. Piano is really my instrument. You must bring Akiko along to tea, Jamie, and we could play together. My sight-reading is still quite useful. Now, let me see, Nakamasa is an unfamiliar name. I spent some time in the East in my youth, but I've forgotten so much! And do you come from a village like this, Akiko?"

Akiko's smile faded. "No," she replied firmly, and did not elaborate. "I shall be pleased to see your lovely house," she said. "Do you have time to take me, Jamie?"

Lois had seen the change in Akiko's expression, and wondered why. As they joined the group throwing confetti at the church gate, she noted that Akiko slipped her hand under Jamie's arm, and hoped there were no problems looming. Just got one safely off my hands with no worries, and only one to go, she reflected. Jamie, her youngest, had always been special, and as she said later to Derek, she did hope he was not going to take up with a foreigner reluctant to talk about her home. Derek had answered abruptly that not everyone had forgotten the Nips.

AT THE RECEPTION IN THE NEWLY RESTORED VILLAGE HALL, there was relief all round that the ceremony had taken place without a hitch. Lois tried hard to dissuade Derek from filling his glass too often, and when it was time for him to make a speech, he stood up without swaying and delivered his warm and funny lines with no trouble.

The best man, a police colleague, thanked the bridesmaids with genuine warmth, and finally they all settled down to eating and drinking. In due course there was dancing to old favourites for the more mature guests and later on, when the oldies had retired, the young set leapt about to thumping music from Tresham's finest young band.

When most of the guests had gone, and Josie and Matthew were on their way to a brief island honeymoon, Lois collapsed on to a chair and gave a satisfied sigh.

"Happy now, Lois?" It was Inspector Cowgill, present as uncle of the bridegroom and a distinguished guest.

She looked at him, frowning. "Of course I'm happy. And why shouldn't I be?"

He smiled, and patted her shoulder. "No reason at all. Young love is so charming, isn't it. And given a chance, we oldies are quite good at it, too."

"Oh, for heaven's sake, give it a rest, Cowgill," she said, standing up. Then she looked at his crestfallen face and relented. "Sorry, Hunter. Didn't mean to snap; I'm really tired now. See you soon, eh?"

He nodded. "I'll be in touch," he said. "I'll give you a ring. Still happy to go ferretin'?"

Before she could reply, Derek appeared and shook Cowgill firmly by the hand. "Off home, are you, sir?" he said. After all, the man *was* a policeman. "Thanks for coming. Now, Lois, we're off to bed. All the rest can be done in the morning. G'night all," he added expansively, and taking Lois's hand, he led her away.

THREE

After Josie and Matthew left for their honeymoon, Jamie had come to his mother and said quietly that Akiko had agreed to stay overnight in Farnden, if they could find her a bed for the night. Their house was full, except for a tiny maid's room up in the attic, which Lois tentatively offered. Akiko had accepted gratefully, saying that to sleep high up in such a lovely house would be a treat.

"Her English is very good, considering," Gran now said, as she presided over a breakfast pan full of bacon, mushrooms, eggs and tomatoes. "How come, Jamie?"

Akiko had not yet appeared from her eyrie, and Jamie answered that her father had given her a very good education and she was fluent in several languages.

"She don't speak Northamptonshire," said Gran. "But I suppose she's a nice enough girl, for a foreigner."

Derek raised his eyes to heaven and said, "No need to

refer to her like that, Gran. She's a guest and a friend of our Jamie. Now, who's for coffee and who's for tea?"

At this point, Akiko put her head round the kitchen door. "Good morning, everyone. Am I too late? Your lovely bed was so comfortable, I had a really good sleep."

"No mice, I hope," said Gran. "They have races up there sometimes. I can hear them in the ceiling of my room. Now, I expect you'd like something different from our English breakfast?"

Akiko smiled sweetly. "I am sure whatever you cook, Mrs. Weedon, will be delicious. Thank you very much for allowing me to stay."

Jamie was looking daggers at Gran, who refused to lift her eyes from her frying pan.

"We were wondering, Jamie," said Derek, "if you and Akiko would give us a taste of the music you play together. We've got a piano, but no cello, I'm afraid . . ."

"Oh, no problem, Mr. Meade," Akiko said with a big smile. "Jamie has mine safely in his car, which is alarmed in case of burglars! It is very difficult to know how to keep a valuable instrument safe, but we decided this is best, whilst we are travelling together."

Lois wondered about Jamie giving so much of his time as an accompanist, when he was now much in demand as a soloist. Still, he must know his own mind. He was a fully grown adult, and had already come a long way in his career. Over the last year or two, he had introduced them to a number of nice girlfriends with whom he had light and casual relationships. This one was not likely to be any different, was it?

"Perhaps you could give us a tune after lunch, then?" she

said. "I can't guarantee your father won't doze off. But no offence meant. He always does on a Sunday."

"What are you doing this morning, son?" Derek asked kindly. He was warming to the neat features and good manners of Jamie's colleague. "Why don't you show Akiko our lovely countryside? And there's something on in the hall park this morning. Dog show, I think."

Akiko clapped her hands and said she loved dogs, and could they take Jeems to the show and enter her into the dog-with-the-waggiest-tail class? "I used to have a dog at home, but she cannot travel with me, obviously."

"I should think not!" said Gran. "Dogs should have their freedom. I don't approve of them being shut up in flats, an' that."

With this imbalance of conversation, Gran on one side with snide remarks, and everyone else being as nice as possible to Akiko, breakfast proceeded. The rain had returned in the night, but now everywhere was glittering in the sun, and Jamie and Akiko left Meade House with Jeems on a lead, promising to be back in time for lunch.

FARNDEN HALL WAS A PLEASANT STATELY HOME JUST OUTSIDE the village, with parkland and farms attached. Geoffrey Norrington and his wife Melanie had bought the whole package, including farms and a private chapel, from Mrs. Tollervey-Jones, and Norrington had plans for it all, but had the sense not to try changing everything at once. But one thing he did straightaway. He opened the park and house to the public and set up a shop in the private chapel selling Farnden Hall souvenirs and gifts.

"But shouldn't we concentrate on furnishing the hall

first?" Melanie had objected. "We don't want to show people around empty rooms."

"We can use that," her husband had answered enthusiastically. "Hold a competition. Charge people to make suggestions for each room—the main rooms, that is—and give a prize to the best. You and I could judge. Special prize for best child's entry?"

"And what else are we going to put in the shop? Packets of grass seed from the tennis court?"

"Oh, there's plenty of suppliers of bits and bobs. Think how many royal wedding souvenirs were on offer in no time at all."

Melanie had shrugged. Geoffrey made his living thinking up good fund-raising ideas. Some of them were less than kosher, but most had been successful and had enabled them to move from a nearby modern villa to the grandeur of Farnden Hall.

The dog show had not been Geoffrey's inspiration. The local branch of Dogs for the Disabled had approached him with a request to help with their fund-raising activities, and knowing how the British love their dogs, he had seen a good opportunity for publicity. When Melanie had asked him how he thought the estate would benefit from a charity dog show, he pointed out that large numbers of people could be expected. The whole thing was relatively easy to organise and would be fun, as well as doing a good turn to disabled people.

"And will you present prizes to the dogs?"

"Of course," Norrington had replied. "I am giving special bones and half a dozen tins of minced kangaroo to the dogs. I've got a mate in the dog food business. He's happy to do it for the publicity. Won't cost me a penny."

"Sounds good. You'd better think of other friends who

need publicity." Melanie's voice had been sour. Being chatelaine of Farnden Hall was not turning out to be as she had imagined it at all. "Maybe in a year or two, once we've settled?"

"Year or two? I've already made plans for an autumn horticultural show, and by then we should have the children's play area up and running."

Now that the dog show was in progress, Melanie had cheered up, meeting new people and feeling very much the lady of the manor. As she and Norrington mingled with the good-sized crowd, she said, "Do you think Mrs. T-J will come?"

Geoffrey shook his head. "No chance. Wouldn't be seen dead here, now the hall belongs to us. But I mean to show her that this estate can be made to pay its way. Patronising old besom! She'll wish she'd never sold it to us by the time I've shown her the way."

"She's still president of the village Women's Institute. I had thought of joining. Do you think she'll blackball me?"

"Of course not. And there's plenty of WI members you know already. Lois Meade for one, and her mother. And Floss, who comes to clean here from New Brooms, and loads of others. You go, gel, and take no notice of Mrs. T-J. And look, I was wrong—there she is, hobnobbing with the judges."

When Jamie and Akiko arrived at the hall gates, he was not pleased to be asked to pay an entrance fee. He had grown up in Long Farnden and was used to running around the park at will. Not that Mrs. T-J had welcomed village children, but in her time it had been possible to keep out of her way and still have great games around the old barns and clumps of trees.

"I hardly recognise the place," he said to Akiko. "And it seems only yesterday that Mum told me that Norrington had bought the Farnden Hall estate, lock, stock and barrel."

"It is a big estate?"

"Quite big, for this part of the world. There are much bigger ones, especially in Scotland. I shall take you to see one or two when we play in Edinburgh next year."

"I have been to Glasgow several times, to meet my father. He has a house there. But I would like to see some wild countryside. It is all very tidy here."

"You wait till you see the Highlands of Scotland!" Jamie led Akiko and Jeems up to the show ring, where owners were already parading their dogs. The present class was for Best Terrier, and an assortment of small dogs obediently trotted round at their owners' heels. One dog, however, was twice the size of the others, and Akiko pointed this out.

"Is it in the wrong class, do you think? It does not look like a terrier."

A man standing next to them at the ringside tapped Akiko on the arm. "It's a Black Russian Terrier," he said "Marvellous dogs. Giant schnauzers crossed with Airedales, mostly."

"Thank you," she said courteously.

The man came closer, and suggested that perhaps she herself was in the wrong class—where did she come from? "From the land of Nippon?" he guessed.

Not much of a chat-up line, thought Jamie. The man's smile was knowing, and Jamie was not surprised when Akiko responded sharply. "Please go away," she replied, and the man raised his eyebrows, muttering that he was only being polite.

Jamie decided to say nothing, and walked after her, noting that this was the second time today she had shown reluctance to answer personal questions. Perhaps she had been warned by her family to be wary of strangers? He would think of a tactful way of asking her.

"Jamie! How nice to see you and Akiko again so soon!" It was Mrs. Tollervey-Jones, who was marching energetically around the showground, telling everybody that the new owner was ruining the place, but never mind, each to his own. She wished him well, she said, though nobody believed her.

"So when are you coming to play for me?" she said to Jamie. "This evening? I can give you a scratch supper if you like. Not much of a cook, I'm afraid. Used to being cooked for! But I am learning, and New Brooms' cleaning lady comes and does a big bake once a week. An excellent service your mother provides, Jamie. Have you told Akiko about this? And, of course, your talented ma has another side to her activities. Private investigator, Akiko, that's what she is. Do you understand that phrase?"

"Perfectly, thank you," Akiko said. " 'Detective' is another name for it?"

"And I am the latest recruit to her team, my dear. A non-cleaning, investigating member of New Brooms, at your service."

"Akiko has no need of a private investigator at the moment," said Jamie, laughing. "Have no fear, Jamie's here!"

Akiko was not smiling. "Please, although my English is good, I do not always understand what is said. Like the man and the Russian Terrier. He was not being pleasant, I thought. Forgive me if I got it wrong." She would be very delighted, she said sweetly, to accept Mrs. T-J's invitation, if Jamie felt it would be convenient for his family.

"Good-o," said Mrs. T-J. "Stone House, six-thirty? Will that suit? Look forward very much to seeing you then."

"A nice lady," said Akiko, as they watched Mrs. T-J stride off towards the judges' tent.

"So are we staying another night in Long Farnden? Happy up in the attic?"

"Very happy. I feel safe up there. Comfortable and safe. Now, is it time to enter Jeems into the Waggiest Tail class?"

FOUR

꙳

Lois and Gran were watching *Antiques Roadshow* on television when Jamie stuck his head round the door to say he and Akiko were off to see Mrs. T-J at Stone House.

"Shan't be late back," he said. "I'm sure the old thing goes to bed about nine thirty."

"Don't be so sure," Lois said. "She's full of surprises, that one."

"Including being one of your latest recruits? I can't see her down on her hands and knees cleaning the vicar's front step."

"Don't be ridiculous, Jamie," Gran said. "And if you are late, you and Aki-ki-ko must be very quiet. That attic bedroom is directly above mine, and I'm a light sleeper."

"Since when?" Lois laughed, and Akiko added that she always took off her shoes on entering a house. This was the custom back at home.

"So that's why you're always around in stocking feet," Gran replied. "I thought maybe Jamie had been taking you in the wet grass."

"Mum! Now you're being ridiculous. Have a nice time, you two, and give our regards to Mrs. T-J. Are you going in the car? It's easy walking distance."

"But there is my cello, Mrs. Meade. It is almost as big as me! It will be safer in the car."

THE PLEASANT SITTING ROOM IN STONE HOUSE WAS FULL OF evening sunlight, and Akiko looked around appreciatively. A crystal vase full of flowers stood on a table by the window, and the grand piano half filled the room. Placed on it were silver-framed wedding photographs from two generations, and over the fireplace hung an oil painting of a serious-looking man in military uniform.

"My late husband," Mrs. T-J said, noticing Akiko staring at it. "He looks stern there, but he had his moments. Very good father to our Robert. Much missed." She took up a photograph from the piano. "That's Robert with Felicity on their wedding day. Terrible day, rained nonstop."

Akiko opened her cello case and withdrew the instrument, and Jamie handed Mrs. T-J a pile of music.

"Would you like to choose?" he said. "And are you going to play the accompaniment, or would you like me to do it?"

"Oh, you, of course, Jamie! My accompanying days are over. I was joking when I offered to play. Fingers like bananas now, I'm afraid. Here, how about this Elgar piece? One of my favourites."

*   *   *

DEREK, WITH HIS ELDER SON DOUGLAS, WAS PASSING BY STONE House on his way home from the pub, and heard lovely sounds coming from the open window. "Ah, that'll be Jamie and his girlfriend," he said.

Douglas said nothing. He was now a married man, with a small son, and his chief concerns were for his own family. He'd noticed Akiko, said she was charming and given her no more thought.

Derek, on the other hand, had thought hard about Jamie with a foreign girlfriend. Very nice girl, she seemed on first acquaintance. It was a pity Gran could not accept her with good grace. He wasn't sure whether his mother-in-law disliked the girl herself, or found her alien and different, and therefore suspect. He would have to have a private word with her, though unfortunately, private words with Gran usually ended up with her shouting only too publicly that he was wrong and she was right.

His thoughts moved on to the Norringtons. There had been a lot of talk in the pub about the new owners of the hall, and many people thought they might well be good for the village. Opinion was divided, however, between the generations. The old guard could not get used to the idea of so much change. New people at the hall, and obviously nouveau riche, as against the inherited wealth and connections in high places of the Tollervey-Joneses.

Then Douglas, visiting from Tresham, had put a spoke in the wheel by suggesting that the Tollervey-Joneses were not all that aristocratic. "Coal mines in Derbyshire, that's where their money came from way back," he had said. "Exploiting the masses. And they were no better than the rest of us. The old great-great-grandfather was a blacksmith. I suppose," he said, making an effort to be fair, "you could argue they did well by their own efforts, and had a right to be toffee-nosed."

A hubbub of conflicting support and disagreement in the pub had ensued, and Derek decided it was time to leave for home.

"It's the same nowadays," he said now. "Take Jamie and his career in music. No musicians on my side of the family. And no one on your mother's, so far as I know. None of the rest of us are musical, and he didn't have any special encouragement. But look where he's got to! Playing the piano all round the world, and sometimes his name is mentioned on the radio. We shall see him on the telly soon, I'm sure of that."

They had arrived at Meade House, and Douglas opened the gate for his father. "Yeah, but he got given that piano, remember? Maybe none of us got the chance, until Jamie," he said. "By the way," he added, "Akiko is his colleague, not his girlfriend. Haven't you noticed he stresses that?"

"So he may. But I know a girl in love when I see one. We shall find out, son. Now, in we go, and make sure you walk straight. Our gran can spot a man who's had one too many from a mile away."

"Right. Better leave the gates open, so's Jamie can bring in his car. The precious cello, you know. Jamie's a bit of a softy, so I hope he knows what he's doing."

"Don't you like Akiko, then? She seems a really nice girl to me."

"Very pretty, very polite, and a bit chilly. I tried talking to her about her home, but she froze me out. Not one word about her folks. A bit strange, don't you think?"

"I did notice, Douglas. But it's none of our business.

Leave it to Jamie. That's my advice, though I doubt your gran would agree!"

AN HOUR OR SO LATER, AKIKO SLIPPED BETWEEN THE COOL sheets of the bed in the attic and thought about the evening performance at Stone House. Her brain was still fizzing, and she did not feel in the least sleepy. She and Jamie had played well, and she had to admit that her growing affection for him was affecting her playing in a good way. Jamie was a real friend, kind and gentle, and helpful when help was needed.

She sat up in bed and plumped up the pillows. Settling back, she thought about the time she had arrived in England to attend the college of music, knowing no one, and with only her father coming to see her as often as he could manage. He had tried everything to dissuade her from leaving Japan, but in the end he could see a permanent rift between them developing and had given in.

In giving way, however, he had arranged to keep in touch with her in several ways, including visiting her on a regular basis and appointing an employee to keep an eye on her. Her mother had died when she was two, and she had been cared for, by first her grandparents, then by a wonderful nanny and a succession of housekeepers. Money had been no problem, as her father had become very wealthy. He had warned her that she might encounter ill feeling among British students, and she was aware that the two countries had been enemies during the last world war. But that was a long time ago. He had also advised her not to talk about her life in Japan. Being a rich man's only daughter without friends could make her vulnerable to unscrupulous advances. She had soon made one or two friends at college, of course, but otherwise tried to remember her father's advice.

She turned over in the narrow bed, and still sleep refused to come. Jamie had been so kind today, so happy and at ease at home with his family. She remembered when she had first met him, when he came to give a recital at the college, and at the reception afterwards he had approached and offered her a drink. He said afterwards that she had looked like a small, sad child, standing alone in the corner of the room. After that, they met again a couple of times and talked about playing together. She protested that she was still a student, and he was rapidly becoming an international star. He persisted, saying playing an instrument was like a game of tennis. Don't play with rabbits, play with people better than yourself, where there would be a challenge. He made her laugh, and she had begun to rely on him for companionship as well as music.

Jamie was proved right. She had succeeded beyond high expectations, and done brilliantly in her examinations. Their partnership had developed, and now here she was, a guest in the Meade family house, rather too obviously regarded as Jamie's girlfriend. Did it matter? She finally fell asleep without coming to any conclusions.

Jamie was also still awake. Together, he and Akiko had delighted Mrs. T-J, and when he was left alone with the old lady for a few minutes, she had said to him that she liked Akiko very much and he should think about getting his feet in the stirrups. Her meaning was clear and alarming, to him at least. It was much too soon to think about that!

His room seemed stuffy, and he got out of bed to open a window. There was no moon, but a security light at the corner of the house shone on his car. To his irritation, he saw the outline of the cello, resting on the backseat, and realised they had not brought it in with them. They had been chatting away about the evening's success, and Akiko must have forgotten about it. He sighed. It would be safe enough. Probably safer than in the house. The car was thoroughly locked and alarmed, as always.

He turned away from the window, but as he did so, a shadowy movement outside in the garden caught his eye. What on earth was that? He stared down, but the shadow had gone. Maybe a fox after Mum's chickens. He yawned. They could investigate in the morning. He climbed into bed, shut his eyes and was quickly asleep.

NEXT MORNING, THE START OF THE WORKING WEEK, THE MEADES were down to breakfast early. Derek had already left by the time Jamie and Akiko appeared, and they announced that they would be away straight after breakfast.

"We play at a concert tonight," Akiko said. "At the Wilmore Hall. A very important fixture. Fixture? Is that right, Jamie?"

"Could be," said Jamie, smiling, "but it sounds more like a football match than a recital. But the meaning's the same." He patted her arm, and she smiled at him.

"By the way," she said, "I left my cello in the car. I will just go and check it is still there."

"It was at one o'clock this morning! I looked out of the window and could see it safely on the backseat."

But in the next couple of minutes everything changed. Akiko ran back from the car screaming, "It's gone! Jamie, my cello has gone!" She crumpled onto a chair, and burst into heartrending sobs.

Lois moved quickly to comfort her, and suggested Jamie should have a second look. "Did you check the boot?" she said.

"But I saw it on the backseat," he said urgently, also trying to soothe Akiko, who turned on him angrily.

"It is your fault! I always bring it in with me where I am sleeping! You made me forget! What are we to do for tonight's concert?"

Gran bridled. "Hey, wait a minute, Akiko!" she said. "That cello was your responsibility. It's not fair to blame Jamie. You may come from a country with different ideas, but over here we own up to our mistakes."

"Hush, Mum," said Lois quietly. "Akiko is naturally upset."

FIVE

❧

INSPECTOR COWGILL WAS AT HIS DESK, STARING AT NOTHING in particular and thinking about Lois. She had looked fabulous at the wedding, elegant and restrained in a dove grey suit. Her long dark hair had been put up in a silky plait, and her legs . . . This won't do, Inspector, he told himself. Down to the business of policing. But his thoughts wandered on, remembering that Lois had been very busy, trying to be everywhere at once, looking after guests and bridesmaids, and generally not having much time to talk to him. When he had tried to tell how beautiful she looked, she had been impatient and he had felt unreasonably hurt. Surely now they were practically related, she would treat him more warmly?

But then he knew it would not be his Lois. He loved her bright sharpness, and even affectionately tolerated her refusal to treat him with anything like respect. But at least he could call her now with his thanks for her brilliant organisation of the wedding. He stretched out his arm to pick up the phone, but it rang before he touched it.

"Inspector Cowgill here. Oh! It's you, Lois. I was just about to—what was that? What did you say? A *cello*? I don't remember anyone playing a cello at the reception? All right, all right. Calm down, dear. Just repeat the details slowly."

Lois frowned. This was all she needed. Sometimes she thought Cowgill was not hearing so well, but it could equally well be a ploy to slow her down. She explained the situation as succinctly as possible, and ended by saying that as Jamie's mother, and because the cello went missing on their driveway, she felt it her duty to do all she could to recover the instrument.

"The case of the missing cello, eh? Well, I shall certainly put my sleuths on to it."

"Cowgill! Are you taking this seriously? If not, you can forget your special relationship with the Meades. Now, when can I come in to brief you?"

"Now, if you like," Cowgill said blandly. "Not much on my desk this morning. Now I'm semiretired, they tend to leave me alone. But I can still make them jump to it, Lois. Be here at ten o'clock, please. And don't be late. I have an appointment later."

"With a small white ball? You don't fool me, Cowgill. I'll be there."

She grinned as she replaced the receiver, and set her mind to sorting out New Brooms problems. The weekly staff meeting was at twelve, so she would have to be back for that. She did not intend to waste much time with the inspector, but knew from Josie's Matthew that he more or less refused to accept retirement and was still considered to be the best brain at the police station. And, of course, he had the connections countrywide. These might be needed, if, as Lois suspected, the theft of the cello was not a local crime.

TRESHAM WAS CROWDED, AS IT USUALLY WAS ON A MONDAY. Shoppers were no longer starved of shopping opportunities over the weekend, what with supermarkets and even some town shops opening seven days a week. But in town, every Monday, local organic vegetable and fruit stalls gathered in the market square, together with farmers selling meat and milk products and marvellous baking done by their wives.

Lois pushed her way through wonderful smells of fruit and herbs fresh from nearby gardens. Derek grew their own vegetables, and Gran would be offended if she went home with a cake baked by another woman. But the smell of new bread was too much for her, and she bought a small loaf, broke off the crust and ate it before she reached the police station.

"Inspector Cowgill, please," she said to the fresh-faced young policeman on reception duties.

"Go straight up, Mrs. Meade," he said, with a knowing smile.

"You can take that smirk off your face," she said, and marched towards the stairs.

By the time she reached the second floor, Cowgill was standing by his door, beaming at her. "Good morning, mother of the bride!" he said.

"Yes, well, good morning to you, too. It went well, didn't it? Your Matthew was a star, and I thought they looked the perfect pair. Now we've got that out of the way, can we talk about my reason for being here?"

She followed him into his office, and he buzzed reception to say he did not want to be disturbed for half an hour or so.

"That's how rumours get round the station," Lois said. "Anyway, the thing is, Jamie's colleague came to Farnden for the wedding, and she had her instrument with her. She has it with her if possible at all times. They went to play for Mrs. Tollervey-Jones at Stone House, and when they came back, by mistake left it in the car, which in theory was fully locked and alarmed overnight. In the morning the cello was gone. Jamie was up opening his window at one o'clock in the night, and it was in the car then. He could see it. That's about it, so far."

"Was the car taken with the cello in it?"

"No, of course not. The door had been opened, somehow without setting off the alarm. They could have forgotten to activate it, what with the excitement of the weekend. That's what I think, anyway."

"No noises to wake up any of the family?"

"No. Absolutely nothing. Unless Jamie had been woken by a sound without realising it."

"Right, Lois. Leave it with me, and I'll get the chaps on to it at once."

"And meanwhile," said Lois, smiling at him warmly, "I shall be contacting my new colleague to start ferretin'. Immediately, if not sooner, as my dad used to say."

"Did you say a new colleague? Paid help?"

"You know me better than that. Anyway, my new colleague is on a one-case trial. If she's no good, she gets the boot."

"So it's a woman? I can't see this new association lasting long, Lois dear. But be careful who you trust."

"I'm off now," Lois said, making for the door. "Keep me in the picture."

She drove home thinking about her new ferretin' associate. This was, of course, Mrs. Tollervey-Jones, who had proposed herself for the job, soon after she had sold the hall. Not happy with Stone House as it was, she had had builders and thatchers in for weeks, but now it was all finished, with the most beautiful Norfolk reed roof, and inside, all modern conveniences without spoiling the priceless features of the original structure.

The house had been built in the year of the Armada, and had once been named after the famous rout of the Spanish in 1588, but a succession of owners had changed its name until Mrs. T-J came along, and she would on no account live in a house called Olde Timbers. "A good plain name is what's needed," she had said to Lois, and Derek's suggestion had been accepted. With nothing more to do, Mrs. T-J was ready for action.

DRIVING INTO THE VILLAGE, LOIS DECIDED TO TACKLE MRS. T-J straightaway. She would fill her in with the bare bones of what had happened, and leave it there. But, most importantly, she would impress on her again the necessity of reporting at once anything of use she might discover. "I shall expect you to tell me *everything*," she had said.

Stone House front door was open, with nobody in sight, and Lois reflected that Mrs. T-J would have to remember that she was living in the centre of a village with the pavement only yards away, instead of being cocooned inside a large mansion with acres of parkland protecting her from sudden intruders. "Yoo-hoo!" she called, and was answered by a faint shout from the garden at the back of the house. She walked through, and caught sight of a wide, green corduroy-clad bottom bent over a flower bed.

"Mrs. Tollervey-Jones, can you spare a minute?" No harm in being polite, thought Lois. She had not admitted as much to Cowgill, but she was already deeply regretting the whole business of Mrs. T-J joining her ferretin' team of one. New Brooms, yes, but Mrs. T-J had made it clear that she was not prepared to handle mop or duster. As for ferretin', Lois supposed she would have to give her a chance, and then ease her out as soon as possible.

Coffee appeared, quickly and efficiently made by Mrs. T-J in her new kitchen, and Lois sat on the edge of a massive armchair while details of the new case were explained.

"Good heavens!" said Mrs. T-J. "Akiko will be absolutely heartbroken. You could tell by the way she handled it that she loved it dearly. Now, who do I know in the musical instrument world? Ah, yes, Lois, I have it. My late husband was on the board of Bowley and Weeks, the oldest dealers in London. He was very pleased with a new, young board member, who should still be around. He might well have some ideas."

She half rose, as if going at once to the telephone to make the call. Then she remembered that she was very much a new girl, and sat back. "What do you think, Lois," she said. "Would that be a fruitful idea, do you suppose?"

Lois did not reply immediately. She would have to get used to this. Then she considered carefully, and said she could see no reason why this should not be a first step. No doubt Akiko could supply details of the cello, including an estimate of its value. The motive for stealing would be important, she stressed.

Mrs. T-J was tactfully humble, and pretended that this aspect of the theft had not occurred to her. "I see I have a lot to learn," she said, as she saw Lois to the door. Then she rallied. "But ideas are my forte, my dear! Never short of them. I shall be in touch."

Six

❧

Lois was back home just in time for New Brooms' weekly meeting. She had made a big effort to put thoughts of her son's relationship with Akiko out of her mind, but decided to tell the whole team about the theft. Her girls, as she called them, though some were way past girlhood, came from several surrounding villages, and could possibly have heard or seen something revealing.

Sheila Stratford was first. She greeted Lois cheerfully, as always, and said how much she and her colleagues had enjoyed the wedding. "Josie looked so beautiful," she said, "and that young policeman, he's a real catch!"

Lois smiled. "Derek thinks Matthew has made the real catch. You know fathers and daughters! Matthew is a very lucky chap, according to Derek. He stressed the point a bit too much in his speech, didn't you think?"

The door opened, and the rest of the team filed in. They

had met outside the house, exchanged greetings and all arrived at Lois's front door together.

"Ah, good. Now we can get on," said Lois. She knew how they gossiped together, and was not in the mood for joining in. "Now, first of all, before we talk about the work schedules, I'd like your help on an urgent matter. I expect you all noticed Jamie with a new girl at the wedding. She plays the cello, with him accompanying her, and they give concerts an' that."

"Yeah, we noticed, Mrs. M. She's a little bobby dazzler!" said Dot Nimmo. "Looked a bit shy, though. They make another good pair for you, Mrs. M!"

Trust Dot, thought Lois. Straight in with both feet. "It's just a working partnership. He accompanies other musicians besides Akiko," she replied.

"She looked like a foreigner to me," Hazel whispered to Andrew Young, who alongside cleaning and handyman jobs, was a qualified interior designer and combined the two jobs successfully.

Lois, who prided herself on her acute hearing, said shortly that Akiko was indeed from another country, but this had nothing to do with anything. Then she told them briefly about the missing cello, and asked if they could keep their eyes and ears open for any clues as to its disappearance or its present whereabouts.

"Sunday night, did you say?" Andrew asked.

"Yep. After about one o'clock, early Monday morning in fact."

Andrew shook his head, but said he'd keep a lookout. The others were quiet for a moment, and then Hazel said that as it happened, her farmer husband, John, was around the village at that time, cursing and swearing, chasing a sizeable calf that had somehow escaped and led them a merry dance all evening. "I could ask him, Mrs. M, but he came straight to bed from the barn."

"Never mind about calves," said Dot dismissively, "why would anyone want to steal a boring old instrument thing? My hubby, Handy, used to say it was the sound of a cat's innards scraped across . . ."

"Maybe," interrupted Lois, unable to repress a smile, "but it is serious, Dot. Akiko's cello is very valuable, and she's in a dreadful state without it. Anyhow, I know you'll all do your best. Now to work. I've asked Gran to bring me a sandwich, so you'll have to forgive me while I munch. I have to skip proper lunch, as I've a lot to do this afternoon."

"NO NEWS SO FAR?" LOIS HAD FINISHED THE MEETING EARLY, and went into the kitchen as Derek and Gran were about to start eating. The mood was grim. Derek said that he had had a good look round the garden and outbuildings of Meade House to make sure nobody had put the cello away for safety, then forgotten it. But even allowing for the excitement of Josie's wedding day so recently, and minds in general being taken up with the marvellous event, it was still extremely unlikely. A cello was a large instrument, as Lois reminded him impatiently.

"You're wasting time on a useless idea," she said. "As if someone would lug that great thing out of the car and into a shed and then forget about it! No, we should be looking for signs of a stranger in the garden, sometime in the middle of the night."

"The police have already done that. And with much more expertise than we have."

But the police hadn't seen the shadow moving round the

front. Jamie had mentioned it to Lois just before they left for London. A cello had been hired for Akiko and would be waiting for her. She had wailed that with only a few hours to become accustomed to it, she would not be able to play her best. Jamie had tried hard to reassure her, but nevertheless knew that she was right. It would be like asking him to play a Beethoven sonata on a cottage piano in the Albert Hall.

Now, Lois went quietly out of the front door into the garden. Jamie had asked her if all her chickens were safe, and she had been surprised that he was worried about such a small matter compared with the drama of the stolen cello. Then he had told her about the shadow and said it must have been a fox on the prowl. She had agreed, knowing that a vixen came round regularly in the hope that she had failed to shut up the henhouse.

But was it a fox or a swiftly moving person? A flower bed ran alongside the narrow drive, all the way down to the gates. If the car had been parked next to it, anyone trying to open a door would have had to tread in the exposed earth. Derek had recently dug out a spreading collection of lupins, saying they were smothering everything else, and the soil was loose.

It was difficult to remember exactly where the car had stood, but she spotted a small puddle of oil. Jamie had said his old Cortina had an oil leak, which he planned to get fixed. From that tiny patch, Lois could imagine fairly accurately the position of the parked car. She walked very carefully and kept a lookout for prints in the grass. A couple of steps from the oil, she stopped and stared down into the flower bed. She could see a tiny flash of blue, a thread caught on a rose thorn. It could easily have been from Derek's jeans, torn out as he was digging. But from memory she could not be sure it was the same blue. She gingerly lifted the thorny stem and pulled gently. A single thread, faded blue. She found a dog bag in her pocket and delicately inserted it. Then she folded the bag and returned it to her pocket.

"Afternoon, Lois! Enjoying the garden, I see. Well, it's good to make the most of this lovely weather. Have you got five minutes?"

It was Cowgill. Of course it was Cowgill. He was a genius at turning up at the wrong moment. How much had he seen of what she was doing? Nothing, she guessed, to give him an opportunity to mock her ferretin' methods.

"Yes, I can give you five minutes. I'm due up at the hall for yet another conference with the Norringtons. He's bursting with new ideas, and she tries to put the brake on all the time. I feel like pig in the middle. Still, it's all good business for New Brooms."

"Shall we go inside, or do you want to talk out here?"

"Oh, let's go into my office. This village is full of nosey parkers. It'll be all round the gossips that Lois Meade is about to be arrested."

"Right," said Cowgill, when they were safely in Lois's office. "I won't waste your time but come straight to the point. How much do you know about Akiko Nakamasa?"

Lois sighed. "I thought it would be that. The answer is not a lot. We met her for the first time at the weekend. Jamie had told us about her, of course, but only that she was playing the cello, with him on the piano. I guessed from her name that she was Japanese, but until Saturday I had no idea what she looked like."

"She looked like a very pretty girl, what I saw of her,"

Cowgill said. "Did she tell you where she came from? I mean *exactly* where she is living?"

"I asked her, natch, but she just said she was living in London. North London, I think it was. I didn't want to quiz her and annoy Jamie."

"Mm. We are having trouble tracing anything to do with Miss Nakamasa. She is supposed to have been a student at a music college, but there are no records of her attending any of the main ones in London. We are still checking smaller colleges in a wider area. How did Jamie meet her?"

"He was giving a piano recital somewhere, and she was in the audience. She buttonholed him afterwards, I reckon, and that's when it started. Our Jamie has an eye for a pretty girl. Did you notice her hands? Very small and delicate. It's amazing she can get to grips with that big old cello. They're both playing at the Wilmore Hall tonight. You could go along and talk to her there. After the concert would probably be best. She'll be keyed up enough beforehand, what with losing her precious cello and having to play a strange one with not much time to practise."

Cowgill was silent. He was thinking about Jamie Meade. The lad had always been the odd one out in Lois's family. Very talented, but modest and charming with it. He knew Lois adored him, and so far as he was aware, there had never been any lapses in his reputation for being a hardworking, honest young man. Girlfriends?

"Are Jamie and Akiko an item?" he asked now. Lois shook her head firmly. "No, they are not!" she said. "It's like saying that just because your assistant Christine spends a lot of time with you, you must be having it off together. The way some people's minds work, honestly!"

"Sorry, sorry! It's a policeman's job to ask questions, as you very well know. So if Akiko is not his girlfriend, is there someone else in his life?"

"I have no idea! He's away for months at a time, and we hardly ever see him. Obviously he wanted to come to Josie's wedding, but I don't suppose we'll see him again until Christmas. If then. Anyway, what are you suggesting? Is he gay? He's had plenty of casual girlfriends. Sometimes, Cowgill, it's hard to see why you're supposed to be such a supercop."

"Semiretired supercop," Cowgill ventured.

"Oh, all right. I give in. Jamie had a perfectly normal adolescence, had a number of girlfriends, none of 'em serious, and now when he sends us photos, there's always a girl hanging on his arm. His dad says he can tell that Akiko is in love with him, but I think that's just to annoy me. I can't be sure. Satisfied?"

"I merely wanted to know if you had been told anything about her background. As I said, we have failed to trace anything about her musical training up to now, but they're still checking the smaller colleges in a wider area. We've traced her father's business. He has offices in Japan and London, and a slightly unsavoury assistant named Parsons. But if she has a serious relationship with Jamie, then he is likely to know a bit about her private life. Could be a grudge theft. That's all, Lois. I mean no harm. At least, not to the innocent."

Lois looked at her watch. "There's still time for you to get a train to London and go to the concert. You might enjoy it."

"I suppose you wouldn't like to come with me?"

"You suppose right," Lois replied, and then softened. "Maybe some other time," she said.

*   *   *

WHEN LOIS WENT BACK INTO THE KITCHEN, DEREK WAS STILL there, rewiring the plug from Gran's iron. As he bent over the kitchen table, Lois noticed a snag in the back of his jeans.

"Derek, stay there a minute." She pulled the plastic bag from her pocket and found the faded blue thread.

"Hey! What are you doing? This is neither the place nor the time, Lois!"

"Don't be silly, Derek. I am just seeing if this thread matches. And it does, unfortunately."

"I hope you know what you're talking about, me duck," he replied, straightening up. "Because I certainly don't. That's a thread from my jeans, which I snagged when I was digging out marauding lupins."

"Right, so that was a blind alley," said Lois, and threw the thread into the bin.

SEVEN

❧

THE RAIN WAS STEADY, SPLASHING INTO DEEP PUDDLES IN the side streets off Oxford Street in London's West End. A heavy thundercloud hung over the city, and Cowgill found it impossible to hire a taxi. He walked along, fortunately with an umbrella, but with his feet now sloshing about in his thin shoes. He had acquired a ticket for the recital to be given by Akiko Nakamasa and James Meade, starting at seven thirty. With time to walk the whole way from Euston station, he stepped out, hoping that he would spot a vacant taxi before his trousers were wet to the knees.

"Hop in, sir," a smiling taxi driver said, drawing up beside him. "What a night, eh? Where to?"

"Wilmore Hall, please. I'm supposed to be going to a concert, but they may turn me away like an old tramp, too wet to sit down."

"Don't you worry. If you've paid for your ticket, they'll let you in. We'll be there in a couple of minutes."

Safely inside the elegant interior of the concert hall, Cowgill was pleased to find that he still had time for a warming whiskey at the bar. He perched on a stool and looked around. Chattering crowds were gathering, and he could see that the concert would be well supported. Some of the young people were obviously students, probably friends of the performers.

"Hunter Cowgill! Well, I'll be blowed. Haven't seen you for years, and you haven't changed a bit!"

Cowgill turned quickly, and his heart sank. He would have recognised his police college chum anywhere. Big-boned, red-faced, bright blue eyes and a mouth full of teeth—more teeth than any normal person, surely. It was Pearson. Now, what was his Christian name? Gareth, that was it. Done well in the Metropolitan division. Ah well, he *was* an old friend.

"Gareth, how nice to see you! Didn't know you were a fan of classical music? How're you doing, you old sleuth?"

"Retired, Hunter, retired three years ago. I couldn't stand the pace, with all these young lads wanting my job. I come here all the time. Graduated, you could say, from the Beatles to Bach."

All this was said as if for the hundredth time, which it probably was, and polished up in the telling. Pearson insisted on buying Cowgill another whiskey, and carried on a monologue until the bell rang, warning that the concert was about to start. Cowgill had chosen a seat in the balcony, well out of sight, and he saw with relief that his cheerful friend marched straight down to the front row of the stalls.

A hush fell in the hall, and then a minion took away the sign reminding the audience to switch off their mobiles. Another pause, and then on came Jamie. He waved to the audience and went straight to sit at the piano. Three more seconds, and then Akiko walked in, carrying the cello as if it was a dead dog. She looked very pale, and Jamie smiled at her encouragingly.

Cowgill settled down in his seat and relaxed. He remembered that Lois had said Akiko would not be at her best. He wished he could communicate to her that she should not worry. She was pretty enough to command a round of applause even before she started to play. And anyway, he was sure most of the audience were tourists visiting London who would have no more idea of the finer points of cello playing than he had.

After a very tuneful first half, the musicians retired, the lights came up, and Cowgill waited until the rest of the balcony audience had gone down the wide steps to the bar. He had other plans, and the main obstacle to these was good old Gareth, who would be keen to seek him out and continue the story of his life so far.

There were two doors leading from the side aisles to where Cowgill presumed were dressing rooms behind the stage. He noticed that a few people from the stalls were now walking away from the main entrance to the hall and disappearing through these doors. He intended to follow them, and set off at speed with his head well down. There was no sign of Gareth Pearson, and once through the door Cowgill relaxed. Walking confidently, he found himself looking at a spiral staircase, and could hear laughter and conversation coming from above. He guessed it was a room behind the stage for entertaining family, friends and groupies.

Looking around, he saw behind him a cupboard, with its door ajar. With practised stealth, he slid inside, avoiding large brooms and a clutch of fire extinguishers. There he settled, eyes and ears wide open.

After a few minutes, he began to realise what a ridiculous sight he would be to anyone discovering him. He was too old for this game, and wished he had, like jolly Gareth, retired and taken up a harmless hobby. But before he had time to return to his seat, he heard quick, light steps coming down the spiral staircase. He peered out and saw Akiko, even paler in the half-light. Then, in seconds, she was out of sight.

He heard her footsteps stop, and her voice, very low and quick. Who was she speaking to? As far as he knew, nobody had followed him in. But then a similar route to the upper room existed on the opposite side of the stage, and there would be a way through. Now a man's voice, nasal and urgent. Cowgill could hear him clearly, and carefully pushed the door a little wider. Akiko's answer sounded close to tears, but he could hear her last words clearly. "Wait outside, Parsons!" she said, and it sounded like an order.

Then she was returning, and as Cowgill eased open the door a fraction more, he saw her ascend the spiral staircase, stumble halfway up and carry on with what sounded like a cry of pain.

The bell for the second half rang, and Cowgill made his way back to the balcony safely. Gareth Pearson had obviously given up on him. He threaded his way past a dithering couple to the end of the row. In the seat next to his, he saw a familiar figure.

"Ah, there you are, Cowgill," a whisper reached him. "I thought you'd done a runner. I was quite late, but sat at the back until the interval. Hush, now. They're on again." It was Lois Meade, dressed in her best, and looking irresistible.

EIGHT

❧

COWGILL COULD NOT BELIEVE HIS LUCK. HIS LOIS! SITTING beside him in the warm, cosy dark of the Wilmore Hall!

He had had little time to ask her questions, or tell her how marvellous she looked and how much she meant to him, before the lights had gone down and the second half began. He felt in his breast pocket and found a pen. Then in the wide margins of his programme he wrote her a message.

She read it in the dim light, and he could have sworn she smiled as she turned her head and looked at him. Then she very gently eased her hand from under his and shifted in her seat, putting space between them. He prayed for the music to go on forever, but the spectre of Derek's angry face rose up before him, and he subsided. At least he would be able to take her out for a meal before she got the train home. How had she managed to get here? And why? He knew Lois well enough to know she would not waste time on a jolly jaunt to listen to her son playing the piano. She would have some information, something important enough to bring her here to find him.

At the end of the concert, Lois was up and making for the stairs, saying to Cowgill that he was to follow her closely. He was alarmed to see her heading for the same door that he had used in the interval, and quickly told her what he had heard there.

"How can you be sure it was Akiko," Lois said, "if it was dark and you were shut in a cupboard?"

"I am sure," he said. Then they were through and ascending the spiral staircase, and there was Jamie, staring at them in delight. "Mum! Inspector! Why didn't you let me know you were coming?"

"Last-minute decision," said Lois, and added, making it quite clear, "Inspector Cowgill was here already, and he didn't know I was coming. I was very late, but got a returned ticket for a seat up in the balcony."

"It was an extraordinary coincidence," said Cowgill. "But may I say how very much I enjoyed your programme. Just my kind of music. And is Akiko around? Such a wonderful musician . . ."

"She had to get off straight after the end of the concert. I'm afraid the theft of her own cello has upset her a lot. She's a professional, of course, and played really well, considering she was playing an unfamiliar instrument. But she couldn't face people afterwards, so she's gone home."

"And that is where, Jamie? I really was hoping to meet her."

"Oh, I'm afraid she doesn't allow the general public to know where she lives. She is a very nervous person."

"I am not the general public," Cowgill said gently. "Although I admire her playing enormously, I am also here on police business, and need to talk to her urgently. We believe she may be in danger."

"What danger!?" Lois butted in, seeing the alarm in Jamie's expression. "Aren't you going over the top, Cowgill? After all, this is only a case of theft of a musical instrument. Don't worry, son, it'll turn up soon, and then Akiko will relax."

The inspector looked at her kindly. "I understand your concern, Lois. But this is not an isolated incident. We have had reports of one or two cases where the theft of a violin has preceded blackmail and once a violent crime. These may be the work of a single criminal."

"A single nutter, you might just as well admit!" said Lois. "A nutter with a back room full of musical instruments? It just doesn't wash, Inspector. What do you think, Jamie?"

"It's a very odd scenario," Jamie said. "But then, as the inspector suggested, if there is some idiot out there with a grudge against music makers, we should be very careful. But surely not our Akiko? After all, she's come from the other side of the world."

"Depends where she obtained her violin. And in what country."

"Do stop being so mysterious, Cowgill," said Lois. "And what do you mean by violent crime? Are you saying they've been attacked?"

"Yes, that's right. In one case, where a ransom was refused, fatally attacked. The blackmailer panicked. It's a clever scam. The valuable instrument is stolen, and then sold on, once a copy of it has been made by craftsmen. The fake is offered to the original owner for a reward, or more accurately, a ransom. It has worked in a number of cases, but in several the first owner has not been fooled by the fake. It's a big operation now, and although we've located one or two fakers, they've been too frightened to talk. Of course, we are pursuing every avenue."

"Oh my God, I'm going to ring Akiko right now." Jamie added that he would be outside, where he could get a good signal.

"Well, well, Inspector Cowgill," said Lois, rounding on him. "You've certainly made a good job of scaring the wits out of my Jamie. Good job you waited 'til the end of the concert! You could have ruined the whole thing."

"Sorry, my dear. I am afraid that scaring Jamie, and if possible, Akiko, is part of my reason for being here. You have to believe me. They need to stay alert."

After a few minutes, Jamie returned, looking worried. "She's not answering. I left a message to get in touch, so I think I'll get going now. I'll go to her flat, unless she rings me first." He scribbled something on a piece of paper and handed it to Cowgill, who slipped it into his pocket.

"Be very careful!" said Lois. "The whole thing sounds fanciful to me. But the inspector is seldom wrong. Ring me later, please, Jamie. I might be on the train, but keep trying."

Cowgill and Lois walked in silence out of the stage door into a small lane at the back of the theatre, and finally Lois agreed to get a later train. "I don't think I can eat much," she said, in answer to his suggestion of supper in a café over the road.

"But we need to talk," he said. "For a start, I need to know your real reason for coming up to the concert."

"That's not too difficult. My son was playing at the Wilmore Hall, a venue with a top-grade reputation. Naturally I wanted to be there."

"Mm. Not the whole truth, is it, Lois. Were you following up a hunch? Or is there something you should be telling me?"

"I tell you what. Let's have some soup and bread, and by then I'll have thought of something convincing. More convincing than Akiko chatting up a man under the stairs. In we go."

Akiko's flat was in North London, and Jamie knew exactly how to get there. He bought a ticket and boarded the train. It was only a few stops to where he would alight, and emerging into dark streets, he marched at speed to Caliban Road, one of several named after Shakespeare characters. He calculated that she would have reached home an hour at the most before he followed her.

With a degree of confidence that he would find her, he knocked loudly at her door. Akiko had a ground-floor flat with separate entrance. He knocked again, and began to worry. The curtains were drawn across all her windows, so there was no way of looking inside. The third time he knocked, a window opened above him. A woman he recognised as Akiko's neighbour upstairs looked out.

"Have you seen Akiko?" he shouted.

The woman shook her head. "Not since she went out to the concert. Maybe she's gone to bed."

"Have you got a key, please?"

"Well, yes. But I can't just let any old—"

"It's me, Jamie Meade! Her accompanist!"

"Oh well, I suppose it'll be all right. I'll come down. Might be a few minutes. I was in bed already!"

Jamie yelled his apologies, and the neighbour shut her window, saying she'd be down as quickly as possible.

*   *   *

IN THE SMALL CAFÉ, WHERE THE STAFF WERE OBVIOUSLY KEEN TO get home, Lois was sitting opposite Cowgill, making an effort with a bowl of carrot and coriander soup. He had told Lois what he had seen backstage, and they agreed that Akiko's behaviour had been odd, to say the least.

"Is that your mobile?" Lois said now.

Cowgill pulled it out of his pocket and handed it to Lois. "It's Jamie," he said. "He wants to speak to you."

"Yes, Jamie? Not there, did you say? Good heavens, didn't she tell you? What's that? You're breaking up a bit. Going in *where*? Oh, her flat. Right. Ring us as soon as you know anything. Yes, Cowgill's still with me. I'll be getting a train back to Tresham very soon. Unless you need me. Yes, I *have* phoned Dad. Now, take care, son, won't you, and *please* keep in touch."

Cowgill paid the café bill, and they emerged into the busy road. "Taxi!" he shouted, and one drew up beside them.

"Well done," she said. She liked his air of authority and was pleased that they would be at the train station in no time. But to her surprise, he pulled a piece of paper from his pocket and read out an address to the cabdriver, who nodded and said it wasn't far.

"Was that the paper Jamie gave you?"

"Yes. Akiko's address. That's where we're going."

NINE

~

A S THE TAXI DROPPED THEM OFF IN CALIBAN ROAD, LOIS
was relieved to see Jamie's car standing outside. She
and Cowgill made their way to the front door and knocked.
Jamie opened it at once, and they stepped inside.

"I thought you would come." Jamie was looking very
shaken, and Lois put a motherly hand on his arm.

"It was the inspector," she said. "He had Akiko's address
you gave him, and bingo! Here we are. What've you found?
Any clue to where she might have gone?"

"No, nothing. Absolutely nothing. She obviously left in a
hurry. Some of her clothes have gone, but not much else. I
don't know where to look next. She didn't have many friends
in this country. Had some at college, of course, but they all
went their various ways."

"Which college was that?" The inspector's tone was
brisk.

"Um, something to do with the river. Riverside? Not

sure. I suppose I could ask around. I know when I played there it was near the river. Quite a long way out of the city."

"Right," said Cowgill. "Well, as I said, we have checked all the main music colleges in London and they have no record of a student named Akiko Nakamasa."

"How up to date are your records?" Lois said. "I asked her when she was with us, just to make conversation. I think she said it opened up a few years ago. Now, hang on," she added, "it's coming back to me. Riverside College of the Arts, or something like that. No mention of music in the title."

"Ah, well done, Lois. Does that ring a bell, Jamie?"

He nodded, looking shamefaced. "Sorry, Inspector. Yes, that was it. I should have remembered. But the last forty-eight hours have been a bit hairy. This was a special concert tonight in a really well-known venue. I was so anxious that everything should go smoothly, and then the theft happened. I suppose I haven't been thinking straight ever since."

"Don't worry. Mind if I have a look around? I might spot something you missed."

He wandered off into another room, tactfully leaving Lois to calm her son.

"You'd better try that Riverside college," she said to Jamie. "They probably have residential places for students, and Akiko may well have gone back there for a short while. They'd be pleased to see such a star pupil, surely?" There was a telephone directory on the windowsill, and Lois looked up the number.

"There you are," she said. "Try now."

But Jamie drew another blank. They knew at once who he was talking about, and said they would welcome her at any time. But so far they had not seen or heard from her for a long while. When Cowgill returned to the room, he was carrying something gingerly by its tail. It was a big grey rat, and it was very dead.

"Ye gods, Cowgill! Where did you find that?" Rats were not Lois's favourite animal, and she backed away as the inspector came towards her.

"It was on the draining board in the outside washhouse. And next to it, a sandwich containing what experience tells me is a lethal dose of rat poison. Did you notice it, Jamie?"

Jamie shook his head. "Sorry, no. I didn't actually go in there. I doubt if Akiko used it. There's a washing machine in her kitchen."

"Lucky for her," Cowgill said. "I repeat, the poison was disguised in a ham sandwich, and it was half eaten. Come and have a look."

"If the poison was disguised, how do you know it's in the sandwich?" asked Lois suspiciously.

"Instinct," said Cowgill irritatingly.

"Rubbish," said doubting Lois, looking round. "I can see what you saw. There's a rat poison packet up on that shelf. That rat must have eaten enough to kill it. Any fool can see that."

"It's very stale, though rats don't care about that. This looks like a straight case of careless rat poisoning." Cowgill had had enough of the subject and moved towards the door.

The neighbour had insisted on being with them until they left, saying she felt obliged to protect the interests of Miss Nakamasa. Now she looked angrily at the rat. "You wouldn't say we were careless if you saw the number of rats we've killed!" the neighbour persisted defensively. "I might as well take the sandwich and get rid of it," she added, stretching out her hand.

"Don't touch it, please!" said Cowgill.

"Why not? You got plans for it?"

"I shall make arrangements for it to be disposed of safely," he said, showing her his badge of office. "And be more careful in future. Nothing more to be done here," he continued. "Why don't you ring your father, Jamie, and warn him that you and your mother will be coming home in the morning. It's getting very late. I promise to let you know when I have something to report. Akiko will probably show up tomorrow, chirpy as a cricket. Do you need a hotel for the night, Lois?"

Jamie answered at once. "No, no, she doesn't. My pad is not far from here. It's small, but there's room for Mum. I can sleep on the sofa. We'll get going now. And thanks, Inspector. We'll hear from you soon, I hope. Our next concert is in a few weeks. Not much on until then, so I reckon it would be a good idea for me to go back to Farnden with Mum. There's always interruptions here in London. Mates calling to take me out for a beer, that sort of thing. I need to do a lot of thinking."

TEN

❧

THE BELOW-STAIRS MESSENGER, WHOSE NAME WAS EZEKIEL Parsons, had waited outside the concert hall last night in his van, and when Akiko climbed into the seat next to him, he had repeated that his mission was urgent. Her father had been taken very ill, and she was to come with Parsons to Scotland as soon as possible. She had protested that it would be much quicker by train, but he had ignored her and driven slowly through heavy traffic, until she said, "Please stop. Surely I can collect some clothes? If I have to stay with father for a bit, I shall need some things."

"You'd better check your door lock when we get back," he had said, grinning and pointing at a suitcase in the back of the van. "Child's play, that was." He knew her father wanted her back with him for his last few weeks, he said, so he had collected supplies. She was angry and scared, and did not altogether believe his story of her father's collapse. He was old, yes, eighty-seven next birthday, but had been extremely fit and healthy for his age. But she needed to collect her thoughts. She must ring Jamie, first of all, and felt in her pocket for her mobile. It was not there.

"Good pocket-picking skills are essential in my line of business," Parsons said, and laughed.

She ordered him to give it back to her, but he said she would have to wait until the time was right. There was something threatening about him. She had always felt this, even when he had first come to work for her father. In what capacity she had never discovered, but had often heard him claim to be a representative for Nakamasa's business.

She had soon realised, however, that he was far too scruffy and unpleasant to represent anything worthwhile, and she had always suspected he had some stronghold over her father. Ever since she had left Japan, he had shown up at regular intervals with messages, mostly inconsequential, and she suspected he had been sent by her overprotective father to be half minder, half guardian angel, and an unsavoury one at that.

"I've thought of something important," she said quickly now. "I must let my colleague know that I shall be away for a few days. Otherwise, he will send out a search party, and I'm sure you wouldn't want that. He probably won't be back yet, but his flat's just round the corner and I can leave a message."

"No chance," said Parsons. "Tell me where he lives and I'll get a message to him."

"I'll show you," said Akiko.

"Which one?"

"There. Over there. Stop, and let me out. I'll just leave a message with the woman in the ground-floor flat. She's an invalid and is usually there. You can come with me, if you don't trust me."

"Oh, for God's sake, go and find the woman and be back here in two minutes. Or less. We've wasted enough time already!"

Akiko dashed across the road and rang first Jamie's bell, but as she expected, there was no reply. Then she tried the neighbour, but with desperation mounting, she realised that the woman was also out. Gone to hospital, she guessed.

Parsons, losing patience, sounded his horn, and Akiko turned away, now in tears of frustration.

"Good evening, miss. It's rather late to be out on your own around here. Are you in trouble?" A policeman had approached, and under the streetlight she saw that he was young and smiling. She was tempted to tell all, get rid of Parsons, and find Jamie. But then she thought of her father, and realised that if she appealed for help, this might well delay her journey to see him. Parsons could be telling the truth, and she might even be too late. That thought was unbearable, and she shook her head.

"Just a lovers' quarrel," she said, sure that he would go away. But he didn't. He produced an electronic device and said, "Your name, please, miss?"

"I'm not in any trouble," Akiko protested.

"Then I'm sure you won't mind giving me your name?"

"Jacqueline Dupre, then."

"Try again, miss."

"I just told you."

"Home address?"

"New York."

"I see. Big place, New York. If you'll excuse me for a moment, I must just make a call."

"You'd get a better signal over there," said Akiko, pointing to an open space.

"Where?"

As the young policeman turned to look, Akiko was on her feet and running like the wind across to the van. Parsons had the engine running, and they were away in seconds. The policeman shrugged. Lovers! And Jacqueline Dupre? What rubbish. What did she take him for? It would have to be reported back at the station, and he could imagine the scorn of his colleagues. He put away his notebook and proceeded on his way.

Meanwhile, in the petrol-fumed interior of the van, Parsons told Akiko to make herself comfortable. They would be driving through the night, he said.

NEXT MORNING, OUTSIDE TRESHAM RAILWAY STATION, DEREK greeted his wife and son with a stern face. "I've decided to ask no questions," he said, "except what the hell do you think you're doing, the pair of you?"

Lois frowned. "I reckon that's not bad to start with," she said.

Jamie nodded. "Let's get in the car and go back home, then we can have one of Gran's breakfasts and tell all. We made a very early start! But there's not much to tell, unfortunately."

Derek had been at the station a good half hour before their train arrived. He would not tell Lois he had spent a sleepless night worrying about her, knowing from experience that nothing would be more calculated to irritate her. He had been far from pleased when she had set off yesterday, apparently on the spur of the moment, to hear Jamie and Akiko playing on their big night. "We've never been to a single one of his concerts," she had said unconvincingly.

He had taken her to the station yesterday, and she had promised to be back home on the late evening train. He'd worried about that, too. Drunks and layabouts making nuisances of themselves. And then her call, saying something important had come up, and she was staying with Jamie in his flat overnight. Dark suspicions had entered his mind, and he had dialled the police station and asked to speak to Cowgill. Unavailable until tomorrow, they had said, and he had replaced the receiver sadly.

The smell of frying bacon was like a blessing as they all stepped into Gran's kitchen. Without a word, they sat at the table, and she dished up platefuls of her specials. Conversation lurched from polite enquiries about the concert to the efficiency of Virgin railways. Finally Derek pushed away his empty plate, downed his coffee to the dregs, and looked sternly at Lois.

"Time to tell, Lois. Just what did happen? I can see from Jamie's face that it was something unpleasant."

"Yes, well. I'll start. Akiko has disappeared. She seemed nervous during the second half of the concert, and told Jamie she wasn't satisfied with her performance. She had decided to go straight home, not waiting for visitors backstage."

"She's very hard on herself, and an anxious sort of girl," Jamie confirmed. "Finds being in a strange country a bit daunting. Only child, mother died early, doting wealthy father, and all that. Mum and Inspector Cowgill, who turned up unexpectedly, came round to congratulate us, and then the inspector said he was on police business, and—shall I explain, or will you, Mum?"

"It had better be good, Lois," said Derek harshly.

Lois frowned and sat up very straight in her chair. "As I said to you on the phone, Derek, Cowgill turning up was a complete coincidence. But I'm glad he did, because he told us the case of the missing cello could be more dangerously complicated than any of us had thought. And take that stupid look off your face, for God's sake. We've got trouble enough. At least, Akiko has. And Jamie has, and I shall help him as much as I can."

Then she explained as if to a three-year-old about blackmailing scams involving offers to restore musicians' stolen instruments to them in return for large sums of money. Only the returned ones were fakes. One refusal to be blackmailed had been fatal. "It could have happened to Akiko," she said.

Silence followed this revelation, and Derek had difficulty in meeting Lois's angry eyes.

"Sorry, gel," he said. "So what has Akiko had to say about all of this?"

"We told you—she's disappeared. Nobody's seen her since she left the concert hall. And I'm very grateful Mum's decided to help find her," Jamie said with a frown at his father.

Gran suddenly thumped the table, and her face was red and shining from cooking at a hot stove. "Well, I'm not so sure that's a good idea," she said to Jamie, "and I'm fed up with you," she added, turning to Lois. "Who do you think you are? Miss Marple or something? Rushing about and stirring up trouble for the rest of us! Why can't you stick with being a wife and mother, and running a successful cleaning business? What more do you want! It'd be good enough for most sensible women. It's got to stop! Leave it to the police, Jamie."

"Now, now, Gran," Derek said soothingly. "Lois has done a lot of good with her ferretin' in the past. And now this business does have a direct connection with our family. Akiko is Jamie's friend and colleague. Of course we all want to help as best we can."

"Huh! Well, you've soon changed your tune, Derek Meade!"

"Lois knows how I feel, Gran," Derek said patiently. "And I think we should leave it there."

"May I speak?" Jamie pushed his chair back roughly, and stood up. "Seems all this is my fault. So the best thing I can do is go back to London as soon as possible."

"Don't be ridiculous, Jamie! Of course it's not your fault. And this is your home and where you should be." Lois was about to expand on this when Jamie's mobile rang. He rushed outside, and they could see him on the lawn, walking up and down and speaking animatedly.

"Was it Akiko?" Derek asked, when Jamie came back.

"No, Dad. Just a friend of mine, dammit."

"Never mind, lad," Derek said, and got up from the table. "She'll turn up of her own accord, like as not. Now I must get on," he said. "I know it's no good asking you to stop ferretin', Lois. Just be careful, me duck. That's all."

IN HIS OFFICE, COWGILL TOOK A CALL. "OUTSIDE A BLOCK OF flats where?" Someone was testing a police siren in the back-yard, and he could hardly hear the voice.

"Speak up! Who is it?"

The young policeman seemed reluctant, but continued haltingly.

"Your superior told you to ring me?" said an exasperated Cowgill. "So where were you? Address? Go ahead then . . . Of course I know it! And you couldn't catch a small, defenceless girl? Said she was Jacqueline Dupre? Dear God, give me patience. Speak to me later."

He put down the phone, grabbed his jacket, and went to the lift. A notice on the doors informed him that the lift was out of order. He swore, and tackled the stairs two at a time, arriving at the bottom considerably out of breath.

"Leaving," he said to the receptionist, and stepped out into blinding sunlight.

ELEVEN

꙾

"Better have a stop soon," Parsons said. "I need coffee to keep me awake, and you look peaky, Miss Akiko. And this old bus could do with a rest." He had pulled into the car park of a motorway café and turned off the over-heated engine.

They had driven through the night, with the old van in no danger of breaking the speed limit, and now they were more than halfway to Hightoun House. Akiko's father had purchased a large mansion some years ago, partly for invest-ment, but also for business entertaining and a retreat for himself and Akiko in Scotland.

He had adored her from the moment she was born. An elderly father, he had been glad that he had chosen a wife half his age. But then his plan had gone awry. She had con-tracted a virulent influenza bug and had died when Akiko was not quite two years old. Distraught, he had hired a loving nanny who had stayed with her charge until she left school and went to college.

Akiko had had plenty of time on the journey north to think about her father and try to understand why he had endeavoured to keep such a restricting rein on her, even though she was now an independent adult. She recalled how hard he had tried to dissuade her from moving to London, but she had protested that she needed to see more of other cello players and establish some useful contacts, and he had given way. As an extra precaution, he had calculated that by using Parsons as a monitoring device, and arranging to come to Britain and use Hightoun and his office in London much more often, he could keep a protective eye on her.

"Should be there in another couple of hours," Parsons said after a long silence. Akiko had slept fitfully, waking every so often in alarm, for a moment still lost in troubling dreams, and Parsons had done his best to reassure her with a kind voice. He had relaxed now that the end of his mission was in sight.

They walked into the café, and Parsons collected a tray with two coffees and sandwiches, taking it to a table only partly occupied by an elderly couple.

"Don't try anything," he muttered to her as they sat down. "I can run faster than a frit rabbit. You'd get nowhere."

"I'm not even thinking of it!" she protested. "All I want is to get to see Father as soon as possible. And please treat me with respect, Parsons. I shall already have enough to tell Papa to cause trouble for you," she said.

"Oh, I couldn't allow that, Miss Akiko," he said, his kind voice turning sharp. "You wouldn't want to risk losing a chance to see your father before he dies? No, best to be grateful to me for a safe journey. I am, after all, doing your father's bidding."

She shook her head. "I hope so," she said, "otherwise Papa will be extremely annoyed."

With a steady hand, he tore the top off a twist of brown sugar and emptied it into his coffee. He turned and smiled at the couple at their table. "Lovely day again," he said politely.

He patted Akiko's hand fondly, and the couple smiled. She moved her hand in disgust. "Eat up, girl," he said quietly. "There's nothing worse than a cold fried egg." He lowered his voice even more. "Though come to think of it, I know many things that are worse, and one of them would be the result of not doing exactly what I am about to instruct you. You will tell your father that everything has gone extremely smoothly, and that your escort—me—has been most helpful and comforting."

Akiko felt anger rising. "Oh, for God's sake," she said, and put down her knife and fork, saying she had had enough.

THE ELDERLY COUPLE SAT IN THEIR CAR. IT WAS HOT, WITH THE sun beating down whilst they had had their lunch. "Better be off, Tom," the woman said. "We'll get the air con going and cool down."

"Right you are then. All set for another couple of hours? We should be there by then. Oh look!" he added. "There's that girl we saw, and the scruffy chap who was with her, walking out together. What does she see in him, d'you think? Look, he's taken her arm."

"She's getting into that black van with him, too! Honestly, Tom, young people these days, they don't seem to have any sense, carrying on like that. Mind you, I'm surprised at that girl. He didn't seem to be making much headway with her in the café."

"None s'queer as folk. Ready then? Got your sunglasses? Off we go, then."

TWELVE

✎

"COWGILL RANG," GRAN SAID, AS LOIS CAME THROUGH THE kitchen door. "Said to ring him as soon as you came in."

"Where's Jamie?"

"Gone out. Everybody went out, except me and Jeems. Good job there's somebody here to hold the fort."

"Yes, well. Thanks, Mum. I'll go and ring Cowgill. Let's hope he's got some good news about Akiko. Jamie's falling to pieces, I reckon."

"No, he's not. I sometimes think I know your children better than you do. He'll be all right. He may look worried— and who wouldn't?—but he's strong inside. You'll see."

"Well, thanks for telling me," answered Lois, and disappeared into her office before she should find herself in another fight with her mother.

Cowgill answered the phone straightaway. "Ah, Lois. I have news, but not good, I'm afraid."

"Akiko? Has something happened to her?"

"Well, that's just it. We don't know. We had circulated her particulars, of course, and asked for an eye to be kept open for her. One of the lads, quite by chance, saw a girl on some steps outside a block of flats, rather late on Monday night, looking lost and frightened. It was Jamie's address. Our lad spoke kindly to her, but she refused to give him any sensible details about herself. Told him she'd had a lover's tiff, and then ran off."

"Not Akiko, then? Is that what you rang to tell me?"

"Yes and no. We think it probably *was* Akiko. I recognised his description of the girl straightaway, but of course it was dark, with a dim streetlight, and his impression is in no way conclusive. Nevertheless, Lois, I think we should be following this up."

"You mean to say a fine, healthy young policeman, fully trained, could not catch a mere slip of a girl, all alone and unprotected?"

"My reaction, too. He's been told, but said she ran across the road to a waiting van, and they disappeared at speed. He judged that she had been fooling him, and left it there. But how polite you are this afternoon! In the old days, you'd've yelled at me that I knew nothing about anything and a child of five could've caught her! But still, the answer's the same. He didn't catch her, and we are continuing our enquiries."

Lois ended the call.

"Mum? Can I come in?" It was Jamie at her office door, and Lois nodded wearily. "Come on, boy, sit yourself down. Where've you been? Is Gran still in the kitchen?"

"I just went for a walk and a think. And yeah, Gran's getting tea things out. Says I look like something the cat brought in." He smiled wanly.

"I've just had a call from Inspector Cowgill. Seems they had a sighting of a girl who might have been Akiko. She ran faster than the policeman, and they have not yet caught up with her."

"So we know she's alive!" He leaned back in his chair, took a deep breath and managed a smile.

"Did you think she might not be? Is there something you're not telling us, Jamie?"

He was silent for a minute or so, then said that perhaps he should tell her something Akiko had told him. Lois nodded and waited.

"She said that when she first came to London, her father, who is so old that he was a young soldier in World War Two, warned her to keep quiet about her origins and not answer idle questions about what her daddy did in the war. He also told her not to flash her money about, nor let on that he was very rich. Said it would make her vulnerable to predators."

"Sounds very overprotective to me!" Lois replied. "Did she say anything else?"

"Nope, nothing more. I've told you all I know. Anyway, I'd better go back to London soon, now I know she's alive. I'm much more likely to find her there than if I wander about Farnden like a fart in a kettle."

"A *what*? You'd better go and see how Gran's getting on with tea."

JAMIE'S RELUCTANT MENTION OF AKIKO'S ORIGINS CAME BACK TO Lois when she set off to take Jeems for her evening walk through Farnden Hall spinney. Here there were interlinking footpaths, and she was familiar with all of them. Mrs. T-J, in her time, had kept these private, except for friends, and Lois was on her list. Now Norrington had put up signposts with twee names, like Piglet's Home and Rabbit Town. The first was an old clearing where a long-dead cottager had kept a pig in a now-disintegrating pigsty, and Rabbit Town was, of course, the rabbit warren, a mass of burrows. She had once sprained her ankle when her foot had disappeared down a rabbit hole.

So, Lois thought, as she climbed a stile with barbed wire threaded across the top, Akiko had come from Japan, whose soldiers seventy-odd years ago had invaded Burma and set up grisly prisoner-of-war camps for incarcerating the enemy, using them as slave labourers to build the notorious Death Railway. And the enemy was us, Lois thought. Thousands of British and Americans and their allies. When they died of malnourishment, disease and neglect, they were put aside like dead dogs. No, not like dead dogs. Dogs would be better treated.

But for now, her concerns were for Jamie, her precious son, who could be mixed up with all of that, though for the life of her she could not see why or how.

She walked on, head down on the lookout for rabbit holes and traps. Norrington had hired a new gamekeeper. He was neat and tidy, but kept himself to himself. Derek had reported that he'd seen him in the pub on his own, not making any attempts at friendship. He lived in the gamekeeper's cottage, and was reputed to have an attractive blonde with him. He had apparently been employed by Norrington to set up a commercial pheasant shoot, and had claimed experience in various locations around the country. He had not mentioned his name in the pub, as far as Derek could remember.

"Good morning, madam!"

Lois stopped suddenly, startled by the loud voice. He was there, wearing the kind of muddy green that renders countrymen almost invisible, and was blocking her way. He carried a gun in the correct manner, and smiled at her.

"Morning," Lois replied. "Sorry—I don't think I know you?"

"Just call me Mellors," he said, and burst out laughing.

"I've read it," said Lois flatly. Conceited idiot! Thinks he can turn on the charm, just because I'm female.

"Ah, well done," he said. "Lady Chatterley, I presume?"

"Oh, for God's sake, man. I'm in a hurry, so could you please let me through."

The path was narrow, with high nettles on either side. Lois hadn't bothered to change into thick trousers, and was determined not to be stung.

"There's just one thing," he said. "I believe you are trespassing. This is private woodland, except on days when Mr. Norrington opens it to the public. And this isn't one of those days. And then there's the pheasants. I'm here to protect these valuable birds from dogs such as yours." He pointed at Jeems, who sidled up close to Lois and growled.

"I always keep her on a lead," said Lois, though this was not strictly true. Many local people had for years walked their dogs in the spinney, chiefly because it was a wonderful place for snuffles and sniffs, and setting up clattering pigeons.

"Right, well, on you go then. Just find another place to exercise your dog, please."

"Oh, don't worry. I shall get permission from Mr. Norrington, if that's what's needed. I'm sure he'll be pleased to hear his gamekeeper is so keen on his job."

"Then we may meet again, Lady C," the man said, and strode off, whistling.

"Yeah, yeah, very funny," Lois said aloud to Jeems. "Too clever by half. One to watch, I reckon, don't you?" Jeems pricked her ears and growled again. She was good at recognising an enemy.

Thirteen

THE TRAIN TO LONDON WAS HALF EMPTY, AND JAMIE CHOSE a window seat. He had a paperback that his father had thrust into his hands at the last minute, saying it would take his mind off Akiko. It was a collection of Matt cartoons, and in spite of himself he began to smile and feel more cheerful.

By the time he reached London, he had decided that they had all been worrying about nothing. The theft of the cello was serious, of course, but there were other cellos, and Akiko had it insured. Then all that stuff about a poisoned sandwich. Talk about melodrama! Really, Inspector Cowgill could see trouble everywhere.

Akiko would turn up. He was sure of that. After all, although the two of them had been playing music together for some while, she had kept her personal life very separate from her professional relationships. Until recently, maybe? Yes, of course he cared about her safety. Who wouldn't? She was as beautiful as fragile porcelain, and was always pleasant and considerate. The perfect colleague, then? But nothing more, as far as he was concerned.

He was almost chirpy as he reached his flat and inserted the key in the lock. But the minute he stepped inside, he knew something was wrong. The hairs stood up on the back of his neck, and he listened hard. No sounds, no footsteps, nothing. He clutched the Matt cartoon book like a talisman, and walked slowly into the kitchen. Everything in order, just as he had left it. He turned and made for the sitting room. His large windows had a view over half of London, and there, standing with his back to him, was a man.

"What the hell do you think you're doing?" Jamie's voice was shrill with panic.

The man turned to face him. "Hi, Jamie," he said. "I've been waiting for you."

RELIEF FLOODED THROUGH JAMIE. IT WAS HIS FRIEND FROM WAY back, a violinist who had been at college with him and was now playing in a string quartet based in Manchester. He had shared the flat with Jamie when they were students, and, of course, he still had a key. They had kept in touch with emails and texts, and occasionally met for an evening of catching up.

"Alan! Wonderful to see you. Forgive my lack of a welcome, but I didn't recognise the smart suit!"

"You okay, son?" It had been a joke between them that Alan was a year older and more mature, and had adopted the role of proxy father to Jamie. "You look as if you'd seen a ghost."

"No, no, I'm fine. Just not expecting to find someone in

the flat. How are you, Alan? Bookings good? Still filling the concert halls in the provinces?"

"Very much so. Manchester's a good place these days. Now the Beeb has come to town, I reckon it rivals London. We get the flags of all nations some weeks. You name a country, and I can give you at least three visiting soloists."

"Great—now, let's open a bottle and fix ourselves some food. I assume you're staying the night? Sofa's quite comfortable. Goodness, Alan, I am really pleased to see you."

So there *was* something wrong, Alan said to himself. He had lived with Jamie long enough to read his face. No doubt he'll tell all over supper.

IT WAS AFTERNOON BY THE TIME AKIKO AND PARSONS REACHED the tiny village that acted as a dormitory for wealthy tycoons in business in Glasgow. About a couple of miles outside the city boundary, it was placed strategically on a hill, less than a mile from the main road, and with good views of the countryside and impressive new industrial buildings springing up all round. She guessed that Parsons was keen for a conversation and so decided to keep silent. She did not trust him one inch. They turned into a long drive and drove slowly for what seemed like at least another mile. A tall building loomed up, and the car halted outside an arched porch, itself almost as large as a small house.

The driver got out, walked round to her door and opened it. "Here we are, Miss Akiko. You will be wanting to go straight in to see your father, no doubt. I will see to your case. Just be wary of the new wolfhounds your father has installed."

He laughed loudly, and Akiko told him to stop talking

nonsense and to take her case indoors at once. She followed him up a flight of stone steps to the door, which now stood open, with a liveried servant waiting.

"I know the way perfectly, thank you," Akiko said. "I shall go straight up." She ascended the wide staircase and knocked at a heavy oak door.

"Come in, my child," said a faint, precise voice. She entered and looked round the high-ceilinged, softly lit room. There were dark red velvet curtains and deep matching armchairs, in one of which, well supported by cushions, sat a small tubby man with Asian features. He was very old, but his eyes were young and bright, and when he looked up at her, they twinkled.

"My precious daughter. How lovely to see you," he said warmly. "I trust you had a comfortable journey in that dreadful van? Parsons's idea. We had something of an emergency, and I am sorry it was perhaps a false alarm. The doctor is hopeful, I am glad to say."

Akiko bowed slightly. "Don't worry, Father," she said. "The van was adequate. But how are you now? Should you be out of bed?"

He didn't answer her, but motioned to Parsons, who had followed her into the bedroom, carrying her case. "Thank you, Ezekiel," he said. "Well done. That will be all now."

When he had gone, Akiko walked to an armchair opposite her father and sat down. "Papa," she said gently, "I was so worried. Parsons was not my ideal companion, but I realise there was little time to arrange things. How are you, really?"

"I have been quite ill, but you must not worry," he replied. "I have an excellent doctor and he has given me the green light. If I am sensible, I can go forward into a contented old age."

"But, Papa, you are already in your old age. It is time to

retire completely. Why don't you hand over to your deputy and take a long-deserved rest? I know you are happier back in Japan. You could stay over there now and catch up with old friends. And what's more," she added with some feeling, "we could get rid of Parsons. He is not a good person. With me he is disrespectful, rough and unpleasant!"

She was answered by a blank stare from her father. "Not at the moment," he said eventually. "I cannot discuss Ezekiel. Please do not mention it again."

Unwilling to upset him, she dropped the subject, and her father reached for a glass of water.

"And if I did what you suggest, what about you, my child?" he continued. "When would I see my only beloved daughter if I give up spending time in this country? We have the office in London where you can more easily visit me, and keep me in touch with everything you are doing, until you decide to return to Japan. Then we can go together. This recent illness has made me even more concerned for your future than I always have been."

Akiko shook her head. "There is no need, Papa," she said gently.

"But when I am gone, you will be quite alone," he continued. "There will, as you are aware, be no problem with finance, but money does not replace old friends and relations in your own country. It is my hope that you will find a nice Japanese boy and make your own family. Come, give me a kiss and say you understand and agree."

Akiko stood up, frowning. "Papa!" she said, forgetting about upsetting him. "Is that the real reason you have brought me up here and frightened me out of my wits? To make sure I return to Japan? Have you really been near to death, as Parsons told me?"

"I have explained, my dear. There is life in the old dog yet, as the English say. Parsons is not a blessing, I agree, but we do not discuss him further."

"If not now, when?" Akiko said, quietly now.

"In good time. One day, I will tell you, but not now."

"Then I suppose I must wait," she said. "But now that I see you are not in immediate danger, I have to explain why I must return to London as soon as possible."

This explanation took some time to convince Nakamasa that his daughter was serious. He had been so used to organising her life, and still could not really accept that she had cut herself free from him. Now, however, when she assured him she must find a way to return to her colleague and her career as quickly as she could, he suggested she should leave him to think for a while, and get some food from the housekeeper.

"Come back when you have finished, my dear, and we will talk some more." Nakamasa put his hand to his heart. "And remember," he said, "my excellent doctor did emphasize that I should take care of myself to enjoy my remaining years with my beloved daughter."

"I *am* hungry, Papa," Akiko said, ignoring this blatant emotional blackmail. "I will be back shortly."

FEELING STRONGER WITH GOOD FOOD INSIDE HER, AKIKO returned to her father, determined to make it clear to him that she did not intend to return to Japan on a permanent basis. Her life was now very much bound up with her feelings for Jamie, but she knew better than to mention an English boyfriend.

"Ah, there you are. You look much more rested and happy," said Nakamasa. "More like my little Akiko."

"Yes, well, Papa, I am not so little anymore. This is what we have to talk about. You see, my career is all-important to me. I am doing well, making progress, and becoming known for being a fine cellist."

She wondered whether to mention the stolen cello, but decided not. Her father would immediately arrange for her to have another equally good one, but that would come with more strings attached.

"The life of a solo player is a peripatetic one," she continued. "We must go wherever the opportunities are, and this means concert halls all over the world. This does not trouble me. I love travelling and do not find it at all onerous. This I must have inherited from you! You are a much-travelled man, Papa. So you see, it is not worth you risking a setback by trying to follow me around the globe."

Nakamasa frowned. "That is for me to decide, Akiko," he said, a stern note creeping into his voice.

"Of course, Papa. But for me, I must return to London and take up my cello again. I am committed to concerts almost straightaway, and I must not let people down."

"Including one James Meade, pianist of distinction?" said her father, his voice growing stronger by the minute.

Akiko coloured. "Including my accompanist," she agreed. "So I will catch the train in the morning. I will telephone you every day to make sure you are keeping up the improvement."

There was a long silence, and then Nakamasa said, "There will be no need for a train. Parsons can take the Bentley, and you will travel in comfort. Please send him to me."

"But I am perfectly happy to take the train, Papa," Akiko protested.

He sighed and put his hand once more to his heart. "Do this for me, daughter," he said. "I shall know you are safe with Ezekiel."

Akiko shivered, though the room was very warm. "Very well. But please speak to him about his attitude. You are his boss, after all."

When she had left the room, and Parsons was sent for, Nakamasa covered his eyes in despair. He had done his best, would always do his best for his daughter, but felt that he had not this time succeeded.

"You wanted me?" said Ezekiel Parsons, coming in as silently as a rat.

"Sir," said Nakamasa.

"You wanted me, *sir*."

"Yes. We shall take Miss Akiko in the Bentley back to London tomorrow morning. We leave early."

"We? I thought you were nigh unto death? Sir."

"The car is very comfortable, and you will drive carefully. Please do as I instruct."

"Yes, sir," said Ezekiel, turning on his heel and leaving as quietly as he came.

FOURTEEN

ॐ

LOIS HAD SPENT YESTERDAY EVENING LOSING HERSELF IN New Brooms paperwork. The business had grown to a point where she would soon have to start looking for a new cleaning member of the team. She seldom advertised the job, but relied on recommendations from her regular cleaners, and from friends in other villages. This had worked well so far, and only once had she taken on a bad apple, and he wasn't very bad.

For all her hard work yesterday, this morning there was still a huge pile of filing waiting on her desk. She decided to tackle it today, and endeavour once more to forget all about lost cellos and stolen Japanese girls. Or the other way round, she thought, and smiled.

GRAN CAME INTO THE OFFICE EARLY, AND ASKED LOIS WHAT SHE would like for lunch.

"I don't think I'll be in for lunch, thanks," Lois replied. "You can have a rest. You certainly deserve it, what with one thing and another!"

"Huh! Well, I'm glad somebody appreciates me. And I might as well say now that I just hope you know what you're doing," said Gran. "If he was my son, I'd be worried sick."

"Which son?" Lois said in a tightly controlled voice.

"The one all mixed up with stolen cellos and a fancy foreign girl, and playing music that nobody wants to listen to all over the world. Why couldn't he have settled down with his father, learning a trade, and got in with one of those rock bands in his spare time?"

This all came out in a rush, and Lois realised that her mother had been brooding on Jamie for some time. She had to hand it to her. Gran had in the past managed not to voice her disapproval of the way Jamie had been encouraged and lauded for his decision to make a career in music.

"Do you know *why* he didn't learn to be an electrician like his father?" Lois replied. "Because his father didn't want him to! Both of us, Derek and me, we were really proud that Jamie took to music like a duck to water. Even when he was a little lad, if you remember, Mum, he loved to play that toy piano you and Dad gave him. Could have been the thing that started him off."

Gran shook her head. "Well, I don't know, I'm sure," she said huffily.

"No more do I," said Lois, "but Jamie says we're not to worry, and so I am not going to. I'm taking Jeems for a walk in half an hour or so, to get my thoughts in order. Don't worry if I'm not back for lunch. I'll take a sandwich. Might go as far as Fletching. I'll take my mobile and let you know when I'll be back. Derek knows. I told him before he went off to work. And thanks for worrying. But don't."

"And now there's something else to worry about! You tramping off with that little dog. Anything could happen to you if you're going through the spinney."

"Jeems may be small, but she's got sharp teeth and knows an enemy from a friend. I'll be fine, Mum. Might even find some mushrooms for supper."

LOIS HAD THE PERFECT EXCUSE TO CALL AT THE HALL. SHE WOULD check that the Norringtons were still happy with Paula's work. Paula had been cleaning there for some time, and occasionally a job would become too routine and she would need to switch the staff around. She could use this to ask permission from the Norringtons to walk Jemima through the park and spinney.

She was pleased to see that the big Range Rover was not in the stable yard where cars were parked. Geoff Norrington must have gone up to London to his office. Sometimes he worked at home, but not today. That would make it easier, as Mrs. Norrington was a much more sympathetic person. Norrington could be smarmily pleasant when he wanted something. Otherwise he could take ages to decide what was in it for him.

"Mrs. Meade! Do come in. You are just the person I wanted to see. I shall put on the kettle and we'll have a coffee. Do you want Paula to be with us?"

Lois said no, that would not be necessary. This was just a check-up call. She left Jeems tied up in the yard and followed Mrs. Norrington into the kitchen. Were there any problems with Paula's work? On being reassured that all was well, and Paula still the best cleaner they'd ever had, Melanie Norrington and Lois sat down at the table to drink their coffee.

"It's nice to have a chat," Melanie said. "If you can spare a few minutes. The truth is, Mrs. Meade, since we've been here I have felt a bit lonely. It was fine for a while, when there was masses to do, but now, unless there is some event or meeting, I'm desperate for the sound of a human voice! Thank heavens for the chapel shop!"

Lois said she supposed it was a different lifestyle. "In your last house, you had neighbours, and people going by along the road. Some folk would give their eyeteeth to be undisturbed!" she said.

Melanie shook her head. "Not me. I like a bit of life going on around me. Anyway, enough about me. How are you doing? And your family? I saw your Jamie at the dog show. Was that his girlfriend?"

"No, Akiko's a cellist, and Jamie accompanies her on the piano. They've known each other for a while now, and seem very good friends."

"But no more than that?" Melanie grinned conspiratorially.

"We're not sure. He's fond of her, I suppose. Not as fond of her as she is of him, I suspect. I personally think that on Jamie's side friendship is all there is to it. Derek doesn't agree, but then that's him."

"Did you say cellist? Wasn't there some talk of a cello being stolen? Geoff heard about it in the shop. From your Josie, I expect. I don't know what we'd do without the village shop. She must do well, your Josie. Is she carrying on, now she's married?"

"Oh yes. She won't give it up. It's her baby, as they say."

"But there may be a real one soon?"

"We shall manage," said Lois, getting to her feet. "Now, I must get along. But there was just one other thing. Is it okay for me to take Jemima through the park and woods, like I always have? Your gamekeeper was a bit unfriendly about it."

"Oh, don't worry about him. I'll have a word. He's a bit of a liability at the moment. Comes and goes without telling us. Geoff employed him a few weeks ago. Goodness knows where he came from! I leave all that sort of thing to Geoff. No, I'll have a word with him, or ask Geoff to, and you just carry on as you always have."

LOIS AND JEMIMA CROSSED THE PARKLAND, THE STRONG SUNLIGHT burning the pale skin exposed on Lois's bare shoulders. She was relieved when she and Jemima reached the cool spinney, where dappled sunlight was pleasant. She had not thought to bring a jacket, and decided to walk round the perimeter and then across a small field shaded with large chestnut trees. From there she could go swiftly into Fletching by a lane lined with mature oaks. She put Jemima on her lead and thought maybe she would have a refreshing lemonade at the pub, though she still felt reluctant to go into pubs on her own. She could hear her mother's voice: "What will your father say, Lois Weedon?" Old habits die hard.

It was not until she had left the spinney and started across on the first field, keeping to the edge in the shade of the chestnuts, that she saw him. Jeems barked a sharp warning, and the gamekeeper looked round. He started to walk quickly towards her. Her heartbeat quickened, and she told herself not to be silly. She had permission, didn't she?

"Ah, I thought so," he said. "And have you the right to roam, as they say? I am glad to see the terrier is on a lead."

"Excuse me," said Lois firmly. "I've got permission to go where I like on Norringtons' land. Now let me pass."

His smile faded, and he made a move towards her. Jeems was on him in a flash, her teeth sunk deep into his thick leather boots.

"Get off, you little bastard!" he shouted, hopping round, trying to dislodge the sharp terrier teeth. Jeems hung on, and Lois began to laugh. "Oh dear, dear!" she said. "Do you suppose she doesn't like you?"

"I'll ring the little bugger's neck!" he yelled, but she twisted away from him, still hanging on to his boot. He finally shook her off, and she retreated, growling ferociously.

"I'll see that you don't," said Lois calmly, pulling Jemima away. "It wouldn't look too good in Mr. Norrington's eyes, would it? Tough gamekeeper attacks small pet dog? I advise you to go home and have a cup of hot sweet tea. Good for shock. I must be getting along. Good morning!"

Still chuckling, Lois continued out of the field and into the shady lane that led to the village of Fletching. As she approached the pub, she saw a family with two small boys sitting in the garden having a snack lunch. They smiled at her, and she decided to buy a lemonade and join them, but not at their table. They might not want her, and in any case, she had come away from home to think without interruption.

"Are dogs allowed in the garden?" she said to the landlady, who nodded.

"We're not called the Dog and Duck for nothing, dear. No ducks, though, except on the menu! Just keep her on a lead. Here, doggie, a complimentary biscuit for all canine visitors."

Settled in a shady seat, Lois relaxed. Quite an eventful morning! First the lost and lonely Melanie Norrington, and then the wicked gamekeeper seen off by the fierce hound at Lois's feet. She was just drifting into a suitable frame of mind for serious thought when her mobile rang. Jamie. She considered not answering, but sighed and said hello.

"Mum? Just thought I'd give you a ring. Alan's turned up, and we're having lunch by the river. No, still no news of Akiko. But I reckon she'll ring in a day or two. So you're not to worry anymore. I'll let you know when she turns up. And thanks for everything. Bye, Mum."

Lois smiled. He was still the same old Jamie. Down in the dumps one minute, and in no time fully restored and back to his usual optimistic self. Takes after his dad, she decided. She looked across at the young family arguing over whether sugary drinks were bad for their teeth. The father said they were to settle it with their mother, and let him know the answer.

Same applies when they're grown up, she thought. Mother will settle it. Mother will find the missing cello, and discover what was troubling Akiko Nakamasa. She thought back to the scene Cowgill had witnessed in the Wilmore Hall. Akiko in conversation with a strange man under the spiral staircase. Had this rendezvous been planned? Something to do with the missing cello?

A blackbird flew to the table where the family had been and began pecking at leftovers. Such a beautiful bird, with its glossy black feathers and bright yellow bill. Concentrate, Lois!

Right. Hunter Cowgill, then. He had thought it worth

his while to sit with wet feet through a recital of music which she was sure he would not have enjoyed. He was a Wagner fan. Big scenes and big noise. Presumably he was there to keep his eyes and ears open for gossip about instrument theft. Or was there more to it? He had been very unforthcoming.

A gang of boys, five or six of them, came jostling into the garden, opened bottles in hand, and one with music blaring. Time to go, thought Lois. She reckoned the purpose of her walk was achieved, and she knew where to go next. Conversations with Cowgill and Mrs. T-J to be set up, and a tactful questioning of Jamie, when and if Akiko returned.

If she ever got the chance, she would like to question Akiko about her cello. But this was unlikely. For a start she was missing, and even if she wasn't, she would be most unlikely to talk about anything except the weather.

FIFTEEN

No time like the present, thought Lois, as she set off back to Farnden. I can call on Mrs. T-J on my way, and hope to find her at home. Since the old thing had moved to the village, Lois noticed that almost day by day the former dragon of Farnden Hall had mellowed. On her daily visits to the shop she had warmed up with Josie, and came in regularly for a catch-up on local affairs along with her purchase of tins of Heinz soup.

"Does she live on soup?" Josie greeted her mother as she walked in and sat down heavily on the stool by the counter.

"Who?"

"Mrs. Tollervey-Jones. She's just gone home with a bagful of tins. And what's up with you? You look exhausted."

"I walked to and from Fletching. Exercise for Jeems. She's on the dog hook outside."

"Sounds like you're roasting her on a spit! Anyway, what can I get you?"

"Three minutes' rest in your shop, thanks. I'm calling in on the old duck on my way home. Should I take some sausages for her? It'd make a change from soup."

"No, she just bought some. I was exaggerating."

"I must say you're extremely chirpy! What time did you get back? Married life obviously suits you. It's a pity you had to come back after such a short break. Comes of marrying a policeman, I suppose. Still, you can have a proper holiday later on. It's wonderful to see you so happy, love. Everything all right with the shop in your absence?"

"Perfect, thanks. The team coped brilliantly. Sorry I missed Jamie, though. How long did he stay? And did you find out if he and Akiko *are* an item?"

"Ah, thereby hangs a tale. Here's somebody coming up the steps. We'll get together later."

GRAN HAD SEEN LOIS WALKING UP THE ROAD WITH JEEMS. FROM her observation post in the sitting room at the front of the house she could see down the street as far as the shop. It was her favourite pastime. When they had moved in, Gran had chosen the best of two large rooms for general family use. The sun streamed in much of the day, and she had her precious collection of Catherine Cookson's novels on shelves filling alcoves by the fireplace, and handy for second reading.

Lois's office was the other side of the house, with much the same view, but shaded by tall silver birches, and was often chilly. Gran pointed out that an electric heater would warm her up in no time, and in any case, it wouldn't do to be too comfortable when she was working.

Now she walked back to the kitchen, shaking her head.

That daughter of mine! She'll be completely done in when she finally deigns to come home from her walk.

Lois, meanwhile, was sitting in welcome comfort in Mrs. T-J's house, opening a conversation that she hoped would lead to some fruitful discussion.

"How's Robert?" she said. "Very busy in the courts, I expect?"

"Oh yes, he's doing very well. And Felicity has matured into a really good wife. I had my doubts at first. Very frivolous, was Felicity! But with the two girls, she has necessarily improved. Any news of Jamie? And Akiko's cello? I had a word with those instrument dealers I mentioned. They were helpful. Said that if it is found, and turns out to be one that has a history, they can probably identify it. Once they find it!"

"Oh well. Very useful," said Lois, trying to sound enthusiastic.

"Of course, we have very little information about her background, other than that she comes from Japan. I do hope this won't upset her relationship with Jamie. They seemed such happy colleagues. Colleagues, if nothing else."

"She's disappeared. Or did I tell you that?"

"No, you did not. But my spies informed me. No, don't look so grim, my dear. Josie in the shop mentioned it when I asked about the cello. She didn't seem too worried. Mind you, just back from honeymoon, and the world looks rosy! All she said was that Jamie was back in London and trying to contact Akiko."

Lois nodded. "Thanks for the instrument report. I've heard from Jamie that he's not worrying too much about the cello, or her disappearance. He reckons Akiko's father is loaded, and will probably buy her another. He's had an old mate to stay, another musician, a hardheaded violinist. They've chewed it over, and now they think she's gone away for a bit to get over the shock. I must say I am wondering if she's had a breakdown and gone off back to Japan. Anyway, now I must go. My mother is a great one for punctuality, and I'm at least three hours late. Thanks a lot. And just remember to shut your front door!"

Mrs. T-J frowned, and thought of reminding Lois of her own undoubted seniority, if only in years, but remembered in time that she was, for the moment, a junior partner in the ferretin' business.

JOSIE WAS ABOUT TO CLOSE THE SHOP, PLANNING TO GO QUICKLY up the road to ask her mother for more on Jamie and Akiko, when a police car drew up, and Matthew got out.

"Early closing day?" he asked, as he gave her a big hug.

"Hey, you're the early one! It's shop closing time. And let go of me! Our boys in blue do not hug strange females in the street."

"Strange? A man can hug his wife at all times. Section forty-three of the police procedure act."

"Idiot. Are you off duty now?"

Matthew shook his head. "Nope. On my way to Waltonby. Theft of a garden sundial, very valuable. Owner heartbroken. Not exactly the crime of the century, but we have to show willing. I shouldn't be long."

"I might still be up at Mum's. She's ferretin' again. It's all to do with the missing cello. That girl who is Jamie's concert duo, with him on the piano. Apparently she's gone missing now, but they're not too worried. Probably gone away for a break without telling anyone. She was pretty shook up, poor kid. Apparently musicians get ridiculously fond of their instruments. Mum may know a bit more, so I thought I'd go up. Get a bit of exercise! Standing in the shop all day is not really the same as a good walk. But I shall be back before you."

"Sounds like Jamie would be well advised to find someone else to play with. Missing Japanese cellists are rare birds, and could be hard to find. Anyway, see you later, wifey dear."

NOW MORE THAN EVER, JOSIE WAS SECURITY CONSCIOUS AND locked, bolted and barred the shop before she left. Matthew had some time ago converted and improved a cottage a couple of miles outside Farnden, and she had moved in with him. The flat above the shop was more or less empty, though she still had a few of her things to carry down to Sycamore End. She planned to do this at the weekend, and then think about a tenant for the flat. The shop was much more vulnerable with nobody living there. She supposed the word had already gone round the village, so she expected to find a suitable person shortly. She arrived at Meade House, and poked her head around the kitchen door.

"Hi, Gran. How you doing? Is Mum around?"

"Hello, dear. I'm fine, and your mother is in the office on the phone. Why don't you put your head round the door and let her know you're here? And how's Matthew?"

"No change," said Josie, smiling. "Still the same old policeman."

Gran sighed. A chip off the old block, this granddaughter of hers. "Have you got time for a cup of tea? Or coffee?"

"Love one. Tea please, Gran."

Lois, still in her office, looked up to see Josie, and was

glad of the interruption. She was tired after her long walk, and wished she could be like Jeems and curl up in a basket to sleep. But there were messages waiting for her, and she had only just finished dealing with them.

"Come in, do. You don't have to knock! Sit down by the window. I'm just checking messages and having another talk to Jamie."

"Has he heard from Akiko?"

"Ah, so you know she's gone missing?"

"Jamie rang me, too. I am his only sister, you know, and we talk quite often. He wasn't too worried at that point. Is that what you were going to tell me?"

Lois shook her head. "No, I've had another message from him, and I rang back. He sounded completely different. Nervous and much more worried this time. Didn't say much. Maybe hiding something, d'you reckon? Can't remember what I was going to tell you in the shop, but it'll come back. But Mrs. T-J has been investigating. Nothing very exciting, I'm afraid. She has an informant in the music business, who says that when the cello turns up, they will be able to identify it. Just to make sure it's not a fake."

"Amazing," said Josie, unimpressed. "I should think Akiko would be the best person to do that."

Lois folded up her papers and put them in a heap, ready for New Brooms' weekly meeting next Monday.

"Let's hope we can get back to business as usual soon." Josie stood up. "I've got heaps of thank-you letters to write. We've had some gorgeous wedding presents, some from very distant members of Matthew's family. All very exciting! I'll be off now. See you soon. Bye!"

After her daughter had gone, Lois thought some more about Jamie's call, and about his confidence in her being able to help, if necessary. And why was he now sounding really worried? She guessed he had had some kind of a message, and it had not been good. After all, the girl's behaviour after that concert had been very odd. It would have taken only a few minutes to let Jamie know what she was doing, and where she could be reached. Maybe Gran's instincts were right, and she was not to be trusted.

On the other hand, as everyone continually reminded her, Jamie was a grown man, and perfectly capable of managing his own affairs. Parents should step back and let their adult offspring get on with it, shouldn't they?

Sixteen

❧

NAKAMASA'S OFFICES WERE IN A SPLENDID VICTORIAN Gothic building in the city and had once been a convent. Planning regulations were imposed on the conversion, but with limitless financial resources, he had made a very good job of it. Akiko, who had been there many times to meet her father, had always sensed in the narrow corridors and cell-like rooms an atmosphere of almost tangible loneliness, and found it depressing. The nuns had belonged to a silent order, and she could not imagine how anyone could voluntarily want to remove themselves from music, and love and laughter, and the rewards of friendly conversation.

As she looked around the small cell which her father had arranged to be decorated and frilled especially for her, she once again thought she could hear the shuffling footfall of unhappy women, enclosed in their own thoughts. And prayers for deliverance, maybe?

The journey down from Scotland had been uneventful,

staying halfway in a comfortable hotel in the market town of Appleby. She and her father had had a good dinner in the restaurant, while Parsons went out to find a pub. It had been an opportunity for Akiko to attempt once more to get her father to tell her more about the man she so disliked, but he had clammed up, as he had done so many times before.

She had tried to ring Jamie from the hotel phone, but there had been only the message voice. She was about to tell him to ring her on the hotel number, but had been interrupted after saying only "Jamie, it's me." Not much of a message, but at least he would know she was somewhere. She would wait until they got to London, when she could be sure of being private.

Now arrived in London, they had settled into the convent, and Nakamasa insisted on going to his office at once to check for messages. Akiko had remonstrated with him, reminding him of what his doctor had said. Or was alleged to have said? She had watched him carefully, in case he should need help, and though he walked more slowly than usual, and looked pale and tired, he was cheerful.

He had installed a live-in housekeeper when he had taken over the convent, and now he looked at his watch. Time for dinner. He sniffed. Good smells were wafting over from the kitchen. He would walk along to the dining room and see if Akiko was there. She had been so quiet on the journey, except for sharp remarks addressed to Parsons. He supposed sooner or later he would have to tell her about Parsons and his ruthless hold over him. Years and years he had suffered from what could only be called blackmail. It had become a way of life, and so far Parsons had kept his side of the bargain. A relationship of mutual respect had developed between the two men. One day he would explain the bargain to Akiko, and hope she would understand. His relationship with his daughter was by far the most important thing in his life.

A thought struck him, as he entered the dining room and saw Akiko waiting for him, sitting quietly reading a magazine. If he could persuade her to return to Japan with him, he would organise some quiet removal of Parsons, which he could justify by saying he did not need him once they were back home. He knew that she would be immensely pleased. And once he was rid of the man, permanently rid of him, Akiko need never know his dark secret.

Retirement had begun to seem a desirable option. He tired more easily now, and although for his own purpose he had exaggerated the severity of his recent illness, he did genuinely feel the need of a more restful life. A peaceful retirement, with his daughter to keep him company back at home.

"Ah, there you are," he said merrily. "All well? Parsons has reminded me about the stolen cello, and I have made some enquiries already about a replacement for you. I shall look forward to a private recital for one old man!"

Akiko did not answer for a minute or two, and then said, "Tomorrow, Papa, I must go back to my own flat and continue my career. I shall naturally keep in close touch with you whilst you are in London. Peace and quiet, the doctor said, and I know you will find that difficult. But you must be sensible. I presume the faithful Parsons will be at your beck and call, and you will be able to contact me at any time."

"Tomorrow is another day, my darling," said Nakamasa. "Now let us eat our delicious dinner."

And tomorrow, Akiko said to herself, I shall be in touch with Jamie again, and we can be together.

SEVENTEEN

❧

PARSONS RETURNED TO HIS UNCOMFORTABLE FLAT IN Bayswater, having been given a sizeable handout from Nakamasa for the safe completion of his duties. He had had plenty of time to think about his master plan for making a great deal more money, before Nakamasa gave him the push.

He had a strong feeling that Miss Akiko would finally persuade her father to get rid of him, now that his usefulness was waning. He knew from years of experience how Nakamasa's daughter had become the old man's overriding concern, bordering on obsession. Because of a lifelong need for control, and also a deep love for a child who had grown so like her tragic mother, Nakamasa had made sure of monitoring almost all her waking hours. Until, that is, she left Japan to study in London. Parsons had been a vital tool in those earlier years, and as a result had found Nakamasa an easy victim for blackmail, based on what he knew about him.

Now, opening up his damp and dingy quarters, chosen because of its anonymity, safe from prying eyes and unwelcome callers, he unpacked his meagre shopping and took out a sandwich. He put the kettle on the gas ring that served his cooking needs, and sat down to finalise his plan. He made a strong cup of tea in a cracked mug, and stirred in three spoonfuls of sugar. One day soon, he told himself, I shall have a comfortable home and, with luck, a family of my own.

And now to the plan. He listed in his head three easy steps to becoming a millionaire.

One, make a final demand, a lifetime promise never to divulge what he knew and never to ask for more. But would Nakky trust him to keep his promise?

A fresh thought struck him. Why bother with the old threat? It was wearing a bit thin. In a world drowning in information technology, it was unlikely that Akiko would still know nothing about the history of the prisoner-of-war camps in Burma.

Two, he could simply abduct her. No problem there. He'd done it before. Then a straight person-to-person demand to Nakky, with a threat to eliminate his daughter if he didn't pay up. But he knew the answer to that one. In seconds, before he could move three paces, Nakamasa, in order to save her life, would act swiftly. Every morning, the first thing he put in his pocket was a small but deadly gun. His faithful servant wouldn't stand a chance. Then, with all his resources and the aid of the police, Nakky would find Akiko in no time.

Three, keep the blackmail anonymous. He would get untraceable messages to Nakamasa saying that unless he paid up a million pounds, his daughter would be eliminated. Nakky's first move would be to enlist Parsons's help to find the blackmailer. This he would pretend to do, meanwhile playing him along. At the right time he would name a safe collection point.

Then, with money in the bag, he could release Akiko, and run, fast and far, forever. Foolproof!

He looked at his watch. Time for a pint, and a swift game of cards with some innocent punter in the pub. Then tomorrow, all systems go!

IN MEADE HOUSE, LOIS AND DEREK WERE PREPARING FOR BED, and as often happened, launched on a discussion safe from interruption by Gran.

"Well, I'm very worried about him," said Lois. "You know our Jamie, he was always very stubborn. Pleasant about it, but whatever advice we gave him, he did exactly as he'd meant to do all along."

Derek nodded. Lois and Jamie had always been especially close, and he trusted her to get it right. Lois had suggested they consult, and after listening, he said, "I'm sure you're right, me duck, but he's a grown man. He doesn't want his mother rushing about after him. I know you won't agree, but it sounds to me like a job for the police. And is it really any of our business? The girl is obviously having a bit of a breakdown, and we'd do well to stay out of it. Leave it to Jamie. He'll calm down, and realise his abduction idea is a load of rubbish."

"You could be right, I suppose. And that's why I am going up to talk to him face-to-face, and then leave it alone. I'll not be rushing about. I shall be cool as a cucumber."

"So much for consultation," said Derek sadly. "I might as well go and eat worms. I think you are being absolutely

ridiculous, duckie. You're usually the one with good common
sense, and here you are, behaving like a neurotic teenager."

That did it. Lois was silent for a few minutes, then went
over to Derek and put her arms around his neck. "I love you,
Derek Meade," she said. "And you're quite right. You know I
hate to admit being in the wrong, but this time I own up. I'll
stay at home and have a good talk to Cowgill. After all, he's
family now."

Next morning, Mrs. T-J was preparing to catch a train to
London. Jamie's odd request about relaying messages to his
mother had puzzled her. Something more behind it? She
had decided impulsively to go up to see Robert and family,
and arrange a meeting with Jamie before she came home.
She had every right, she told herself, as a member of the ferretin' team.

Now, this morning, she was not so sure. She had not slept
well, revolving in her mind various approaches she should
take with Jamie. Perhaps better not to go at all? But waking
early, she decided it was too late to change her plans. Robert
would be expecting her, so she might as well go. They had
all been pleased to hear she was coming and Robert's voice
had grown noticeably warmer when she had replied that she
would be going back to Farnden the same evening.

Once on the train, travelling first class as always, she
began to feel the excitement of a journey out of the village.
Before her husband died, they had travelled widely, spending
weeks at a time in faraway places. He had retired early, and
spent a great deal of time managing the hall estate, which he
loved. She had filled her own time being a magistrate, chair
of the Bench and in the family courts. But they had both

made sure of good holidays, and train journeys were the ones Mrs. T-J liked best.

She thought back over countries they had visited, and soon her eyelids drooped and she fell into a light doze, dreaming she was once again in the California Zephyr club car, cocktail in hand, and gazing with wonder at the beauty of the Feather River valley, the Utah desert and a procession of changing landscapes.

"We are now approaching Euston station," said the anonymous voice, loud in her ear, and she woke feeling refreshed and looking forward to the day.

As she queued up to leave the train, she thought perhaps it would be best to ring Jamie more or less straightaway, and ask when she could call to have a little chat. She had intended to take him by surprise, but now reconsidered. After all, she might turn up later this afternoon and not find him at home. Then her journey would have been wasted. She stepped out on to the platform, found her mobile and dialled his number.

Jamie was at home, still in his pyjamas and ready to take a shower. "Hello? Oh yes, Mrs. Tollervey-Jones? You're going to be in London? Well, really, there is nothing more to tell you at present. But, of course, you are always welcome to come and have a coffee before you catch the train home."

How was your journey, Mother?" Robert said, as Mrs. T-J arrived. He was looking well, she thought. Business must be good. Always plenty of criminals to defend, she supposed. Well, perhaps he would give her some tips on how to proceed in their efforts to save Akiko Nakamasa.

The day passed pleasantly enough. She was shown photographs of the family's recent holiday in the Faroe Islands, mostly shots of the girls against a background of black basalt humps in the sea. Around four o'clock, as they were having tea, Felicity looked at her watch and said they must not leave too late to get to the station. Of course, she insisted, they had plenty of room for Grannie to stay overnight. But if she had made other plans?

"I should like to catch the five o'clock back to Farnden if possible," Mrs. T-J said firmly.

"Then I shall certainly run you to the station. We don't want you held up the underground!" Robert said.

"Absolutely!" said Felicity, and she hushed the girls when they interrupted with urgent pleas to their grandmother to stay.

Mrs. T-J got to her feet and proposed leaving. She had had a good day, she said cheerfully, but there were things she had to do. She climbed into Robert's car and waved goodbye. Then, as the car purred along, she wondered if she should have taken the tube? Robert might insist on putting her on the train to Tresham. When they reached the queue of cars outside Euston, she said quickly that she would alight right here and he could drive on home. She was getting old, she reflected sadly. Always changing my mind, being unsure what to do next. Definitely symptoms of old age.

"What a pleasant flat, Jamie! And a lovely view right over London. You must be doing well with your concerts?"

He assured her that his diary was comfortably full, but Akiko's disappearance had meant that he had had to cancel one or two bookings. The conversation limped along, until Mrs. T-J said, "Now, Jamie, your message was a little mysterious, my dear, as you must admit, and I have popped in to clear things up."

Jamie's offers of tea, coffee, or a small sherry, were all refused, and he collapsed into an armchair. He truly had nothing more to say to the old duck, and regretted his previous impulse to ask her for help.

"Under what circumstances," she continued, "could you possibly need to telephone me instead of your mother, or, come to that, if it is an urgent matter concerning Akiko, get hold of Inspector Cowgill. He is the most efficient policeman, you know. I have known him for many years, from my work on the Bench. And then, your family all have mobile phones in their pockets wherever they are, haven't they? But Mother first, is my advice."

What he really meant was obvious to Mrs. T-J. He might need his mother to be informed, but he did not wish to listen to her reply.

"Of course," he said. "Mobiles are a boon and a blessing to men. But there is always a time when some are switched off and others run out of juice, and I would love to think of you as backstop, if it is not too much trouble."

"Ridiculous, my dear," she said magisterially. "Either get on with it, and risk the consequences, or if you need help, ring your mother or Inspector Cowgill."

With a feeling of having been let off the hook, Jamie got up and walked to the window. "I honestly believe," he said, "that Akiko is out there somewhere, held against her will. And I shall find her, you can be sure of that."

"You might, and then again, you might not. It is for you to decide how much to be involved. It only remains for me to tell you to be cautious and sensible. Perhaps you would think of doing that before you rush in, all guns blazing? Anyway, I shall say goodbye now, and be on my way."

Jamie shook her hand. "Safe journey, Mrs. Tollervey-Jones," he said. "I'm grateful for your advice, but I must find her as soon as possible."

Stubborn, just like his mother, thought Mrs. T-J.

EIGHTEEN

༂

THE ATMOSPHERE AT THIS SPECIAL MEETING OF NEW Brooms was unusually sombre. Sheila Stratford, Floss Cullen, Dot Nimmo, Paula Hickson and Andrew Young had arrived on time, and at once realised that Lois was not in a happy mood. The team had been with her long enough to know the signs. No smiles, no pauses for a short gossip while they drank their morning coffee. Business only. Their rotas were gone through at top speed, and the general impression was that Lois was anxious to end the meeting as soon as possible. She had explained that she might not be available on Monday, and thanked them abstractedly for turning up on a Saturday.

Hazel Thornbull, who managed the New Brooms office in Tresham, arrived fifteen minutes late, and was treated to a glassy stare from Lois. Her apology seemed not to register with the boss, and she sat down quietly, listening to the others' contributions.

Finally, a long silence was broken by Dot Nimmo, the most cocksure of the lot, who said in a loud voice, "Right. Now, Mrs. M, time to tell us what's up. You never know, we might be able to help."

The rest held their breath, waiting for an angry outburst from Lois. Instead, she slumped in her chair and sighed heavily.

Floss was first on her feet. She went over to Lois and patted her shoulder. "Come on, Mrs. M. Take your time, and don't worry about Dot. You know what she is. She means well. If we can help, you know we will."

Sheila, an older woman, said that perhaps Lois would like her mother to come in? Lois sat up straight, rubbed at her eyes and cleared her throat.

"For God's sake, no!" she said. "Home truths from my mum are the last thing I need. Sorry everyone. I will just explain a bit."

In a few short sentences, Lois explained that she had heard from Jamie saying he had at last received a short message from Akiko. Her voice had been strained, and although she insisted she was fine, she would not be able to see him for a while. "He's convinced that she's locked up somewhere," she added.

"And I suppose Jamie's determined to find her? Is that what you're thinking, Mrs. M? Jamie getting out of his depth and in danger? I suppose the fuzz aren't on to it?" asked Dot. From a lifetime of encounters between her gangland husband and the police, she had no great faith in either criminal or cop.

Lois did not answer. She thanked the team for their support, and sent them away in a very worried frame of mind.

*   *   *

"NEVER MIND ABOUT DOT NIMMO," DEREK SAID AT LUNCHTIME. "You knew what kind of a person she is when you first took her on. I want to know what news there's been from Jamie. How did he sound, and have there been any developments?"

"He was all right, but jumpy," Lois replied. "Naturally enough, considering how worried he obviously was. He wouldn't tell me much. When he got the last message from her, he hardly recognised her voice, she was so stressed. He still thinks the most important thing for him is to find her, and I didn't get much further with telling him it was madness to try and tackle it on his own. Everybody has bad patches, I tried to tell him. Give her time, I said."

Gran had kept quiet for as long as she was able, but now burst forth. "Why doesn't he go to the police?" she shouted. "We've got a policeman in the family now, and Lois's admirer is a top cop. Isn't that enough? For two pins I'd go to Tresham myself and demand to see Cowgill. I shall tell him everything."

"No need for that, Mum," Lois said. "I have already made an appointment to see Inspector Cowgill. He'll be here late this afternoon."

"But what will you tell him?" said Derek. "Everything? Or are you going to tell him not very much, and carry on ferretin'?"

"I shall keep him informed," said Lois sniffily. "So, can we get on with our work now?"

"I'll say n'more," Derek answered. "But just promise me you won't go getting yourself mixed up with violent criminals. Leave it to them that know how to deal with it. Promise?"

Lois said that she would do her very best not to get mixed up with criminals of any kind. "I have quite enough to do keeping my clients and my girls happy," she said. "There's this complaint from a client about Dot Nimmo that I have to deal with. And don't look like that, Mum. I've told no fibs, nor shall I tell any. You can be satisfied with that."

There were indeed no lies in Lois's report, but she was expert at adjusting the truth. If pursuing her ferretin' saved her youngest son from harm, she would not hesitate to do it.

IN LONDON, JAMIE HAD HARDLY SLEPT, AND THIS MORNING decided to make a start by going down to the Wilmore Hall. That was where Akiko was last seen by him, and there were one or two people there who might help in his efforts to trace her. She had been particularly friendly with one of the women who acted as chair shifters on stage.

He remembered the woman well. She was tall and blonde, what his Gran would have called "bottle blonde," and no longer young. She had obviously taken to Akiko, and said frequently that the foreign girl needed taking care of. More care than most performers, she had confided to Jamie. "She looks scared most of the time," she had said. But the woman had left, given in her notice, and the manager had no forwarding address.

Disappointed, Jamie got himself a sandwich and coffee and took them to a seat in the corner of the restaurant, where he could observe the comings and goings. He had brought the *BBC Music Magazine* with him, so that he could eavesdrop whilst pretending to read.

"Jamie Meade! What are you doing here?"

Jamie looked up and saw a familiar face. "Inspector Cowgill! I could say the same to you. Are you here for the afternoon concert, or on duty?"

"The latter," said the inspector. "But seeing you is a bonus. I have to get back to Farnden by four, to keep an appointment with your mother. I've other business in London, but thought I'd take the opportunity of doing a spot of investigating backstage. Our missing persons people are on the job, of course, but I am pursuing the stolen cello at the moment. My belief is that Akiko has taken off somewhere to get away from questions and pressures. That cello was probably like a child to her. Such an important piece of her life, you know. If we can get it back, it would mean everything to her. I'd give her time, if I were you. This is an odd place, isn't it? All corners and cupboards and stairs."

Jamie nodded. "You're right. But it's an important venue. I have had to cancel another performing date, unfortunately."

"Perhaps that is just what Akiko needs," Cowgill said gently. "Time to recover. I must be away now. Meeting your mother at four for a conference, which should be productive. Keep in touch."

"Um, yes," Jamie said noncommittally. "Mum's always keen to help."

"I have great faith in your mother," Cowgill said seriously. "She has a gift for what your father calls ferretin', and most times she knows when it is time to bring in the police."

After the inspector had gone, Jamie thought about what he had said. He had been at pains to give the impression that he did not regard the Japanese girl's absence as a first priority. No doubt he would persuade Mum to take the same view.

NINETEEN

꧂

Cowgill rang the bell at Meade House just after four o'clock, and, as he expected, Gran opened the door.

"Good afternoon, Inspector. Does my daughter know you're coming? She doesn't tell me anything, as you know."

Cowgill smiled his cool smile, and said that Lois was expecting him. At this point, Lois appeared.

"Thanks, Mum. You can get on now. I'll take the inspector into my office."

Gran scowled. "Dismissed, eh? Well, I suppose you won't mind if I bring in a tray of tea?"

"That would be very nice," Cowgill said, warming up. "I have had a tiring journey coming down from London. Leaves on the line, or some such ridiculous excuse."

Lois said nothing until they were safely settled in her office, Gran had brought in tea and was back in her kitchen.

Cowgill looked at Lois's frowning face, and opened the conversation.

"So here I am, Lois. Sorry I'm a little late, but it is good to see you again, and looking as lovely as ever, if I may say so."

"You can say what you like. But I'm in no mood for compliments. I asked you to come because I think Jamie may be acting foolishly in trying to find Akiko. He is convinced she is being held somewhere against her will, and means to find her."

Cowgill nodded wisely. "As it happens, I met him in London this morning. Extraordinary. Bumped into him at the Wilmore Hall. He seemed in reasonable spirits, considering. Told me nothing. But you can tell me more."

Lois took a deep breath and, comforted a little by the thought of Cowgill being on the job, began. "I am worried that her family might be involved in all of this. Jamie has said that her father dotes on her, and he may well be suspicious of her falling for an Englishman. Do you think that may be so?"

"Could be, my dear. But doting fathers are not confined to Japan. I remember feeling very worried about my own daughter marrying a struggling artist, but they're doing fine. Not all of us have the good fortune to welcome a policeman son-in-law into the family!"

"Okay, okay! I know we're lucky with Matthew. But returning to Akiko, she has disappeared for some reason, and Jamie is convinced that it was not her own idea."

"Right, Lois dear. I must say that I got that impression from him. We have two courses of action. First, we must advise Jamie not to try to contact Akiko's father. He could well spread unnecessary concern there. If he does get a lead on where she might be, and in danger, he is to contact me. As I said to Jamie this morning, we have to remember that she may well be missing in the sense that she does not *want* to be found. Many of our so-called missing persons have vanished deliberately for a variety of good reasons. Naturally we shall keep our ears open, but at the moment we have no real evidence that she is in trouble."

"Yeah, well. She's Japanese, isn't she?"

"What difference does that make?"

"Think back, Cowgill. You must be old enough to remember. Burmese prison camps? Japs defeated? Honour needing to be defended? All of that?"

"I haven't forgotten," he answered sharply. "And old grudges are passed down from generation to generation, I know that. Has Jamie ever mentioned Akiko's family being connected to wartime prisoner-of-war camps? Maybe grandparents, or other members of her family?"

"Just once. And then it was a passing reference. She had mentioned something, but he hadn't really registered what she meant. I am afraid we still know very little about her. But if this is what it's all about, we have to consider it, I suppose."

"I am considering it, but there is no need to spread alarm unnecessarily. We shall pursue the subject discreetly, I can assure you. Meanwhile, you must try to find out exactly what Jamie intends to do, and make sure he is not acting foolishly."

"Easier said than done," said Lois gloomily.

A knock at the door produced Gran to collect the tea things. "Still chewing things over?" she said. "It's my opinion that we should leave it to you, Inspector Cowgill. I have always had absolute confidence in the police. When I lost my cat, years ago, they found it for me in a couple of days. You should be able to find a foreign girl cellist without too much trouble. Then we can all get on with things, and stop footling about with other people's lives."

Inspector Cowgill smothered a smile. He could see Lois was boiling, and attempted to intervene. "Thank you for your vote of confidence, Mrs. Weedon," he said. "You can rest assured we have matters in hand. I am sure things will be sorted out very soon."

"Here, Mum, take this and leave us in peace." Lois thrust the tray at her mother and all but pushed her out of the room.

"God, as if I haven't got enough trouble, without a mother with loopy opinions under my feet the whole time. Sorry about that, Cowgill."

"Not so loopy, my dear," he said mildly.

TWENTY

❧

THE CONVENT OF ST. IGNATIUS AND ALL ANGELS HAD BEEN built around a courtyard, well protected by huge double doors that screened the nuns from the main road outside. At all four corners of the building there were Gothic-looking towers, three used for storage and one originally as a retreat, accommodating a single nun who needed to be by herself for a given period of time. When Nakamasa moved in, he had been told that it was haunted by a suicidal nun who had starved herself to death there, and being a superstitious man, he had ordered that it be kept permanently locked.

Ezekiel Parsons had long been familiar with this story, and decided it would be the perfect place for his prisoner. He was always in and out of the offices on Nakamasa's business, and nobody would even notice his presence as he went to and fro. It had been simplicity itself for him to steal the key, have it duplicated and returned, and the new one slipped on to his bunch of usefully copied keys.

When he had opened up the tower cell to check on its contents, he found only two hard chairs and a narrow iron-framed bed. He remembered Nakamasa ordering the builders not to disturb the spirit of the starving nun, but to leave it exactly as they found it. The perfect place, then.

Late in the quiet Sunday night, he had brought in a struggling Akiko, a gag over her mouth, and locked her in with an assurance that if she behaved herself, no harm would come to her. Then, padding softly along to Nakamasa's office, he had placed on his desk a ready-written note, his handwriting heavily disguised, demanding a ransom of one million pounds for the return of his daughter. Instructions where to leave the money would follow.

It had all been so easy, Ezekiel Parsons had congratulated himself. Safely back in his own bed-sitter, he had waited for his mobile phone to ring.

AT EIGHT O'CLOCK IN THE MORNING NAKAMASA HAD CALLED, swearing and cursing, blaming Ezekiel for not keeping an eye on his wayward daughter, and saying she had left the building. "Gone to that Meade and run away with him!" he had shouted. "Stupid blackmail demand to put me off the scent!"

Ezekiel was to present himself at the convent immediately and receive instructions.

The day had gone by without sight of the truant, and despite the ransom demand on his desk, Nakamasa had now convinced himself that she had run away to join her lover. He had decided that the notes were part of an amateurish diversionary plan, and had screwed them up in a fury and thrown them into the bin.

"I should have seen it coming!" he had screamed. "Wretched

Meade is not content with stealing my daughter! He wants my
fortune as well!"

Ezekiel had been sent for again and instructed to pursue
every possible option for retrieving her. He had had to invent
places where she might have gone, lie about investigating
these, and report back that he had found no trace. Nor had he
any news of Jamie Meade, he had confessed apologetically.

Later that night Parsons had taken in a stale bread roll
and bottle of milk for Akiko, but she would eat nothing,
though she was awake. She had turned away from him, not
speaking. She had not bothered to get up from the bed and
he was worried. He had reckoned on Nakamasa's quick
agreement to the demand. After all, one million pounds
was peanuts to him. But now the old man was reacting in a
completely unexpected way, discounting random abduction
and fixing venomously on Meade as the guilty party.

Parsons supposed he could keep up the demand notes,
making them more and more threatening, but how long
was it going to take? He had no stomach for allowing his
prisoner to die! Not only was he squeamish, but there would
be nothing in it for him.

Still, no need to be so ridiculously melodramatic, he told
himself. I can play a waiting game as well as the next man,
providing I can persuade Miss Akiko to buck up and eat
some grub. He realised the food he had given her so far was,
to say the least, unappetising, and he planned to buy something more tasty. Perhaps that would cheer her up. If chal-
lenged, he could always say it was for himself.

Jamie, meanwhile, was also anxious to get things moving. Digesting Cowgill's advice in the Wilmore restaurant,
he reckoned giving Akiko more time was all very well, but
it did not mean that he had to do nothing. Surely he could

pass the time with some preliminary searching around? He doubted very much that he was being followed. There would be no need for that, if Cowgill was right in advising him that Akiko was secretly recharging her batteries somewhere else, known only to her and her father. Knowing how much she cared for her father, he was sure she would have kept him informed. Perhaps he could approach Nakamasa? But Cowgill had cautioned strongly against that.

A little surreptitious research? That could do no harm. He knew that Akiko's father had London offices in the former convent of St. Ignatius, or a name similar, and he had surfed around until he had found it. He could work out ways and means of getting inside the building in a bona fide role. As a tourist, maybe? Nobody would recognise him. Once inside, he reckoned if he kept his ears open, and casually mentioned Akiko's name, it shouldn't be too difficult to pick up some clues as to where she might have gone. Then he could retreat and decide what to do next.

Tomorrow, then, he would be up with the lark and make an early start. Feeling much better, Jamie retired to bed and went straight to sleep.

BRIGHT AND EARLY NEXT DAY, LOIS'S PHONE RANG. "LOIS, MY dear! How are you this fine morning?" Cowgill sounded irritatingly jolly.

Lois groaned. "Oh no, not the golf club captain again."

"I cannot think what you mean. It *is* a fine morning, and you *are* very dear to me."

"Hunter Cowgill! That is quite enough. What do you want?"

"Just to tell you that we've had another report of an instrument theft, a violin this time, and are following it up. The more we know about this one, the more likely it is that Akiko's cello will be traced."

"Bully for you!" said Lois. "I don't know where the police would be without a brilliant brain like yours. I'm sure the whole case will be mopped up by teatime. Hope you win. At golf, of course. Bye-ee!"

OH, FOR HOME SWEET HOME! JAMIE WAS FEELING HOMESICK. How tempting it would be to relax in the bosom of his family and forget all about stolen cellos and Akiko Nakamasa herself! But then her gentle face rose up before him, and he knew he could not desert her, unless it was proved to him that she really did want to be left alone.

His father had rung and this in itself proved to Jamie how worried they must be. It was almost always Mum on the phone. After some preliminaries, he asked, "How's Gran?"

"No improvement," his father had said, and they both laughed and assured each other that everything was fine and promised to keep in touch.

"SO WHAT DID HE SAY?" LOIS ASKED.

"Not a lot," Derek said. "Asked after you, Gran," he added, smiling at his mother-in-law.

"He's a good boy," said Gran. "I've always said he is a good boy. Not one to let other people do the dirty work. Has that ever occurred to you, Lois? As long as you go on interfering with other people's lives, your family are always at risk of being hurt."

"It wasn't me that got Jamie involved with Akiko!" Lois

said defensively. "He did that on a professional basis, all by himself. I don't see how you can blame me for that."

"It's no good going all round the houses and thinking you'll get round me," said Gran, her colour high. "I don't know where we went wrong in your upbringing, but you're nothing like either me or your dad! And you can take that smile off your face, Derek Meade. If you were any way half good as a husband, you'd've given her a smack bottom long before this!"

Lois looked at Derek's horrified face and began to laugh. "I might enjoy that," she said in a whisper to him.

"And I heard that!" Gran continued, sitting down heavily at the table. "I don't know I'm sure, what to do for the best."

"All you usually do," said Derek, reaching out a hand to pat her arm. "We'd be nowhere without you. It's just too late to change people, once they're past a certain age. But we do take notice of what you say, and maybe act on it afterwards, when nobody notices. Come on, my duck, drink up your tea and we'll stack the dishes, won't we, Lois?"

"Natch," she replied. It was a slang word she had caught from Josie, and found it really useful.

"Oh well. I've had my say," Gran muttered. "Might as well do a bit of ironing. It doesn't do itself you know."

Derek put his elbows on the table and covered his eyes. "Heaven preserve me from the gentler sex," he said.

TWENTY-ONE

COWGILL WAS STANDING ON THE DOORSTEP OF MEADE House, wondering if it was a mistake to call unannounced. When Lois answered the door, he smiled fondly at her.

"Sorry to be a pest, my dear," he said. "I was passing, and as I had one or two more questions to ask, I decided to stop off and hope to catch you at home. Can you spare a few minutes? Is Derek here? It would be useful to have him in with us, if you don't mind."

"And me," said Gran, coming up behind Lois. "I'm an indispensable part of this household, you know, Inspector."

He laughed. "And you, of course, Mrs. Weedon, if you can tear yourself away from your kitchen."

"In other words," said Gran, pursing her lips, "you'd like a cup of tea. Well, I can manage that, so come on in and sit yourself down."

Derek appeared then, and frowned. "Wouldn't it wait

until tomorrow, Inspector?" he said. "We have had a busy day today, arguing and disagreeing over the Jamie and Akiko nonsense. Very tiring. Still, you'd better come in and get it over with."

"Hard work, isn't it," Cowgill answered sympathetically, "keeping all the members of your family happy."

"Most of the time it's a waste of time trying," Lois said. "Anyway, sit down. When Mum's brought in tea, we'll ask her to sit in with us. She means well, you know. Meantime, how's Matthew getting on, now he's a married man?"

"Exactly the same. He is a very competent young police officer, and if anything, more dedicated than ever. Your Josie is a lovely girl, and has her head screwed on right. Takes after her mother."

"They do seem to make a good team. I expect she's told him all about the missing cello and cellist. Nothing escapes my Josie. And being in the shop all day, she hears a lot of local gossip. But this is something different. Not much to do with locals, I reckon. Except for one new local, possibly."

The door opened and Gran came in with a tray.

"Please join us, Mrs. Weedon," said Cowgill politely, and Gran replied that as far as she could see, they weren't coming apart. None of them laughed, and she sat bolt upright on a hard chair and folded her arms.

Lois said that they should cut the cackle and concentrate on talking about Akiko Nakamasa, her cello and what had happened to both. If they exchanged what they knew up to date, then something new might emerge.

"I'll begin, shall I?" said Cowgill.

"Okay," said Lois, "but try not to tell us what we know already. There's a telly programme I want to watch soon."

Cowgill nodded. "So shall I begin? Just a quick summing

up first. Always useful, even if we know it all already. So, I heard about the case from you, Lois. A valuable cello had gone missing from a car parked in the driveway of Meade House. It belonged to Akiko Nakamasa, who has disappeared and not been traced, so far. She played regularly with Jamie Meade, pianist, and they had performed many concerts together. Almost the last time she was seen was at the Wilmore Hall in London, when I saw her backstage talking to a strange man. There was subsequently an unconfirmed sighting of her by one of my men the same evening. We have put into place the usual procedures, but have not as yet found either the cello or the cellist."

He came to a halt, and looked at Lois. "Anything to add? Something about the one new local person talked about in the shop?" asked Cowgill.

Still no slouch, thought Lois. Even if he is semiretired. "It doesn't sound much, but it is the only unusual thing that has happened around Farnden since this whole thing started. It's the new gamekeeper at the hall."

She described her encounter with him and said she had mentioned him to Melanie Norrington. "Neither she nor Geoff seem very sure of him. He apparently applied for the job about three weeks ago, and was taken on. On probation for a couple of months, says Geoff. Although already he seems to come and go as he chooses."

"But what might this have to do with Akiko?"

"Maybe nothing, but as I'm sure you know, Cowgill, anything out of the ordinary in villages is worth noting. He was weird and went on about *Lady Chatterley's Lover*. Then sort of warned me off when he thought I was trespassing. Jemima was growling and he seemed scared of her. Not much like a gamekeeper!"

"Quite right," said Cowgill. "We'll make a policeman out of you yet. But I can put your minds at rest about the gamekeeper. We know all about him. Foster, his name is. Slippery customer, but not dangerous. Destructive thieving is his thing. Let's hope he's learnt his lesson and is a reformed character. Now, the reason I called in is to see if there is anything new from Jamie about what he intends to do. Am I right to think that in spite of good advice, he is not willing to do nothing about Akiko for the moment?"

Lois nodded. "I reckon you're right there. That's the impression we've been getting, haven't we, Derek. And no, we've heard nothing more about his intentions."

Cowgill frowned. "I am anxious to know if he has tried to get in touch with Akiko's father. I have told him, maybe more than once, that this would be a mistake. The old man has had a heart attack, apparently, and should be taking things easy."

"How do you know that?" said Lois sharply. "Have you spoken to him?"

"No, but we have a contact who works in his office. I am reliably informed that he worships the ground Akiko walks on, and would never dream of allowing any harm to come to her. At the same time, he would not hesitate to take action if he thought she was in danger. All this points to her being safe and her father knowing where she is. But he is unlikely to tell Jamie, as we believe your son is persona non grata as far as Nakamasa is concerned."

"In other words, he don't take to our Jamie?" said Gran. "Well, I must say I don't take to *him*, either. Keeping that girl under his thumb all these years. It doesn't do, you know. They break out eventually."

"Quite right, Mrs. Weedon," Cowgill said. "So you see

my point. Jamie must not try to get in touch with him. I
am sure you can stress this, Lois. Or Derek? He might take
it more seriously coming from you?"

"He listens to both of us," Lois answered huffily, "but
whether he takes any notice is another matter."

"NOT SUCH A BAD CHAP," GRAN ANNOUNCED, AFTER COWGILL
had gone. "Quite a gentleman really. Now, what do you fancy
for supper? Early yet, but I'll cook, and you and Derek can
watch the telly. My quiz show is on later. We do really all
work together very happily, don't we?" she added, and stalked
off, leaving Lois and Derek speechless.

TWENTY-TWO

⤜

E ZEKIEL PARSONS WAS IN A PANIC. AKIKO HAD REFUSED TO eat or drink, and seemed unable to wake up properly whenever he took her food. He realised with dismay that he would be forced to release her if this went on. Nakamasa was still furious, and rejecting all suggestions from Parsons that he should meet the blackmailer's demands. He persisted in his certainty that Akiko had run off to a secret location with James Meade.

Parsons had placed the latest anonymous message, naming the point where the money should be left. He had thought long and hard about this, and in the end named a hollow behind the statue of William Huskisson, who was killed in the first railway accident, commemorated in Pimlico Gardens on the Thames embankment. He had used this hiding place before, and as far as he knew, nobody else had discovered it.

He had been thinking desperately of some way of dealing

with his rapidly declining prisoner. It would be disaster if he had to deliver up a lifeless body to the boss! Then he remembered something Nakamasa had said in his fury. He had blamed "that upstart English pianist," and had cursed and said he was sure that if they found him, they would find Akiko also.

The old man had searched around in his daughter's bedroom and found an address book with Meade's details. "Find him, Parsons," he had said triumphantly, and now Ezekiel could see a possible solution to his problem. He would find Meade and persuade him that Akiko needed to see him, and offer to take him to find her. If Meade fell for it, and he could get him into the nun's cell, then lover boy's presence would surely cheer her up. After that, what? Hand Meade over to Nakky?

He was finding it difficult to think straight. All those years living in comfort at Nakky's expense had softened his brain. More thinking needed, but for now, immediate action was more important. He must keep a watch on Meade's flat, and nab him as soon as possible. It could be a matter of life or death.

IN HIS FLAT, JAMIE DOZED IN AN ARMCHAIR, EXHAUSTED FROM anxiety alternating with optimism, and now was awoken by his telephone ringing.

"Hello? Who is it? Mrs. T-J. Sorry, didn't recognise your voice. How can I help?"

"It's I who can help you. Now, please listen quietly. I have a friend who lives in North London, with an address very near to your flat. Remember I called on you? Well, it seemed familiar at the time, but I could not recall who I knew living in the same postcode area. Then, as often happens, when I was least expecting it, the name came to me. I have telephoned him and asked how near he was to your address. Very near, it transpired. In fact, he lives just around the corner. I explained that I was looking for a Japanese girl who might have been outside your flat some days ago, and he remembered immediately."

"Which day?" Jamie reached across for an apple and began to munch.

"The right one. Now, if I may continue? He said he was about to cross the road and ask if he could help. She looked very upset, he said. A policeman appeared and began to talk to her, and then she suddenly stood up and with an admirable burst of speed, sprinted to where a car was waiting with the engine running, jumped in and the car drove off. All this happened in less than five minutes, and my friend walked on home. Until I questioned him, he had forgotten it completely."

"And do you think it was Akiko?" said Jamie, already sure it was her, but wanting to humour the old dear. After all, she was going to a lot of trouble on his behalf.

"Unquestionably. Jamie, are you eating something? Frightful noise. Anyway, you will know what to do next. I shall keep looking out for clues," she said enthusiastically. "I think your mother is finding my contributions quite helpful, you know."

"Um, yes. Thanks a lot. Really interesting and useful." Jamie looked at his watch. He was still hungry, and got up to look in the fridge. "I do appreciate all you're doing on my behalf, Mrs. T-J," he said.

TWENTY-THREE

F EELING IN NEED OF FRESH AIR, LOIS HAD ASSURED GRAN she would be back in time for supper, and set off to see Josie. They could sit in her garden and have a chat about this and that. It would make a much-needed break from Gran's endless advice on what should be done about Jamie.

Now she was admiring all the latest additions to Josie's new home, and was amused to see her daughter, previously a very casual housekeeper, now a house-proud wife. There were fresh flowers carefully arranged for the small sitting room, and pleasant prints had been hung in the tiny hall. Josie and Matthew had taken to hunting around antique fairs at the weekend, and had found several nice pieces of Royal Worcester porcelain.

"I suppose you've never spotted a valuable cello on your bargain hunts?" Lois said, gratefully downing a large gin and tonic.

Josie shook her head. "You don't see many musical instruments at the kind of events we go to. Car boot sales, charity auctions, that kind of thing. Cellos would be in specialist fairs, I expect. Anyway, I wouldn't know a cello from a banjo! Do you really think it'll turn up?"

"Who knows? I suppose it might. But sometimes things are stolen to order, and it's more likely to appear at a recital, being played by an up-and-coming musician with money to spend."

"Well, we can still go on looking. You never know. And, by the way, Mum, I've been thinking about that gamekeeper. I reckon he's a red herring as far as we're concerned."

Lois laughed, and said Cowgill obviously thought that he was. "But I've always reckoned that in villages, anything out of kilter is worth looking at, and he's certainly out of the usual run of gamekeepers. Of course, the Norringtons wouldn't have a clue what to look for. They should have asked Derek to give him the once-over. Mind you, we've got enough to worry about, without dodgy gamekeepers on our patch."

"Poor Mum! Your ferretin' has landed you on your own doorstep, hasn't it. What's new with Jamie?"

"Nothing much. Just the odd call to say he was all right, and getting back to practising ready for a solo concert. I tried to find out if he was planning anything stupid, like bearding the giant Nakamasa in his den. But you know how stubborn Jamie can be. He sidestepped most of my questions, and said that he was sure Akiko would return, singing and dancing, and with a perfectly good explanation for her absence. I didn't believe him for one minute, but I think he was trying to shut me up."

"He's an idiot in some ways. Always was a bit of a mother's boy."

"Josie! You know that's not true. I admit I worried about him when he was trying to get started as a professional pianist. But he's made his way by himself. You have to give him that. Anyway, he said not to worry. Some hopes!"

"Oh dear," said Josie. "*Should* we be worried, Mum?"

"I never stop, about any of you," said Lois. "You'll find out one day. When you have kids you'll find out worrying don't end when they're grown up. Well, thanks for the drink, love. I must be getting back, else Gran will accuse me of slacking. It's been very nice, Josie, and I'm glad you and Matthew are so happy."

MELANIE NORRINGTON WAS WORKING LATE IN THE CHAPEL shop, totting up her accounts. It had been a good day, with plenty of visitors. Although she had reservations about opening all week, she was still feeling her way to running a business and never knew when an idle shopper might come in for a look around. Any day could be good, especially when they had an event in the park. She was still tidying up and counting up the takings when a call came in from Geoff.

"Hi, Mel," he said. "Forgot to tell you this morning. The gamekeeper has imported a woman. Introduced herself as Diana. I went round to his cottage to tell him arrangements for next weekend, and there she was. No sign of him. She said he would be back, but they were both going away for a day or so. Not so much as a by-your-leave!"

"Thank God for that," muttered Melanie. "Good riddance, say I. I didn't take to that Foster at all. You can tell him not to bother to come back. Was the woman his wife? I don't think he mentioned that at interview?"

"Did you say something, Mrs. Norrington?" asked Dot Nimmo, popping up from cleaning behind the shelves. She had insisted on doing overtime to finish sorting out the vestry.

"No, Dot. Just a piece of good news from Geoff. Makes a change, I can tell you!"

"I don't mean to be nosey, but do I gather that the handsome gamekeeper has got a fancy woman installed?" Dot was incurably nosey, but had a knack of getting away with it. Most people ended up liking her a lot, and as a long-service member of the New Brooms team, she considered it her duty to be also on the lookout for snippets of information that might help the boss in her ferretin' activities. Needless to say, she did not approve Mrs. T-J as Lois's new deputy.

Melanie, always glad of someone to talk to, answered that the gamekeeper had indeed gone off without a word to anyone. His fancy woman, Diana, was on the point of following him, she said.

"I should check to see if he's taken anything with him," said Dot wisely. "That sort are very fly. They look around, make a plan and before you can say Jack Robinson, they've disappeared with the best silver."

"Do you really think so? I must say it has occurred to me that when I'm here in the shop, the house is often quite empty. I always mean to lock up, but the chapel is so close, I think I'll know if someone is hanging around. But I wouldn't, would I?"

"No, you wouldn't," said Dot firmly, and began vigorously polishing the top of the counter. "I should go and check now, if I were you. I'll wait while you're gone."

TWENTY-FOUR

❧

W HEN LOIS ARRIVED BACK AT THE HOUSE, GRAN WAS simmering with excitement and spluttered that she had something very important to tell her.

"Not Jamie?" said Lois immediately.

Gran shook her head. "No, no. The lad is fine, as far as I know. No, it was Mrs. Norrington. She rang to say she was talking to Dot Nimmo in the chapel shop, and they got on to the subject of the gamekeeper. Foster, his name is. You know, him what started work at the hall. He's run off, and Dot sent Mrs. Norrington out of the shop to check the silver and her jewellery. You know, Lois, she's got some really good stuff."

"Mum—get to the point. When did she ring?"

"While you were at Josie's. In a dreadful state."

"Did he take the lot?"

"No, worse than that." Gran paused dramatically.

"Mum!"

"Well, when she got back into the house, her eyes met a dreadful scene . . ."

"Mum!" repeated Lois, beginning to smile.

"It's no laughing matter, young woman," said Gran. "The poor thing was distraught when she rang. Not ten minutes ago. If you'd come back on time, you'd have talked to her."

"So what had happened, Mum?"

"The house had been trashed. At least, the kitchen and the dining room. He was obviously looking for silver, but the Norringtons had the sense to keep it hidden safely. But everything had been pulled out of cupboards. All broken pottery and glass. And wine spilt everywhere, mixed up with tomato ketchup and milk. Ugh! I can just imagine it. Enough to unhinge anybody, that was!"

"Sounds like a deliberate mess," Lois said. "Was anything valuable taken?"

"Well, that's the peculiar thing. Nothing she has discovered so far. She's sent for the police, of course, and rang here to see if you or one of the girls could possibly help to clear it all up."

"Certainly will. But first I'll go straight over there and have a look around. Thanks, Mum. I'm sure you gave her good support. She'll need it. This is the second time she's been burgled, remember? The first time was before they moved. And by the way," she added, "did she have any idea who could have done it?"

"Not really, but she did say that on top of all that trouble, their gamekeeper had disappeared, so naturally he is number one suspect."

FOSTER WAS CONGRATULATING HIMSELF ON HIS LUCK. MRS. Norrington had left the house unlocked when she went up to the chapel shop, and he had been in and out in fifteen minutes. Trashing was one of his special skills, and he was particularly proud of this one. It was like an addiction, he had been told by a no-good shrink. At least nobody ever got hurt in his trashing forays. But he usually took the precaution of getting away for a bit until things calmed down.

He had left the hall and made straight for Last Resort House at Waltonby. He was an habitual client and was certain he would be taken in. Fortunately, he knew of certain questionable deals involving musical instruments, part of a lucrative scam worked by the man in charge, Solomon Grundy, who would not have wanted this information made public.

Over the years, ever since his first transgression, when he had trashed his grandmother's magnificent Georgian drawing room in South Kensington, he had returned periodically to the safe house run by the quasi-religious organisation Last Resort. This had originally been set up by a weird character who claimed to be a kind of maharishi, an inspired sage, who took in sad people who were unable to cope out in the big, bad world, and gave them protection and a home. At a price. They handed over all their worldly goods as a nonreturnable deposit, and were seldom able to escape.

The first person he had met there on his initial visit had been Ezekiel Parsons, an older man and already a devious operator. The two had become friends, and had worked a scheme together which enabled them to come and go as they pleased, unlike most of the residents. It had been years now since they had met, though he had heard from Parsons from time to time about his cushy billet with a Japanese tycoon. He was therefore extremely surprised to receive a postcard of Big Ben addressed to him at Last Resort House, suggesting a meeting in London. "Need help," Ezekiel had written enigmatically, and had scribbled the name of a café and a time and day to meet.

TWENTY-FIVE

❧

JAMIE WAS AWAKE EARLY, STRETCHING AND YAWNING AT HIS window, when he saw in the sunlit street a single person loitering outside. An empty house with a high fence and a FOR SALE notice stood on the opposite side of the road, and as he watched, the loiterer vanished into the tangled front garden of the property. Oh dear, thought Jamie, squatters. The area had been a poor one, but was on the up, and the presence of squatters would inevitably lower house prices. Not that Jamie was thinking of moving, though he had begun to feel he had had enough of London. A nice peaceful cottage in the country, like that of his sister, Josie, seemed a better option right now.

He had a quick breakfast and, looking at his kitchen clock, decided that he would walk to the city and St. Ignatius convent. It was a lovely morning, and he would go along the route by the river and up into the city. He felt optimistic about the chances of gleaning some information on the whereabouts of Akiko. He showered and found some clean clothes, pocketed his mobile and opened the door. He stood at the top of the steps for a few moments, staring across the road for signs of more squatters. But all was quiet and still. Soon the rush-hour traffic would be in full flow, but now it was pleasant and cool.

Ezekiel Parsons, concealed behind the fence, watched Jamie set off at a cracking pace. Was lover boy intending to walk far? The long trek from the convent, after he had taken food to Akiko at dawn and she had rejected it, had depressed him. But needs must, and he followed at a suitably distant interval, waiting for an appropriate moment to grab him. But where on earth was the lad going? They were well on their way to the Thames embankment, now busy with people on their way to work. They soon came to Pimlico Gardens, and to Ezekiel's astonishment, Jamie went in, and with his elbows propped up against the river wall, he gazed across the fast-flowing water. Already a number of people about. Ezekiel cursed. He waited for a few minutes, and then Jamie was off again.

The temptation was too much for Ezekiel. He dashed across to William Huskisson's memorial, and to his huge relief, his hand touched a sealed envelope in the hollow. He hurried back to the path, relieved to see Jamie still sauntering along towards Westminster, and he continued to follow. His relief started to ebb when he realised the envelope contained only a small sheet of paper, with one sentence in Nakamasa's handwriting. "Come home, my darling daughter," Ezekiel read. He swore, crumpled up the message and flung it into a rubbish bin. "Same stupid old Nakky," he muttered. He rushed on, determined not to lose sight of Jamie, although crowds were now streaming across the bridges.

*   *   *

THE EMBANKMENT ROAD WAS LOOKING ITS BEST. THE SUN glittered on the Thames, and all the historic buildings along its course seemed to have been cleaned up for the day. Throngs of tourists and office workers were beginning to collect in queues for the commuter boats, and Jamie's spirits rose higher. He turned up away from the river, making for the city.

Finally, when Parsons saw that the convent was just around the corner, he realised Jamie had been doing some constructive thought. Then his quarry stopped outside the large, heavy doors, still shut against intruders, and looked around. Parsons halted in the shadows. This solution to all his problems must be a gift from God! His failure to nobble Meade somewhere out of sight of passersby was no longer important. Lover boy had walked right into a trap.

The smaller entrance door to the offices was ajar, and members of staff were arriving and chatting on the doorstep. Jamie hovered, then approached an attractive girl.

"Excuse me," he said. "Was this once a convent? I'm an architectural student," he explained. "Doing a project on the Victorian Gothic buildings of London."

She stared at him. "That's the best chat-up line I've heard for a long time," she said, laughing, and then took pity on him as he coloured with embarrassment. "Yes, it was a convent years ago. Creepy old place in some parts. You should make an appointment to see Mr. Nakamasa. He's the owner, and is very proud of the improvements he's made. Must go now. Late already!" she said, and disappeared through the door.

Perfect, thought Ezekiel, who had overheard this conversation, and now approached Jamie. "Good morning," he said. "I couldn't help hearing what you said to our Marjorie. I work here for Mr. Nakamasa, and could show you round, if that's what you would like? It is a most interesting old place. Have you noticed the Gothic turrets? Apparently the nuns used to say the pinnacles were like prayers, winging their way to Heaven." Oh, you wicked man, he said to himself, and grinned. Perhaps God was really on his side this morning. Certainly things seemed to be going his way at last.

TWENTY-SIX

❧

"**P**LEASE FOLLOW ME," SAID EZEKIEL PARSONS, SELF-APPOINTED tour guide, and he beckoned Jamie towards the great double gates. A small door cut in one of them was locked, but Parsons fished his bunch of keys from his pocket and they were soon inside the courtyard of the convent.

It was an attractive sight, full of flowers, with a central fountain playing, sparkling in the sunlight. "Mr. Nakamasa has taken a deal of trouble to maintain this place," Ezekiel said proudly. "It makes a very good impression on important clients. He likes to show them around and tell them the history of the convent. The turrets are used as storerooms, except that one over there." He pointed to Akiko's prison. "We keep that to show visitors what it was like originally. Come along with me, please."

This was much more useful than Jamie had hoped, and his eyes darted everywhere. He looked up to the second storey, and thought he saw a bulky figure staring down at them from a beautiful mullioned window. Their eyes met, and then the figure disappeared. Ezekiel had seen it, too, and knew it was Nakamasa. There was no possibility that he would know the visitor was Jamie Meade. His boss had some time ago made it clear he would not attend any concert where his daughter was playing with an Englishman.

Nevertheless, he did not want Nakamasa to see him entering Akiko's turret. "Oh look!" he said, stopping suddenly in the middle of the courtyard. "Isn't that one of those green parrots? They've invaded the whole of the south of England apparently. Noisy beggars, aren't they?"

When he was sure it was safe, Ezekiel continued to the door of the corner turret. "Up we go," he said brightly. When they reached the door of the cell, he turned the key and stood back. "You first, please. You must get the real authentic impact!"

Jamie took a step forward and opened the door slowly, then suddenly he was pushed from behind and the door closed with a bang. He heard the key turn in the lock and an unpleasant laugh from Parsons, who called softly, "See you later." His voice faded as he retreated down the spiral stairs. There he waited until the coast was clear, and then sauntered casually out into the courtyard, locking the turret door behind him. A wrought-iron seat circled the fountain, and he sat down to think.

INSIDE THE HALF-LIGHT OF THE CELL-LIKE ROOM, JAMIE SAT ON the narrow bed, his arms tightly around Akiko, who was sobbing and smiling at the same time. "I'm so pleased it's you, Jamie!" she said, over and over again.

"Akiko, you poor little thing! I can't see you very well,

but you mustn't cry! Are you ill?" said Jamie, still holding her in his arms. "How long have you been here? And what happened? There's no window in this horrible place. No wonder that old nun did herself in! Oh God, I *knew* you must be in trouble somewhere."

After a while, when she had calmed herself, they talked about what seemed to be their hopeless situation. Locked in a tower where nobody ever ventured, and with only Ezekiel Parsons to bring food and water, what could they do? And what did their captor intend to do?

"It is all due to Parsons. He is my father's unpleasant assistant," she replied. "He is responsible for everything. I have tried and tried to persuade my father to get rid of him, but the horrible man has some hold over Papa. Has had for years! He will not speak of it. Just changes the subject. But I think now if we can get out of here, we will have no trouble in seeing the last of Mr. Parsons! My father will be so angry that I fear for Parsons's life."

"When will he be coming back? Does he bring you food regularly?"

"Very early in the morning, and late at night, after dark. I do not eat it. He stole the key from my father's office, but replaced it after having a new one cut for himself. He is trying to blackmail my father, I am sure of that. He has more or less said as much. But my father, though extremely rich, is not likely to give him any large amount of money, even if he believes that I am held prisoner, which I very much doubt. Papa is so obsessed with preventing me from going back to my career with you, he probably thinks I have run away and we are together! Parsons is quite stupid, and will not be able to conceal his identity as blackmailer for long. Sooner or later,

I am sure there will be a violent scene, and . . ." She was in tears again, and Jamie silently squeezed her hand.

"Sounds like Parsons is not that stupid. He followed me from the flat, though I don't think he could have expected I would come here. Must have had another plan. But he's chosen a good hiding place. People who work here would be scared to see a ghostly nun! But what were you going to say, Akiko? What do you think will happen? Please don't worry about us getting out of here. I shall think of a way, and very soon."

"Jamie, if my father realises that Parsons is the blackmailer, one of them will end up, well, probably badly hurt or worse. Father always carries a beautiful little gun. It is a habit with him. And I have seen Parsons flashing a dreadful knife around, teasing the girls in the office. It is illegal, I know, but he is not worried. Everything about Parsons is illegal."

"So he is your father's right-hand man, right? And there is some reason why he cannot be given the push?"

Akiko nodded. "He has watched me for years, on my father's instructions. Sometimes I know he is there, sometimes I don't. But he is always around. And when Papa fell ill, Parsons persuaded me to go straight from the concert to Scotland to see him. It was Papa's idea, and Parsons was, as he said at the time, doing my father's bidding. The next move, I am sure, will be to take me by force away from England and back to Japan. Papa wishes me always to be close to him. I have tried many times to explain to him that much as I love him, I must live my own life."

"And he does not accept that?"

Akiko did not answer, but hung her head.

"I see," said Jamie, who was beginning to wish he had never heard of Nakamasa or Ezekiel Parsons. "Well, that is for you to deal with, Akiko dear. All I want at present is to stop playing games and get out of here and take you with me, so that we can decide what to do. If you must return to Japan, then that is that. We must cancel all our concert engagements, and I shall wish you well."

TWENTY-SEVEN

❧

"ARSENAL MATCH ON THE TELLY SHORTLY," SAID DEREK. "Are we all watching?"

"It's a bit hot for football, I'd say." Gran remembered the days when football was an autumn and winter game, and now the season started in the middle of summer.

"Forecast says rain later," Lois said. "That should cool them down."

"Rain?" scoffed Derek. "Did you see the sky today? Not a cloud in sight. But they'll be playing, whatever." He looked at Lois's miserable face and added, "Why don't you drop everything and watch with me?"

Lois had clearly been worrying about Jamie ever since she last spoke to him. She had tried once or twice to ring him, but he had not answered. She had threatened to go and catch the next train to London today, but Derek had persuaded her against. "He's only been gone a day or two! He did warn you he was going to be out and about. For goodness sake, think of something else, like football," he said.

Lois sighed. "I'm just worried that he might still be trying to find Akiko and has got into real trouble somewhere. I wish there was somebody we could ring, who might be able to check on him. A neighbour, maybe, or an old friend. But he's never needed to give us contact numbers, what with mobile phones an' that. And yes, why isn't his mobile switched on?"

Derek squared his shoulders. "Now then, Lois, me duck," said Derek, "I've changed my mind about those two. They've been thrown together, playing their music, but Jamie's no fool. He's not going to get serious about a girl who's so determined to make a global career. It'd never work, and I suspect he knows it. He's probably decided to forget all about her and get on with his life. Now, don't snap my head off, Lois love, but I've got an idea." Derek reached out and took Lois's hand.

"It was you," Lois replied accusingly, "who was originally so sure he was in love!"

"Well, as I said, I have changed my mind. Now, are you going to listen to my suggestion? Mrs. Tollervey-Jones—no, let me finish—she's supposed to be some kind of assistant to you, isn't she? Didn't she have friends who lived around the corner from Jamie's flat? Well, I'm sure they would pop round and see that he's all right. Would that put your mind at rest? He probably won't like it, but that's a risk we have to take."

"Quite right," said Gran. "Might as well make use of the old trout, seeing as she's so keen."

Lois forbore to point out that Mrs. Tollervey-Jones was probably much the same age as Gran, but agreed that contacting the old trout was a good idea.

* * *

"EVENING, MRS. TOLLERVEY-JONES. I DO HOPE IT'S NOT TOO late to have a word?" Lois had decided to walk down to Stone House, to see if Mrs. T-J was working in her garden. It was the most likely place to find her.

"Not too late for me, Lois dear," came a voice from the vegetable patch. "Come in, my dear. My best thinking is done in the evening. So what can I do for you?"

"It's rather difficult to explain," Lois said. "You remember Akiko? The one who's gone missing? Well, Jamie's still in London and I can't get hold of him. I am a bit worried, because of all the hoo-ha surrounding that cello theft, and I know that you've friends living just round the corner from Jamie's flat."

Mrs. T-J thought fast. Perhaps not a good idea to say she'd already contacted them. She had quite forgotten the rule about telling Lois *everything*.

"So you would like me to ask them to check?" she said. "Leave it to me. I'll ring them first thing tomorrow, and then let you know. Try not to worry. I remember with my Robert, once he had left home and had a flat of his own, I might just as well not have existed! They remember us when we're useful, in my experience."

Lois did not agree with her for one minute, but said nothing except to thank her and her friends in advance. "Derek thinks I am making a fuss about nothing," she said. "But—"

"I know exactly how it is, my dear. I will certainly do what I can and be in touch with you very soon. Ah!" the old lady added. "Is that the telephone in the house? Must dash. Expecting a call, you know."

Lois had never seen Mrs. Tollervey-Jones move so fast. Must be an important call, she guessed, never dreaming that it might be from Jamie.

"DOESN'T SOUND AS IF SHE'S THERE," JAMIE SAID TO AKIKO. HE was about to sign off when he heard a voice, puffing and panting, calling his name.

"Hello, Mrs. T-J," he said. "Sorry about this, but try to cool down. No hurry, we're not going anywhere. Akiko and I are locked in a gloomy, haunted cell, living on bread and water. I have just managed to retrieve my mobile from our captor's pocket. If my mother mentions not having heard from me, tell her I called with a quick message about the cello. Say I'm terribly busy but will ring soon for a chat. And don't mention imprisonment! I have a master plan, and we should be out of here very soon."

"Are you making this up, Jamie Meade?" Mrs. T-J frowned. He sounded almost jaunty, and the whole message was ridiculously melodramatic. "Have you remembered what I said about being cautious and sensible? I think this must be a joke."

"No joke," said Jamie. "Must go. I don't want to speak to mother at the moment. She has a genius for wheedling everything out of me. But reassure her, if she asks. Thanks very much indeed. Bye."

TWENTY-EIGHT

❧

ROBERT TOLLERVEY-JONES DROVE INTO LONG FARNDEN feeling decidedly resentful. Thanks to both his mother and wife, he had been manoeuvred into leaving all the things he had planned to do with his evening, in order to spend half of it in a car.

Mrs. Tollervey-Jones had telephoned him to ask for help, refused to say what it was about, and announced her intention of coming up to London again. Felicity had said he must not allow it. "Go down there," she had said. "Today, if possible. She sounded very worried, and she *is* an old lady, darling."

Ever obedient to his wife's wishes, Robert told his mother he would be with her by late suppertime. As he made his way down the familiar High Street, he passed the shop where, as a boy, he used to buy sweets. He sighed. He had thought that once his mother had left the hall and was settled in Stone House, she would relax into a contented retirement. He should have known otherwise.

He cruised into the drive, and switched off the engine. It was all Lois Meade's fault, he thought. Her rash involvement in solving local crimes had landed his mother in this latest muddle. Perhaps he should have a word with her? He could suggest she would do better to concentrate on her cleaning business and leave his mother to a quiet retirement. Some chance, he thought, as he saw Mrs. T-J rounding the corner of the house at speed.

"Ah, there you are, Robert. Don't sit there brooding on the misfortune of having a troublesome mother. Out you get. Supper is ready."

As they tucked in, Robert heard the whole story. As far as he could make out, two people and a cello had disappeared, and his mother had had a message from one of them saying they were incarcerated in a prison cell. Without the cello.

"Sounds like a bad dream," he said, helping himself to another glass of red wine. "If I didn't know better, I would worry that Alzheimer's had taken hold of my beloved mother. No, Mother, no! I don't mean you *have* got it, just that it sounds like that. More than likely your associate in Long Farnden has an over-fertile imagination. There is probably some quite simple explanation. Jamie Meade and Akiko have gone secretly up to Gretna Green and got married. Very likely they had too much celebratory champagne and thought it a hoot to play a trick on you. As for the cello, it will turn up, I'm sure. She should have taken greater care of it, if it was a valuable old one. A cellist on the radio was saying he always books an extra plane seat for his instrument. Never lets it out of his sight. Dates back to sixteen ninety something. Made by a man named Kapper, or some such."

"Very interesting," said his mother. "And more or less what I expected you to say. But it is possible that both are in danger, and I have promised Mrs. Meade I would do something. That something was to have been a call to our friends, the Oakes, to see if they could check Jamie's flat. But I've spoken to them already and don't want to be a nuisance." She did not add that so far she had not told her boss. It was not that she had actually forgotten about Lois's rule, but she wanted to choose the right moment. She had almost convinced herself that this was true, but not quite.

"I suppose there is no point in asking you whether you or the tiresome Lois Meade has been to the police about all of this?" Robert felt a little more cheery after the wine.

"Lois is constantly in touch with her friend, Inspector Cowgill. He values her participation very highly."

"Mm. I wonder how highly he would rate her if she was old and ugly?"

"Neither here nor there," snapped his mother. "I am beginning to wonder if it was a waste of time asking for your help."

"Sorry, Ma. Now listen. I have a sensible suggestion to make. You give me Jamie's address, and I will shoot back up there and knock on his door. I shall have to think of a convincing reason for appearing at midnight. But when he answers, I shall ask him to contact his mother at once and set her mind at rest. Will that do?"

"No, it will not. I don't believe he is there. And anyway, I could have asked you to do that without your coming all this way, nice as it is to see you," Mrs. Tollervey-Jones replied. "I had been intending to ask for your help in finding disused or converted nunneries, or places where there are small cells with no light."

"Prisons? Police stations?" suggested Robert, with the ghost of a smile. "London is a big place. I think the needle in the haystack would apply. But," he added quickly, seeing his mother's expression, "I will certainly do my best. I'll report back in a day or two. Now, will you promise me you won't do anything more yourself? I don't want to fish you out of the Thames, strangled with a cello string."

"Robert! This is no joke! Now, if you've finished, I'll make some coffee."

IN THEIR BARE CELL, AKIKO AND JAMIE SAT HUDDLED TOGETHER on the tiny, hard bed. It was evening, and they had had nothing to eat but sandwiches curling at the edges, and water to drink. Jamie, for one, was hungry for some real food. Ezekiel Parsons had brought them this minimal sustenance, and had dumped it on the floor of the cell without speaking. During his last appearance, Jamie, with commendable stealth, had managed to lift his mobile from Ezekiel's jacket pocket before he left again, mumbling that he'd forgotten to refill the water jug and would be back soon.

Jamie had just had time to make the call to Mrs. T-J before Parsons surprised them by returning almost immediately. He seemed distracted, left them a jug of clean water and disappeared again. Jamie held his breath, and listened. He was almost certain that Parsons had forgotten to lock the door behind him.

Akiko began to speak, and Jamie hushed her. "Listen!" he said. They heard loud voices raised in anger, followed by banging doors and a revving car engine. Then an uncanny silence.

"Something's happened!" Akiko said, grabbing Jamie's

arm. "Those voices were my father's and Parsons's, and they were having a terrible argument. You remember what I said about the gun and the knife? I am frightened, Jamie, really frightened. We must get out of here!"

"No problem," said Jamie, and opened the door.

They fled, Akiko leading the way. "We must go to my father's office," she said, "to find the key to the side door. It is late now, and we have to risk meeting one or other of them. We will see if the Bentley has gone. If it has, both will be gone. Papa does not drive. We need a key to get out, and I know exactly where it is hanging."

Jamie was reluctant to go through the offices, but they would need a key, so Akiko said, and he had no alternative but to trust her. There was no turning back now, and he duly followed her along the convent passages. They met no one, and the Bentley was not in its usual place.

"Quick!" Jamie said. "They've gone off somewhere. Must have made up the quarrel. Don't be frightened, Akiko, we are out now, and can go straight to my flat."

They found the side door, and had no trouble opening it. Then they were stumbling into a quiet, dark alley down the side of the convent, and Jamie realised that Akiko was shaking from head to foot. "I am frightened for Papa," she said, beginning to sob. "What has Parsons done with him?"

"Or what has he done with Parsons," Jamie replied grimly. "Come on, we'll get a cab. Give me your hand now, and hold on. You'll be safe with me."

TWENTY-NINE

A S JAMIE PAID THE TAXI DRIVER, HE HEARD SOMEBODY CALL his name from the top of the block steps. It was his neighbour, and he rushed up to apologise for waking her at this time of night.

"I've already been woken up by your friends calling a short while ago," she said.

"Friends?" said Jamie, his heart sinking. "What did they look like?"

"Only one got out of a big car. He came and knocked, until I got out and swore at him! He said he needed to find you urgently. I said you'd gone away for six months and wouldn't be back until after that. Sorry, Jamie, but I really was outraged at his behaviour! Very impolite, to put it mildly."

"So what did he do?"

"Got back into the car and drove off with squealing tyres, like some film gangster."

"I'm so sorry. It must have been a practical joke. I don't

believe any of my friends would be so barbaric. Off you go, back to bed now. We'll talk more in the morning. Good night, and sorry again!"

"DID YOU SEE EZ'S KNIFE WHEN WE WERE IN THE TURRET?" Akiko was stretched out on Jamie's sofa, a pillow behind her head and a mug of cold camomile tea by her side. He had told her about their so-called friends disturbing the sick lady on the ground floor, and she had agreed that it was almost certainly Parsons and her father. Her father would have insisted, she said. It was a lucky thing that they'd gone before the taxi arrived, they both agreed.

"What knife? Do you mean Parsons?" Jamie sat beside her on his one comfortable chair. As soon as they had settled in, he had insisted that Akiko should try to rest. She had drifted off quite soon, and was still half asleep. Jamie looked at his watch. This was the first thing Akiko had said for three hours. She had whimpered in her sleep, and twice he had caught her when she suddenly jerked towards the edge of the sofa in what seemed to be fright. Now it was completely dark, and he desperately needed some sleep himself. But he was reluctant to leave her, and decided to make a quick coffee.

Her question was an odd one. Of course, it could be the continuation of a dream, or, more likely, a nightmare. "You told me he had a knife, but I didn't see it," he said gently.

"It was in his pocket. Didn't you see it when you got your mobile back?"

Jamie was not sure how to proceed. It was likely that she was still worried for the safety of her father, but he did not want to alarm her if she was half in a dream. His dilemma was resolved by a knock at the door.

"Jamie! I must hide," she said, suddenly awake now. "Please wait a moment, and I will go into your bedroom and hide in a cupboard."

"Relax, Akiko," he said. "It's probably some mistake. It's very late."

He went out into his hall and shouted through the locked door. "Who's there?"

"Robert Tollervey-Jones. You know my mother. Apologies for calling so late. I had trouble getting past your guard dog!"

Jamie sighed and opened the door. "Come in, please. It is not exactly a convenient time, and that poor lady has been pestered by others looking for us. But how can I help you?"

Robert entered and was led into the small sitting room. It was empty now, but there were telltale signs of a second occupant. The chair drawn up to the sofa, the pillow, with one dark hair left behind, the mug full of cold camomile tea.

"Where is Akiko?" he said.

"Safe," said Jamie shortly. "What is it you want? Did my mother send you?"

Robert shook his head. "No, *my* mother sent me. Where would we be without mothers?"

His tone was so heartfelt that Jamie smiled briefly. "She wants to know where we've been, I expect," he said. "Well, I can't tell you at the moment. Perhaps you would kindly report back that we are both safe and well? I really do appreciate all the trouble you've taken, and your mother's concern for us. I probably shouldn't have sent that message to her. I'm not thinking too straight at the moment, but as soon as I've had some sleep, we shall be off to Farnden. We can tell your mother—and my mother—the whole story then."

"Don't worry, old chap. Is there anything I can do for you now? Or later? Just let me know. Here's my card. Get some rest, if you can. Oh yes, and one thing you can do for me. Could you possibly ask *your* mother to dismiss *my* mother from her new job? What does she call it? Ferretin', that's it. Good night, then."

Next morning, Jamie woke Akiko early. She had elected to continue sleeping on the sofa, saying that her upbringing would not allow her to occupy a man's bed. Jamie was tempted to say that any bloke feeling as deeply tired as he did could guarantee that her moral code would not be compromised. But he had finally given way to her insistence that she would have the sofa and he his own bed, where he had slept the sleep of the innocent.

Now he made a quick cup of tea, and toasted a couple of pieces of bread. "More later," he said. "We must get away from here as soon as possible."

"Where are we going?"

"Down to Long Farnden, to my mother's house."

She sat up, frowning. "But surely, Jamie, that is the first place they will look for us?"

"I presume you mean Parsons and your father? It is by no means certain that they will be together now, or will even continue trying to find us. We don't know where they've gone, or why, nor do we know if your father had discovered we were in the turret. If they do turn up in Farnden, I shall be ready for them. And so will Inspector Cowgill and his men. I mean to tell them the whole story as soon as we reach home. I daresay Mother has had them combing the countryside for us already. Now, please hurry, and we'll be off. We'll take the train, and then a bus from Tresham to Farnden."

"Shouldn't we tell your mother we are coming?"

"No, I don't think so. It'll send her into a spin, rushing around. Think of poor old Dad! If we just turn up, then we can explain at leisure. Now, be as quick as you can."

"Please may I borrow a toothbrush? Then I am ready."

Jamie frowned. "Sharing a toothbrush is even more of a commitment than sharing a bed. Did you know that?"

"I know that you are laughing at me. Please turn away, and I shall tidy myself."

"GUESS WHO I'VE JUST SEEN, GETTING OFF THE BUS," SAID JOSIE. "At least, I think it was them." There were no customers, and she had been gazing out of the shop window, thinking about ordering more stock.

"Not—?"

"Yep," Josie said, "Jamie and Akiko. Looked like they were heading your way."

"Oh, good heavens! Are you sure? You're not kidding me?"

"I wouldn't be so cruel, Mum. They'll be there in a couple of minutes, so better compose yourself. And don't fire questions at them straightaway."

"As if I would!" Lois rang off, and rushed into the kitchen with the news.

Gran took off her apron and filled the kettle. "They'll be thirsty," she said, as if they were just coming home from school. "Now, Lois, clear those dirty dishes off the table. We don't want Akiko to think we're slovenly, do we?"

They fell silent, listening for the gate to click open. When it did, Lois could wait no longer, and rushed out of the back door and into the drive. She held out her arms and embraced Jamie, and then, on a sudden impulse, she approached Akiko and gave her a gentle hug.

"Welcome, both of you," she said. "Come on in, and no, I'm not going to ask you a single question until you are ready. Have you told Cowgill you're here? Please, Akiko, make yourself at home. Gran is longing to start cooking a huge breakfast for us all."

"Lovely morning, darling," said Geoff Norrington, as he looked out of the bedroom window. The hall park was at its best, with the sun lighting up the spreading chestnut trees. Rare breed sheep, newly acquired, grazed calmly, and Geoff felt the satisfaction of a man who is monarch of all he surveys.

"Busy day?" said Melanie. "Are you going into the office?"

"Afraid so," he said. "The usual mound of paperwork, I expect. The pundits all say paper is a thing of the past. The internet has made it slow and unnecessary. But if you ask me, there is just as much junk paper as before, if not more."

"Ah, well, I hope we shall get some replies to the gamekeeper ad. I'm sure we will. After all, it's a nice, healthy job, and could be more or less what you make of it. Am I right?"

Geoff nodded. Then he stiffened, and peered more closely out of the open window. "Hey, there's a strange man coming down the long drive. But no, he isn't strange. I'd know that jaunty stride anywhere. You won't need to bother about your ad, Melanie. Our gamekeeper is back."

"But you won't take him on again, will you? I mean, what about the burglary?"

"No proof that it was Foster. There was nothing missing, although it was such a mess. Now, don't worry. I'll give him a stern talking-to, and warn him if he doesn't pull up his socks, he won't get another chance."

THIRTY

꙳

"Lois, my dear? How are you? Any news? As always, lovely to hear from you. And how are our newlyweds? Matthew is positively bouncy, in spite of the usual teasing in the canteen."

"Never mind the newlyweds, Cowgill," said Lois. "We need to see you on a very important matter. Will you come here, or shall we come into town?"

Inspector Cowgill's tone changed immediately. "I'll be in Farnden in twenty minutes. Or less. Don't go out before I arrive. Bye, Lois."

Lois put down her phone and leafed through a pile of New Brooms papers on her desk, but could not concentrate. After a second breakfast, when they had all exchanged commonplace conversation, Jamie and Akiko had come into her study and told her the whole story.

It had clearly been very difficult for Akiko to describe the sounds of violence between her father and Parsons. She explained again that there was some kind of secret that gave Parsons a hold over her father. She had repeatedly tried to get him dismissed, but her father would not even discuss it. She suspected there was something so appalling about her father's past that he would do anything to keep it from her. It must have been something Parsons had discovered and had for years used as blackmail. Since then, his constant presence in their life had become routine, and Parsons had maintained a comfortable, if subservient, life for himself as a result.

Lois had thought again of Japan's past history in the Second World War. Was that anything to do with Nakamasa's secret? She had thought all this over before, and had decided it was too long ago. But only this morning she had heard an old man, a surviver from a Japanese prisoner-of-war camp, talking on the radio about a book just published recounting his bitter experiences.

Now in her office, waiting for Cowgill, she turned over the next week's cleaning schedules without reading them, hardly knowing what she was doing. All she could think of was a convent in London, where for years nuns had spent their lives in prayer, and where now it was an ex-convent occupied by criminal and possibly murderous characters, with her precious Jamie in their sights.

When the knock came at the door, and she opened it to see the reassuring bulk of Inspector Cowgill, she felt she could kiss him for being there. So, to his extreme delight, she did. Fortunately, since Gran was close behind her with her usual offer of coffee and an unofficial listening ear, she then collected herself sufficiently to ask him in and show him to her office.

"Shall I bring in Jamie and Akiko?" Lois was struck by Cowgill's concerned expression. He probably knew some of what she had to say already. There was now a legitimate channel of communication to him through Josie and Matthew. Whatever she said to Josie stood a good chance of being passed on to Cowgill. But that was fine. She would never dream of asking Josie to keep anything from her husband.

"No, I'd just like to hear what you have to tell me, and then we can get the other two in. Are they staying long?"

"I honestly don't know," Lois said. "It was such a relief to see them turn up safe, and then to hear them out, that I haven't really had time to take it all in. All I knew for sure was that we needed to get you here. They know you're here, and seem quite willing to talk."

"As I am always saying, Lois, we have not been idle. A certain amount of interesting information has emerged on the disappearance of musical instruments. These have led us to an unlikely connection with an underground organisation operating worldwide. Valuable instruments and paintings are stolen to order. These are passed on to customers, but the victim is led to believe they will be returned on payment of a large amount of money. In this way, thieves double their money. Clients pay up for the genuine instrument, and when the original owners pay the ransom asked, they then receive a fake violin, or cello, a replica of their own. Obviously the organisation has very skilled craftsmen, as nine out of ten of the musicians are convinced."

"And, as you said awhile ago," said Lois, "some violence, even one death, has been associated with all this?"

Cowgill nodded. "Yes. It seems that if the victim argues, or threatens retribution for being deceived, other methods of keeping him quiet are used, namely threats of violence to him or his family, and once or twice a threat has been carried out."

"And you have no idea who the villains are?"

"Oh yes. And we have one or two doing time and unwilling to talk. But they are the tip of a large iceberg. When Akiko's cello is found, it will, we hope, lead us to more discoveries, and it is important that she lets me know at once if she is approached with a ransom demand. Of course, it may be that all this is quite coincidental and has nothing to do with Jamie and Akiko being held prisoner. The theft could have been merely opportunistic."

Lois sighed. "Though I couldn't say it to them, I personally think they left the car unlocked," she said. "How easy it would have been for the thief!"

"We'll see, my dear. Would you like to ask them in? Gran could bring us all coffee to warm things up."

"Watch me," said Lois, with a smile. She opened the door suddenly, and there stood Gran, a guilty expression on her face, bearing a tray loaded with coffee things.

"Ah," said Cowgill, "there you are, Mrs. Weedon. What wonderful service! Let me help you with the tray."

WHEN ALL WERE SETTLED, LOIS INTRODUCED AKIKO, AND explained that Inspector Cowgill was an old colleague, and completely trustworthy.

"I've told him some of what we are here to talk about, but not all. For one thing, I don't know all. But there is no doubt that the two of you could be in danger, because of what you may know. I'm blowed if I know what that is, but Akiko particularly may have been a target because of her cello. We need the inspector's help, and must tell him all we know."

"Perhaps a question or two from me would be a good start," said Cowgill. "So, Jamie, how long have you known Akiko, and how did you meet?"

The conversation proceeded on these formal lines for quite a while, until the inspector suddenly interrupted Jamie's description of the kind of music they played, and said with force, "Is your father living in London, Akiko? In a converted convent in the city?"

She turned and looked at Jamie for help. He began to speak, but was interrupted.

"No, Jamie," Cowgill said. "Let Akiko answer for herself, please."

"My father does occasionally live in London in an apartment in his offices, which are in a converted convent. But possibly not at the moment. He has a house in Scotland and, of course, his main offices in Japan. But he has been in London, with his assistant and chauffeur Parsons. We heard them quarrelling and shouting violently whilst we were shut up in the turret, and they were not around when we escaped. My father may have wanted to go back to Scotland for some reason, and does not drive, so perhaps he was ordering Parsons to take him. Why do you ask?"

"I am very sorry, Akiko, but your father has been found in an abandoned Bentley on a slip road from the M1 going north."

"Cowgill!" Lois interrupted fiercely. "What on earth are you saying?"

"The truth, Lois. My chaps have found Mr. Nakamasa. And I believe it has nothing at all to do with a cello."

"But is he—?"

"No, he is not dead. He had apparently suffered a severe heart attack, was left to recover, or not, and has now been brought back to a hospital in London."

Akiko was trembling violently. Jamie took her hand, and said that perhaps it would be best if they had a break, whilst Akiko recovered herself. Cowgill nodded agreement. "Your father is not allowed visitors at the moment, but the prognosis is good," he added.

Lois quietly poured more coffee, and pushed a box of tissues towards the now-weeping Akiko. "These two have had a grim time, Cowgill, so go easy, please," she said.

"Of course," he answered. "My apologies. I should stress that Mr. Nakamasa has been very poorly, but is receiving the best possible attention."

"What about the other man, Parsons, who guarded us and probably attacked my father?" said Akiko. "I think he was blackmailing Papa, demanding much money for my release. He knew I was persuading my father to get rid of him, and he no doubt thought he would take a good chunk of money with him when he left. As we told you, he hid me in the convent building, in a cell almost never entered, and as far as I know, Papa was unaware of this."

She shuddered at the thought of it. "Papa would not have believed the blackmail threats. He would think I had run off to join Jamie, I am sure," she continued. "Poor Jamie was coming to look for me, and he too was imprisoned. I think this unnerved Parsons, and he did not know what to do next. He was so bemused—is that right?—that he left our cell door open! Perhaps Papa had realised that Parsons was his blackmailer, and faced him with it. They were both shouting so loudly. You must find Parsons, please. I shall be happy to identify him. Very happy."

"The search has begun already to find him. It will not take long, we hope. He is known to us, and known to be ruthless. Perhaps it would be best if you returned to London, to be near your father for when he improves? Do you have a friend you could stay with?"

He looked at Jamie Meade, and recognised in his face his mother's stubborn expression.

"Akiko will stay here with me," Jamie said. "I can look after her, and we will see what happens next."

"Very well." Cowgill frowned, and added, "You must report to me immediately if there are any developments here in Farnden. In the meantime, it would be advisable to keep a close eye on Akiko, in case Parsons should make an approach. He will undoubtedly need to know whether your father is dead or alive. I presume you mean to stay here with your mother, Jamie? Please let me know at once if you intend to leave. I need not stress how important this is. And one more thing. When we found your father, Akiko, he was handcuffed."

EZEKIEL PARSONS HAD WITNESSED NAKAMASA HAVING HIS first small heart attack in Scotland, but this time it was different. His face had been a terrible colour, and he had clutched his chest. Then he seemed to pass out completely, moaning and writhing with what was obviously a very severe pain.

Parsons had panicked. He had driven off the motorway into a deserted slip road leading into open country, taken Nakamasa's gun from his pocket, then got out of the car. He had locked it and run as fast as he could until he had got a lift from a passing lorry going his way. When his own heart had stopped beating wildly, he had considered his position. Pity old Nakky had twigged that the blackmailer was in fact his faithful servant, Parsons himself! Still, he had been able to take him by surprise and get the handcuffs on him before he could reach for his gun. The cuffs that he'd been carrying in his pocket for immobilising Nakky and had seemed so useful! He should have removed them. Idiot! It had been relatively easy at first. He had got him out of the convent and into the Bentley with a bit of pushing and shoving, then on the road to Scotland, where the old man would be out of the way. The offices were deserted, and he was fairly sure no staff heard them leave. Once out of town, he had planned to drive through the night, dump Nakky back at Hightoun House, force him to hand over his cash, and scram. Jump before he was pushed!

Then the heart attack! Should he have tried to resuscitate him? Yes, and risked him blabbing to the police? After all, his threat to destroy Nakamasa in the eyes of his precious daughter still held. It was too late now though, and sitting next to the lorry driver, who was a big, bald man, evil-looking and covered in tattoos, Parsons had decided to spend the shortest possible time in his company. They had slowed down through a village, and Parsons asked to be dropped off. He had made his way to the church and, in the waning light, curled up in the porch and tried to sleep.

Now, next morning, he was awake, stiff and hungry. He looked out across the churchyard to see that the coast was clear. The lorry had driven away after leaving him. He was in vaguely familiar countryside, and had recognised a name on a signpost. He knew he could find his way to the main road and once there, with a bit of luck he could pick up a lift that would take him straight to Waltonby and Last Resort House. It was a shame about his proposed rendezvous with Foster in London, but it was entirely possible that his old friend would still be in the community, where they could talk without interruption.

THIRTY-ONE

❧

A FTER COWGILL HAD GONE, AND JAMIE AND AKIKO SET OFF for a walk, Lois sat in her office, trying to make sense of notes she had scribbled earlier, but subsequent events had removed all recollections of a conversation with Dot Nimmo. Something about a possible new client, but she had not been clear about the woman's address, or whether she had definitely decided to hire New Brooms.

She grinned as she remembered Cowgill surreptitiously taking her hand as he left. He was a naughty old thing! She looked at her watch. Dot had a clear morning today and would be at home, so she put in a call. The messaging voice was interrupted by Dot, who yelled, "Hello! Hello! Don't go! I'm here!"

Holding the receiver away from the bellowing in her ear, Lois's grin widened. Thank goodness Dot would never change. She was comic relief in dark times. "Hi, Dot," she said. "I'm just going over my notes from the last meeting and can't read some of it. You know you told me about a possible new client? Can you go over that again?"

"Yeah, sure. It was a woman I met at the bus stop. She was very respectable, and said her car was in for service so she had to take the bus. We got talking—"

"As you do," said Lois.

"—And when she heard I worked for New Brooms, she said she was moving house and would need some help, cleanin' up an' that. I said I'd tell you, and you'd get in touch."

"Details?" said Lois.

"A Mrs. Rowntree, from Waltonby. She's moving to a smaller house."

"When?"

"Next week. It's all happened quickly, apparently. The sale of her own house, an' all of that. She lives at Walnut House, Keats Meadow, in Waltonby. She said she was in the telephone book, so you could look her up. Or would you like me to?"

"No, no, Dot! That's fine. I'll give her a ring. Thanks a lot."

A tap at her office door brought Gran in, with a long face.

"What's up, Mum?" Lois asked.

"It's them two. Akiko and Jamie. Jamie's changed his mind and they've decided to go back to London in a couple of days' time, and I shall never have another minute's peace until we get all that other thing settled. Akiko told me about her father being very ill, and I reckon she's behind this new idea to go back. Are you sure you've told Cowgill everything?"

"More to the point," answered Lois, "has he told everything? Anyway, we'll all talk about Jamie and Akiko over lunch, see what we can sort out. I'll get on to this new client now."

"A new one? Where's she live? You'd think we'd got the entire area covered by now. Is she in Farnden?"

Lois shook her head. "No, Waltonby. Dot met her at the bus stop, and chatted her up. Might not come to anything, but I'll give her a ring."

"Huh! That Dot Nimmo! She'll land herself in trouble one of these days, talking to all and sundry wherever she happens to be. If you'd listened to me—"

"I know," said Lois. "If I'd listened to you, I'd never have employed Dot. And then I'd have lost one of my best cleaners and a good friend into the bargain."

IN FARNDEN HALL, MELANIE STOOD IN THE DOORWAY OF THEIR elegant but only half-furnished drawing room, and looked across at Geoff. He was buried behind the newspaper, and she waited for him to appear. "So did you hire him? And did you give him a warning that one more transgression would see him out on the streets?"

"Um, what? What did you say?"

"I said, did you give the gamekeeper his job back, and did you warn him that this was his last chance?"

"No to both questions," said Geoff. "He was cocky and unrepentant, so I told him to get lost and not turn up here again."

"What did he say?"

"Muttered something about plenty more fish in the sea, and then he turned on his heel and walked off."

"Why did you change your mind? I thought you were going to give him another go at it?"

"The minute I started talking to him, I realised it was a bad idea. He offered no apology, and seemed to assume we would take him on again without question. Oh yes, and the woman's gone. So that's that. There are limits to my patience, Mel."

"Oh, don't think I'm criticising! I never wanted him back in the first place. Thank God you sent him packing. As for empty threats of revenge, I think we can take them for what they are."

"And what are they? More burglaries? House set on fire?"

Melanie shivered. "Not likely. More the words of a weirdo. He's probably used to living on his wits. I doubt we'll see him again. I'll advertise, and we'll make sure we get reliable references next time."

FOSTER HAD NOT GONE FAR. HE HAD CHECKED IN WITH THE Last Resort community, the group of oddly assorted people living in a large farmhouse in Waltonby. They had been useful to Foster in the past, and he intended to turn to them again. One of the great advantages of the community, as far as he was concerned, was their absolute vow of discretion. They released no names or information of any kind to questioners outside the group, and required equal discretion from members about the community itself. According to reports that occasionally filtered out through the invisible walls of silence, once inside it proved very difficult to get out again. Unless your name was Foster or Parsons.

This community had grown, buying up businesses and accommodation in the area. Among the community's members were professionals and skilled persons of all kinds, and whatever they undertook was done successfully.

Now, when Ezekiel Parsons arrived after a lucky lift from a sympathetic motorist, he was desperate and exhausted, and received gratefully the usual welcome of a hot bath, clean clothes, a Bible and a bed, and a repeated lecture on loyalty to the community. He was known to those in charge as an unreliable liar, but the more scrupulous of them argued against banning him. "What would Jesus have said?" had been the comment. "He who consorted with thieves and prostitutes?"

Left to himself in his room, Parsons stretched out on the bed, fully clothed, and thought about his options. If Naka-masa was now dead, however you looked at it, he had killed the golden goose. If only Nakky had not finally guessed that Ezekiel himself, his right-hand assistant, was actually his blackmailer, and had not scorched his ears with an angry diatribe about kidnapping Akiko. If he had not then added threats of what would happen to Parsons if he did not turn around on the M1 and take him back to London immedi-ately, the old fool might not have been provoked into a heart attack.

If, if, if. He had made a mess of it all round. Forgetting to lock the turret door was careless, handcuffing Nakamasa was not necessary with the frail old man. Anybody finding him would know it had been a crime. And worse, he should have stayed and made sure that Nakky was either alive or dead. As it was, he was in limbo.

If Nakamasa was dead, he was a murderer. With Naka-masa alive, he was still an abductor and blackmailer. In order to plan what he would do next, he desperately needed to know for sure whether the old boy had survived. He had never wished him dead. Last Resort House was indeed his last resort, and he knew from his close observations of Akiko in the past that the parents of the Meade chap lived close by, in the next village. Through them, he might find out what he needed to know about Nakky.

He had discovered that Foster was still in the community, but at the moment was out. He had been working locally as a gamekeeper, apparently, but that had come to an end and he was back living in the community. Parsons had on arrival talked to Solomon Grundy, the man in charge, and had reminded him of what he knew about violins and cellos, and their agreed terms, and suggested he would do well to abide by them. Anonymity was essential to Parsons's survival. He was now once again a fugitive from the law.

Grundy's business on the side, trading in old musical instruments, was shady. One of his residents was a very skilled craftsman. That was all Parsons knew about it, but it was enough for his purposes. He looked forward to seeing Foster again and discussing his own plight. While some of Last Resort's residents had families anxiously trying to retrieve them, Parsons had no relations of any kind. His father and mother were shadowy figures in his past, and he had much clearer memories of the orphanage where he grew up.

Then, as he settled for a nap on one of the community's comfortable beds and closed his eyes, all at once he had a subliminal flash of Nakamasa slumped in the car, his old, veined hands still clamped together in his lap. A heavy weight in the pit of his stomach caused him to sit up in fear. For the first time in a life of petty crimes, and some not so petty, he realised there was a strong possibility that he could now be on the run from a charge of murder.

THIRTY-TWO

❧

AFTER LUNCH, LOIS ANNOUNCED THEY SHOULD RELAX AND have a discussion with Jamie and Akiko about when they would return to London after a sensible interval. Jamie had cancelled a number of concerts when Akiko had gone missing, when there had been no clues to where she was or whether she would be able to return to performing with him. As a result, they had three weeks or so before they needed to be in Edinburgh for a concert in a small venue in the old town.

While they were out walking, Akiko had told him her father regarded her English accompanist as "the enemy." She stammered as she revealed this, and Jamie took her hand reassuringly. "He is a very old man," he replied, "and no doubt has his own grim memories of the last world war. When all the survivors have gone, perhaps time will tell whether the memories will stay alive or be slotted into history."

They were approaching Stone House and as they passed,

the front door was flung open and Mrs. Tollervey-Jones appeared, waving and smiling.

"Jamie! Akiko! You are back here safely! Do come in and tell me all about it. I've just made a pot of coffee. There's plenty of time before lunch."

Jamie hesitated. He was not sure about Akiko's reaction. She could well not want to talk about her father or Ezekiel Parsons. But to his surprise she turned back and said they would be delighted, so he followed her into Mrs. T-J's kitchen, where they sat around the table and exchanged pleasantries. A light breeze fanned them through the open kitchen door, and there was a tempting smell of real coffee brewing.

"Let's stay in here," Akiko said, refusing a suggestion that they retire to the drawing room. "I love your kitchen, Mrs. T-J," she added. "It is so peaceful and reassuring."

"You poor child, you must have had a very bad experience?" She patted Akiko's hand and beamed at Jamie. "What adventures have you two been having since we last spoke?"

Jamie gave her a sketchy account of their abduction, thanked her for handling his message to his mother and sending Robert to help them and looked enquiringly at Akiko. She nodded, and took over the telling, haltingly at first, but then as she described the quarrel between her father and Parsons, the rest of the story came out in a rush.

"So how is your father now?"

"I have telephoned the hospital," Akiko answered, "and he is making very good progress. In fact, they said he was demanding to be released! Of course, they are not allowing this."

"But have you a plan what to do when he does come out of hospital?"

Jamie looked at the old lady, and could see from her expression that she was rapidly thinking ahead. Even so, he was surprised by her next words.

"No?" she said. "Then you must let me make a suggestion, Akiko. I have a large house here, with plenty of help and plenty of money to hire nursing assistance if required. I would like to offer a period of convalescence for your father, until he is well enough to make plans for himself. Do think about it, and let me know."

Akiko smiled broadly, and said she did not need to think about it. She said that she had been quite prepared to take on the care of her father in some way. The Parsons man had almost certainly disappeared, and so Papa would need support. She would encourage her father to reorganise his life, once he was better, and then they could make a new start. She accepted Mrs. T-J's offer straightaway, and added that in this way she would be able to stay with Jamie and his family in Farnden for longer, and know that her father was in the best possible hands.

"Of course," she said, "he will want to repay your kindness. He too has plenty of money, Mrs. T-J."

Good God, thought Jamie, stunned into silence. They'll have the old boy proposing to Mrs. T-J in no time! Then money will be sloshing around all over the place!

But Mrs. Tollervey-Jones had not finished. "And now we have to think about finding that wicked man who imprisoned you. I presume it was a serious quarrel he had had with your father. Something to do with money, do you think? He clearly meant to leave him for dead, and could so easily have been wanted for murder by now. He will no doubt have gone into hiding somewhere, but our beloved Inspector Cowgill, ably assisted by your mother and myself, will surely be able to find him in no time. Then he will be severely punished, Akiko, for his wickedness. So is there anything else I should know?"

Akiko and Jamie exchanged a glance. Both knew that the subject of Parsons's longtime hold over Nakamasa had not been mentioned. Akiko shook her head, and said quickly that there was nothing more to tell, and then they all relaxed and talked of happier times to come.

LUNCH WAS ON THE TABLE BY THE TIME THEY RETURNED TO Meade House, and Gran was in a fighting mood. "Don't you two think of anybody but yourselves?" she said fiercely as they walked in. "Your mother's been biting her nails worrying about where you'd got to. You must know we are all on tenterhooks not knowing what's going to happen next."

"Sorry Gran," said Jamie. "But we'll tell you what's going to happen next, the minute you have dished up whatever it is that smells so good. Sit down, Akiko, and don't look so alarmed. Gran's like dog Jeems; her bark is much worse than her bite."

After giving the details of their conversation with Mrs. T-J, and especially her amazing offer to turn her house into a convalescent home, they looked around for reactions.

Lois stood up, scraping her chair on the tiled floor. "Right! That's it then," she said. "Another session with the inspector, and then we make a plan to catch Thingy Parsons, or whatever his name is. Mind you," she added more gently, "I think it would be best if Akiko and Jamie concentrate on getting back to working together and putting their music first. If they can."

"And not forgetting my father," Akiko said softly. "Without him, I am alone in the world. And I remember the good times, when he would come to visit me at grandmamma's and play lovely games in the park with our dog."

Jamie saw her tears and squeezed her hand. "And now he will be taken care of properly," he said. "And don't forget you're not alone. You have me and my family around you." Oh Lord, he said to himself as he saw Akiko's loving look. Perhaps that was going a bit overboard.

Gran's eyebrows shot up, and Lois blinked. "Um, yes, of course," she said. "And your dad, too, when he gets back from work."

AFTER SHE HAD HAD TIME TO DIGEST THIS NEW DEVELOPMENT and discuss all aspects of Akiko's father staying in Farnden, Lois remembered about Dot's possible new client. She had noted the number to call, and went into her office, telling Gran she would put in an hour's work to make up for time lost this afternoon.

"Hello? Is that Mrs. Rowntree?" A firm voice answered that yes, it was, and she had been expecting a call from New Brooms.

"I usually like to come and see potential clients to talk about what you need from us, look around the house and so on. Would that be convenient? Tomorrow morning? Yes, thank you, Mrs. Rowntree, eleven o'clock would be fine. I understand you are moving to a smaller house in Waltonby, so there will be a number of things to discuss? See you tomorrow, then."

Sounds a nice enough woman, thought Lois, as she settled down to orders for new equipment and supplies for the team. There would be a question of who took on the new job.

Perhaps as Dot had found Mrs. Rowntree, she ought to be given first option? The other girls were more or less fully occupied, though possibly a little reshuffling might be a good idea. Floss and Paula, for instance, had been ages working with Mrs. T-J at Stone House, and at the hall before that. Lois made a note in her diary, and decided to leave the rest of her paperwork until tomorrow. She set off to have a shower and change, and steel herself for a conversation with Derek, filling him in with all that had been discussed this afternoon. She could imagine what he would say. No further involvement of the family. Hand over to Inspector Cowgill, and refuse any future part in ferretin' of any kind. Concentrate on New Brooms business and friends and family, and take up singing in the choir or knitting.

"Lois! I'm home!" It was Derek, returning in time to hear the six o'clock news on the radio. She had not expected him until seven-ish, and now here he was, calling from downstairs, thwarting her plans for drowning herself in seductive perfumes before tackling him. Perhaps she was too weary for seduction anyway. And these days, after a hard day's work, Derek fell asleep as soon as his head touched the pillow. Weekends were different, thank God, and today was Friday.

As it happened, Derek was in a very good mood, having just received a request to rewire the entire premises of Tresham football club. Not only was this a lucrative contract, but he would get to rub shoulders with his heroes.

"Very sensible," he said, when he was told Mrs. T-J's offer to receive Nakamasa into her house. "Akiko's father may have been genuine in his strong feelings against the British, but all that was a long time ago," he suggested. "Mind you, a couple of weeks staying with Mrs. T-J could make or break!"

"Papa is a fair-minded man, Mr. Meade," Akiko said

defensively. "Old-fashioned, of course, but not always too old to change his mind. His early days were not happy ones, and he has never wanted to talk about them."

"We shall see, dear," said Gran soothingly. "Now, if everybody's ready, I'll get a very tasty fish pie out of the oven and dish up. You do the vegetables, Lois, and Akiko can get us a jug of water for the table. Right?"

When the meal was eaten, and the dishes stacked, Derek asked Jamie if he fancied a pint to celebrate the football club contract? They could have a jar or two, and be back in time for the news on television.

Jamie looked at Akiko, and said perhaps she might like to come with them? She shook her head, and said she would have an early night. She had not slept much since those awful days in London.

"Of course," said Gran, never one to mind her own business. "Very good idea. I'll do you a hot water bottle and you can curl up safely in bed."

As they all prepared to leave the kitchen, Lois said, "Oh, and by the way, it looks like we're getting a new client for New Brooms. Mrs. Rowntree, who lives in Waltonby, is moving to a smaller house in the village, and wants us to help with the move, and then continue cleaning for her. I'm going over to see her tomorrow."

"Good-o," said Derek. "Well done, me duck. So it's good news all round."

"Well, yes, until the next thing," said Lois.

"Did you say Waltonby?" Akiko said, growing pale. "Isn't that where there is a charitable community?" She had once overheard Parsons talking to her father about his wayward youth, and she was sure he had mentioned a community in a village named Waltonby. He had been trying to persuade Papa to make a donation to help them in their charitable work in providing succour to the needy.

"That's right," said Derek. "Barmy lot. Religious nutters, the lot of 'em. Harmless, though, so far as anyone knows. So come on, Jamie, let's be going. Back soon, girls. Behave yourselves."

"If you ask me," said Gran, "our Derek has been celebrating his new job even before he came home, bless him."

Thirty-Three

❧

HALF ASLEEP ON THE SOFA, AKIKO AND JAMIE HAD TALKED in fits and starts about Parsons and the part he had played in her life. Akiko had described how she had felt, knowing that for most of the time she was away from her father, Parsons would be monitoring her, sometimes visible, sometimes lurking in the shadows.

The mention of Waltonby had reminded her of the community where Parsons had found refuge. She had overheard him more than once telling her father that he had been very young when he first discovered it, and it had saved his life. Always a rebel, he had found a home there, and compared with what he had experienced in an orphanage, it was a good one.

"Later he discovered the truth about the Last Resorters," she had told Jamie. "There were stern rules in the community and restrictions on movement in and out of the premises. But he boasted to Papa that he had turned the tables on the manager and made his own rules."

Now, Akiko had gone to bed early, and Jamie and his mother were in the sitting room, talking quietly. Gran had also retired, and their only companion was Derek, now comfortably propped up with cushions, fast asleep.

Jamie had brought Lois up to date on Akiko's memories of Parsons, and now he said, "We need to set a trap. It is quite likely that he'll turn up at the Last Resort community, judging by what she said."

"You don't mean a trap involving Akiko? That would be cruel, Jamie. That poor girl has gone through enough!"

"Yeah, you're right, Mum, but I know she will want to help. She looks frail, but she is really very tough. Has had to be, I reckon."

"Do you feel you know her really well, love? She doesn't give much away to anybody else, does she?"

"Funny question, Mum! Of course I know her really well. You don't rehearse and practise most days together with someone without knowing them well. And she is getting better about talking to people."

"So you believe everything—no, let me start again—so, you believe she is telling you the *whole* truth? I don't mean to be unkind, but it is possible to select the bits of truth you want to tell, and conceal other bits."

Jamie was quiet for a few minutes, then he said, "I see what you're getting at. Just how much does she know about Parsons blackmailing her father? And you're right. I'm not sure. She knows it's there, lasting many years, but I am not certain she knows what it is. No doubt, like the rest of us, she wonders if it was to do with the last war. She probably doesn't *want* to know."

"Perhaps we shall get to know a little more if Nakamasa comes to Stone House. Mrs. T-J will have the whole story out of him in no time!"

"Not so sure about that, Mum. It's true that I haven't heard much about him, except that he's a very successful businessman, is the only relative Akiko has and is obsessed with her, to the point of being a control freak. I don't think she's seen him regularly recently. But he always kept a close eye on her, usually with the aid of Ezekiel Parsons, as when she was abducted and taken to Scotland."

"Ezekiel? Blimey, where'd he get a name like that?"

"Dunno. Orphan, an' all that. Anyway, there was a big gap when Akiko and her father didn't see each other often. That was between her starting school and going to music college, but Parsons was always around. Akiko has not seen her father since we were shut up. He stayed in the car when they tried to find us after we'd escaped. He's in his eighties, you know, but pretty spry up to now. I suppose he'll have to take it easy after a heart attack?"

"Yes, well, it is not for me to say. We'll leave that to our Gran! But if you could get Akiko to talk to you about things, mostly her recent past, I reckon that would help us a lot. You must understand, Jamie, that your dad and me have been very worried about you both, but specially about you. Precious son and second in line, et cetera, et cetera."

"Cor!" said Jamie. "How much do I stand to inherit?"

"Be serious," said Lois. "I should probably hand over what we know to Hunter Cowgill, and leave it there. That's what your dad would like. But I know you're fond of Akiko, and so I shall do my best to help sort out Mr. Parsons and get you both out of danger. If the cello turns up, so much the better. But I do not intend to waste any more time on that. It doesn't have anything to do with Akiko and her dad. I'll make an appointment to see Cowgill in the morning."

"And Mrs. T-J?" said Jamie. "She's a clever old duck. It'd be good to have her along, especially as she might have Nakamasa as a lodger some time soon."

"Silly old trout," said a sleepy voice from the other end of the sofa.

"Ah," said Lois. "Thank you so much for your helpful contribution, Mr. Meade. Perhaps you'd like to escort me up to bed?"

Derek leapt to his feet, wide-awake, ready and willing. "You bet," he said, and he lifted her bodily in his arms. He got as far as the stairs, before puffing and blowing and setting her down.

"Well done, Dad," said Jamie. "Now for God's sake, go to bed. And don't worry, I'll lock up."

NEXT MORNING, BEFORE BREAKFAST, LOIS PHONED COWGILL on his private line. "Of course, my dear," he said. "What time do you want to come?"

"About half nine," she said. "I'm seeing a new client at eleven, so that should give us time. Jamie has suggested a plan of action, and I want to try it out on you."

"Good. I shall look forward to half past nine, then. Bye."

Lois raised her eyebrows. It was unlike Cowgill, not to have some silly affectionate words for her? Perhaps he was cooling off at last. His assistant, Chris, was certainly a very attractive girl . . .

She had a quick breakfast, took Jeems for a run around the playing field, and then set off for Tresham police station. "He's expecting you, Mrs. Meade," said the officer in reception. "You know the way. I'll ring through and tell him you're here." He winked at her, and she felt like telling him to mind his own business. But this time he reminded her of Jamie, and so she just smiled and set off up the stone stairs.

"Coffee, Mrs. Meade?" Chris stood at the door. "Please come in. The inspector will be back in a minute. He's just gone along to leave a message with one of the team."

Lois frowned. "I haven't got much time, so I hope he won't keep me waiting," she said. Was she imagining a certain coolness in the air? Ah, well, she was here on business, and if that was the way Cowgill wanted to play it, so be it.

He was back in the office with her in two minutes. "Morning, Lois," he said gravely. "You've got a coffee? Good. Now let's hear Jamie's plan."

Lois stared at him. "What's up? Is something wrong?"

"Um, well, not too wrong, we hope."

"What the hell is it, then? *Not Matthew?*"

Cowgill nodded. "I'll tell you all I know at present. It seems there was some sort of a fracas over at Waltonby last night. Just after midnight. At that community place. We do get some bad feedback occasionally from over there, but nothing we can ever pin down or act on. Anyway, last night we got a call from a neighbour, complaining that two men were shouting obscenities at each other in the trees surrounding the place, but loud enough to disturb the nearby residents. Matthew was on duty, and he went out to have a look, taking another officer with him."

"So what happened? Get to the point, *please*."

"It seems Matthew got slightly hurt. When they went in to investigate, Grundy denied everything, as usual. Said they'd had no trouble, and had heard nobody shouting, or causing an affray."

"So how did Matthew get hurt?"

"As they were leaving, walking down the unlit driveway, they saw a shadow moving in the woods surrounding the place. Matthew went in to take a look, and fell over a fallen tree, just grazing his arm and spraining his ankle badly. A nasty sprain, it turned out to be. They both chased after the shadow, Matthew limping, of course, and so lost him."

"So, does Josie—?"

"Of course. We took him to the hospital, and they dressed his arm and treated his ankle. Then we took him home. He'll be hobbling for a bit, but knowing our Matthew he'll not take too much notice of it! I was going to ring you, Lois, but thought it would be best if Josie told you first. Anyway, that's why we're a bit dull here this morning."

"And two great policemen couldn't catch a lone shadow in the woods? Oh my God, Cowgill, this beats everything."

"Matthew's fellow officer was concerned primarily with making sure Matthew was all right," he replied sternly. "Whoever it was knew the territory, and disappeared in seconds. Nothing to follow up, of course. But the past history of that place is tricky. Visitors are not encouraged."

"Except the police, of course?"

"Oh yes, those in charge of the place are not stupid. They apologised. Said they would look into it. They are polite and helpful. On the surface, anyway. Very strange atmosphere there, Lois. I advise you to keep well away."

"Oh dear. Perhaps I should go back straightaway and check that Josie is okay? Why on earth hasn't she told me herself?"

"Didn't want to worry you, I expect. Matthew was a bit shamefaced about the whole thing. They should be coping on their own now, my dear. He will have warned her that such things happen. Leave them be. That is my advice."

Lois sighed. He was probably right. "So I'd better tell you about Jamie's plan, though I don't feel much like it."

"Best to tell me. Matthew is safe and well, so I should put it out of your mind for now." He walked across the room to where she was still standing. "Look at me, Lois," he said. "Do you trust me?"

She nodded mutely.

"I shall never let you down, my dear," he said, and bending forward, he kissed her gently on the cheek. "Come on now, sit down and let's talk."

Her cheeks flushed and, finding it hard to breathe, Lois dutifully sat down and gulped down a mouthful of hot coffee. She choked, and Cowgill silently handed her his big pocket handkerchief. Then he smiled broadly, and said he was eager to hear anything she had to say, including Jamie's plan. She managed a laugh, and began to talk.

"Yes, well, you see, we all decided that now the Parsons man, who seems to be the villain in all of this, may well think Akiko's father is dead, and so won't have anyone to blackmail. On the other hand, he may discover that he is alive, and plot another way of getting at him. Through Akiko, if necessary. He's bound to find out sooner or later that Nakamasa *is* alive and in the care of our old toughie, Mrs. Tollervey-Jones. So with father and daughter both in Farnden, Parsons is bound to show up. That's what we think, anyway."

"And the plan?"

"A trap. That's what Jamie is suggesting. Once Nakamasa is settled into Stone House, we should all be on the lookout for signs of Parsons. He is fairly recognisable. Scruffy and furtive-looking. Then, and here's the difficult bit, we bait the trap. And the bait will be Akiko. Says Jamie."

Cowgill was quiet for a minute or so, and then he said, "Do you remember that night of the concert at the Wilmore Hall? When I hid in a cupboard?"

"And saw Akiko talk desperately to a man standing in the darkness under the stairs? Yep, I remember that. And that is the reason why I have asked Jamie to do what he can to encourage Akiko to talk more about herself in the recent past. She has already told him that the man you saw was Ezekiel Parsons, and that he was the one who more or less forced her to go with him to Scotland. And that him and Nakamasa stopped her from getting in touch with Jamie."

"Mm. So, the plan?"

"Is something wrong?"

"No, no. Please carry on."

"Anyway, we decided Parsons will be around here. If you don't get him first, of course."

"Thanks for the vote of confidence, Lois."

"I have no idea why it should have been him shouting the odds in the middle of the night in Waltonby," she continued, "but it looks likely. Nasty piece of work, according to Akiko."

"And the trap?"

"Patience is a virtue, Hunter," Lois said. "I'm getting there. We wait for him to make an approach to Akiko on her own, when he might even make another attempt at abduction. And then we nab him. After all, if he's still thinking Nakamasa's dead, she will be a rich woman. Have I got it right?"

"Right. And it is about the most dangerous, amateurish plan I have had the misfortune of hearing. I can't forbid it. But then, yes, I can. Presumably you want the entire police force of the county to lie in wait for Parsons, should he appear, and should he approach Akiko, and should she be willing to do it. No, Lois, no! But I know that forbidding Lois Meade to do anything is as good as giving her carte blanche, so I'll just say this. When we have carried out more investigations into the whereabouts of Parsons, which shouldn't take long, I'll let you know if we need your help. In the meantime, I repeat my insistence on being told the minute any of you spot him. And he is not to be approached. Right?"

"I suppose so," said Lois.

THIRTY-FOUR

❧

EZEKIEL WAS IN BIG TROUBLE. SOLOMON GRUNDY HAD hauled him into his office and now demanded to know what he thought he was up to.

"We have a peaceful regime here," he said. "And of course we make sure there is no offending our neighbours or arousing their curiosity. Let alone involving the police! I want a detailed account of how you came to be out in the woods after curfew, shouting obscenities at Foster and attracting unwelcome attention."

"Oh, sod off, Grundy!" said Ezekiel. "Who d'you think you are, standing there pontificating like some tin-pot dictator? Still, that's what you are, aren't you. Just remember who you're talking to, and what I know about a certain fake cello! I'll thank you to treat me with respect, or else!"

"Come, come," said Solomon, backing down. "You surely know I am concerned for your safety? You only turn up here when you are in trouble of some sort. I have every right to be curious on your behalf."

"Oh, give it a rest. If you must know, I saw a fox from my window prowling about in the trees, and that's the truth," said Ezekiel. "I know we keep a lot of chickens here, and sell the eggs we don't need. This fox went over to the run and was digging his way in, and then he'd have been inside the house in no time. They're very clever you know. Like me. They'll keep trying until they get what they want."

"And what do *you* want, Ezekiel? Why have you come here this time?"

Ezekiel grinned. "All right, I'll own up, guv. I came to do penance for my sins, reverend sir. I seek forgiveness for all my wicked ways, and wish to serve you in any way I can."

"Bollocks," said Grundy. "That's quite enough of that. Just tell me the truth."

"I am in a somewhat tricky situation," said Ezekiel, serious now, "I've come to find my friend Foster, and ask him for his cooperation. If that is all right with you, Grundy?"

Solomon was silent, thinking. He didn't believe a word of Ezekiel's story, but he did not wish to pursue it further in case it meant having the police back on the premises.

"Very well," he said. "And don't worry about Foster the fox. I'll say no more. Now go. Go, please, Ezekiel. Just get out!" Grundy turned away from him, and Ezekiel stood at the door, chuckling. "Go! Now!" Solomon shouted.

Ezekiel sauntered off and made for his bedroom in order to think hard about what he would do next. Last night's episode had involved Foster, who had returned to find Parsons in residence, and had been less than pleased. It was a long time since he had seen him, and word had got round circles they both moved in that Parsons was in trouble. When he heard what was proposed, he refused point-blank, and Parsons had gone for him, causing him to run out into the grounds, with his ex-friend in hot pursuit and shouting at the top of his voice.

"So you've given that gamekeeper another chance, have you, Mrs. Norrington?" Janet the postlady had handed over a parcel and a pile of letters, and now stood on the doorstep smiling at Melanie.

"No, certainly not! Mr. Norrington gave him the boot when he came back. A very unpleasant man, Janet, and not one we want prowling about the place. He threatened us with unnamed nasties when he went, and I hope that's the last we see of him."

"I thought I saw him coming out of that Last Resort place this morning," Janet said. "He said good morning in a leering sort of way."

Melanie frowned. "I should ignore him. If he's gone to Last Resort House, he may still be lurking around. Anyway, Janet, how's your mother now? Such a shame she picked up that nasty bug."

The phone rang from inside the house, and Melanie walked off to answer it. Geoffrey was away for a couple of days, and she hoped it would be a message from him. But it was the usual cold caller trying to sell her double glazing, and she put the phone down mid-sentence.

"I've done now, Mrs. Norrington!" called Dot from the kitchen. "Anything else you need? Otherwise I'll see you tomorrow and concentrate on putting stock into the old cupboard in the chapel vestry. It's quite dry. I could open the window and let some air in, and then help you stack the stuff."

"Right, thanks. That's a really good idea. So I'll see you as usual at half past eight tomorrow?"

After Dot had left, Melanie made her way to the shop to relieve the girl from the village who was learning to be a useful assistant. As she walked away from the house, she felt a sudden shiver of worry. So that awful man was still around. And Geoff away overnight. The great house could be quite spooky at night, and when she was alone, Melanie usually locked herself into their bedroom and took a sleeping pill to make sure she did not wake until morning.

"Time to go home now, thank you," she said to the girl. "Any customers this morning?"

"No, just some old tramp cadging a cup of tea. I sent him away with a flea in his ear. I hope I did right, Mrs. Norrington?"

"Quite right," said Melanie. "We're not a hostel for down-and-outs." She smiled, but that scary shiver returned and she tried once more to phone Geoffrey, just to hear his voice.

THIRTY-FIVE

❦

Lois returned from seeing Cowgill in Tresham in time to collect a folder she needed from the house, before setting off for Waltonby and her appointment with Mrs. Rowntree. When she opened the kitchen door, she saw Akiko sitting at the table, and nobody else around.

"Where's Jamie?" she said.

"He has gone to the shop. He will not be long."

Lois frowned. "I thought I said you were not to be left alone," she said.

Akiko nodded. "But I persuaded him," she said. "I feel very safe in Meade House."

"Well, you'll be even safer along o'me in the New Brooms van," Lois answered. "I have to see a client, and I'll be glad of your company. Come on, get your jacket. It's a bit chilly this morning. I'll write a quick note for Jamie."

Akiko smiled. "That would be very nice, thank you. I am ready at once."

They drove through Farnden high street and passed the shop, where Jamie stood at the door and stared as they went by. Akiko waved gaily, and they continued at Lois's usual breakneck speed on their way.

One of these days, thought Jamie, as he made for home, my dear mother is going to get so many points on her licence that she'll be banned from driving completely. And then what will she do? Get around the problem, no doubt. Police connections and all that. And Akiko with her? Well, it was quite nice of Mum, to take her along. Poor girl needs a break.

There was a message on the house phone from Mrs. T-J asking Akiko and Jamie if they would like to come down to Stone House for coffee. Jamie hesitated, but not for long. He was growing fond of the old thing, and decided to go down on his own straightaway.

Without wasting time, Mrs. T-J came to the point. She had been doing some work on Parsons identity, and found that he had come up before the magistrates' court in the northern town of Rudleighton on the edge of the Lake District, years and years ago.

"How on earth did you discover that?" Jamie asked admiringly.

"There are ways," she said mysteriously, now quite into the spirit of ferretin'.

"Mm," said Jamie. "Why was he up before the bench?"

"Petty larceny. Got off with a fine. It was a first offence, apparently."

"So, that is helpful," Jamie said, but could not think why.

"Next, are you absolutely sure he was the one quarrelling with Mr. Nakamasa?"

"Come to that," said Jamie lightly, "are we sure it was Parsons who drove off with Akiko's father?"

"Well, are we?" Mrs. T-J was beginning to think Jamie was not taking her seriously.

"Yes," said Jamie. "Akiko recognised the voice. And she has talked to her father on the phone in hospital, and he confirmed it was Parsons. But well spotted, Mrs. T-J. Important points."

"And here's another one. Does Parsons have a gun?"

Jamie thought for a moment. "I think her father does. Parsons has a fearsome knife, I believe. I don't know for sure, I'm afraid." He looked longingly at the coffeepot, but his hostess did not respond.

"No, nobody seems to know. But it is just one of the many questions I shall ask Mr. Nakamasa when he arrives. There is a lot more we need to know about Akiko's family."

"He may not be up to too much questioning at first. Do you know when he is coming?"

"Monday, all being well. An ambulance will bring him, and I shall have everything prepared for him. I was hoping Akiko would be with you, when we could have discussed exactly what he will need. But perhaps later. Coffee?"

OWING TO MINIMAL DIRECTIONS GIVEN BY MRS. ROWNTREE, IT took some time for Lois and Akiko to find the neat, nineteen thirties detached house. It was up a long private drive on the outskirts of Waltonby, and as Lois's van drew up outside, the front door opened and a small, neat woman stood smiling at them.

"Looks promising," said Lois, and Akiko laughed. "How can you tell, Mrs. Meade?" she asked.

"Oh, long experience," Lois replied. "And by the way, why don't you call me Mrs. M, like the girls on my team? Less formal than the full whack. Right, in we go."

"I shall stay in the van and wait for you," Akiko said. "You can lock me in and I shall be quite safe. Please do not worry. I am used to looking after myself."

Lois frowned. She was not happy about this arrangement, but in the end decided it would be, as Akiko said, quite safe. She walked up the small path to where Mrs. Rowntree stood, introduced herself and went in, determined to keep the interview short.

In the end, it was Mrs. Rowntree who, after fifteen minutes, said, "Right, that seems to be all, Mrs. Meade. I shall be glad of help from your team straightaway in packing up and labelling my goods and chattels for the removals van. Please give me a ring to confirm. Nice to have met you. Goodbye."

All this was said as she firmly ushered Lois to the door, which was now shut firmly behind her. She walked up to the van and was relieved to see Akiko still safely sitting in the passenger seat.

"That did not take long," said the girl. "All went well?"

"Very well," said Lois. "If only all clients were as efficient! Now, I am going to drive round to look at the house she's moving to. Are you happy with that?"

"Oh yes, that would be very nice. I like to look at the English landscape. It is so gentle and well cared for, and very beautiful."

"Depends where you are," Lois said. "But look, look at that flock of birds on the stubble field! I love that. The colours, and everything."

"You are a country person?"

Lois laughed. "Not really. I'm a towny by birth. Grew up in a housing estate in Tresham. Oops! Watch out, squirrel! I do know a squirrel when I see one."

Mrs. Rowntree's new house was in fact three hundred years old, a long, low cottage in the main street. It was separated from the road by a strip of garden and a row of spreading roses trained along a low post and chain fence.

"Come on, let's look around," Lois said. "The house is empty, ready for Mrs. Rowntree to move in."

They pushed open the small side gate and walked round to the back, peering in small diamond-paned windows as they went.

"It looks rather dark inside," Akiko said. "I do not think I would like to live here."

"Nor me," said Lois. "But some people find it cosy in these old houses. Me, I like big windows and lots of light coming in."

"Me, too," said Akiko, delighted with the rapport she and Jamie's mother seemed to have. "When I have a house of my own, I would like it to be exactly like Meade House. Large and light and comfortable."

"Right," said Lois. Alarm bells were ringing. Was this a prelude to an announcement? But no, if Akiko and Jamie were thinking of an engagement, they would do the announcing together, surely? And though she could see Akiko was smitten, she couldn't say the same for Jamie. Not yet, anyway.

"What is that big house in the trees over there?" Akiko said, sensing that she had said something not quite comfortable for Lois.

"Oh, that's the Last Resorters. A mysterious lot. Charitable group, rescuing drug addicts and people down on their luck. They give them a home and work to do. They've been there for ages, but nobody seems to know much about them. They keep themselves to themselves. Sometimes they come into Josie's shop for supplies. Not big supplies. They get those at a supermarket people say they own in Tresham. She says some of them are really quiet and polite."

"It is good to hear of people doing such good work," Akiko said. "Are we going inside Mrs. Rowntree's house?"

"No, I don't have keys," Lois said. "We'd better be getting back now. Gran will have lunch on the table and we'll be in trouble."

"And that will not do! Gran is a very strong person, isn't she?"

"She's had to be," said Lois. "She always says most of her grey hairs are due to me being a terrible teenager."

Akiko laughed happily. "I, too, wanted to be a rebel," she said. "My father was so much older than other girls' fathers, and my mother died young, so I had only grandparents' guidance for behaviour, and I think they spoilt me. But Papa kept a close watch on everything I did. Have I said that right?"

"Quite right," said Lois, putting her foot hard down on the accelerator on a straight stretch of road. "Home again, and there's Jamie waiting for us."

CONCEALED BEHIND THE TALL HEDGE WHICH SURROUNDED LAST Resort House, Ezekiel had watched them pass by with satisfaction. So, Akiko and her boyfriend *were* around. And Nakky? Almost surely dead by now. He had had a quick look through the house newspapers, and there was nothing about a wealthy Japanese businessman left abandoned on the M1. But why should there be? He was not famous, and his grim past was not known to many, if any, apart from himself.

He must move quickly now, and find a way of catching Akiko Nakamasa by herself, so that he could satisfy himself that her father was really dead. Then he'd be off like a rocket.

He made his way to the chickens' field, where the birds were kept in big houses inside even bigger runs. The job allocated for today was to clean out all the houses and runs and put in fresh sawdust. Egg collection was done by the women, presumably because they were thought to have more delicate hands. Cracked eggs were regarded as a transgression, and the careless handlers duly reprimanded.

One of these days, thought Ezekiel, the Resorters are going to rise in a body and revolt. I hope I shall be here to see it, he thought, as he scraped chicken droppings off the perches.

THIRTY-SIX

❧

I N FARNDEN HALL SHOP, MELANIE NORRINGTON WAS PILING
up stock in the now-clean-and-sweet-smelling vestry.
Dot Nimmo was on her knees beside her, and they had nearly
completed the task when the bell over the door jangled.

Melanie struggled to her feet, and turned to see who had
come in. At first, she did not recognise him, but then she
remembered. It was Solomon Grundy from Last Resort
House. She had met him before, but never had a real conversation, and now wondered what he could want with her. She
saw he was carrying a bag which he began to open, unwrap-
ping a number of exquisitely carved animals.

"Good morning, Mrs. Norrington," he said, as he set them
out in pairs on the counter. "I've brought along a Noah's Ark,
the work of one of my residents, and as you see, they are really
something special. I was hoping you might take a look, and
decide to sell them from your lovely shop." He glanced

around at the jewel-bright stained-glass windows and stone faces looking down on him, survivors from Geoff's conversion of the chapel to a shop.

Melanie picked up an enchanting figure of a kangaroo, with a baby joey peering from its pouch. "Oh, aren't they adorable?" she said. "Dot, come and look at these."

"Morning, Mr. Grundy," grunted Dot. She looked at the figures, and said they looked like copies of some she had seen in Marks & Spencer in Tresham. Then she went back to the vestry.

Melanie frowned, and asked if this was so. Solomon Grundy laughed, and said Mrs. Nimmo would have her little joke. And no, of course they were not copies. An old fellow who had spent a good half of his life in the fellowship of the Last Resorters had carved them skilfully in their own workshops. Then he brought out Noah and his family, and the Ark itself. All were marvellously individual, and Melanie forgot about Dot's reservations.

"Well, I would really love to have them in the shop," she said. "I am sure my customers would buy them for special Christmas presents. But how long does it take for your old man to make them?"

"Ah, well, not too long, fortunately. He has other important work he does for us. But we have three sets finished, and I could let you have one more for stock."

"And the price? I imagine the old man will want a tidy sum for such wonderful work. On the other hand, Christmas is an expensive time, so we wouldn't want to overprice them."

Solomon Grundy named a sum which seemed about right to Melanie, and said he would leave them with her, and bring others in as soon as possible. As he turned to go, he stopped and said, "Oh, and by the way, Mrs. Norrington. You haven't seen your ex-gamekeeper recently, have you? I owe him some money, and have no forwarding address." He knew perfectly well where Foster was, but was checking on his version of why he had been sacked.

Melanie shook her head, and shivered. "Not likely!" she said. "My husband sent him off with a flea in his ear, and we don't wish to see him ever again. We thought maybe he was staying with you?"

"Ah, I see," said Solomon, and managed a wintry smile. "Not popular then?"

"Dreadful man! My advice to you would be to write him off and forget you ever saw him. Now, I must get on. Thank you for coming in. Good morning, Mr. Grundy."

After he had gone, Dot came round to the other side of the counter and said she had finished the job and would be getting off home.

"Fine, and thank you very much, Dot. But before you go, can you tell me why you clearly disliked our visitor and his wares? I know I am not very experienced in the retail trade, but I did think those carvings were very special."

Dot nodded. "The carvings were all right. It was the visitor I didn't take to. I apologise if I was rude, Mrs. Norrington, but that man has a very dodgy reputation in Tresham, and I wouldn't trust him as far as I could throw him. But don't take any notice of me. All gossip, I expect. I'll be off now, and see you next week."

For a long time after Dot had gone, Melanie sat on a stool behind the counter and thought about her morning. She had, of course, heard the rumours about Last Resort House, but had discounted them. As far as she knew, they were doing a very charitable Christian job with people who desperately needed help. Perhaps she would have a talk with Geoff about Mr. Grundy. She certainly intended to keep the Noah's Ark and all its lovely creatures, if she had to buy them herself!

THIRTY-SEVEN

W HEN JAMIE GOT BACK TO MEADE HOUSE, NEARLY LATE
for lunch, he saw Akiko already at the table, and was
surprised by her glowing face. She had not looked so happy
for weeks, and he had forgotten just how lovely she was
when not overburdened with worry.

"Hi, Jamie!" she said, and then continued with a rush.
"Where have you been? We have had a very nice morning,
haven't we, Mrs. M? First we went to see Mrs. Rowntree—
well, your mother had a talk with her and I waited in the
car—and then we went on to see the house our new client
will move into, and it was all very exciting."

Gran's eyebrows were raised again, and Lois said that yes,
the morning had been useful, and Akiko had been good
company. Then she glared at Jamie, and said, "And where, if
I may ask, have *you* been? First you leave Akiko alone in the
house, and then just now I thought I saw you coming up the
road from Stone House. I should have thought you could

have waited and taken Akiko with you this afternoon? That
message invited you both."

Jamie sighed. "I could say the same to you, Mum. Taking Akiko off on a jaunt without a word! Well, a scribble on
a scrap of paper! But no harm done. I had nothing to do, so
thought I'd go off and see the old thing. She was pleased,
and rarin' to go with your father, Akiko. She's all fired up to
give him the best possible convalescence." He had decided
not to mention Mrs. T-J's list of questions. "She was proud
of what she has discovered about Parsons, though I thought
it wasn't much use."

"Right," said Lois, sitting back in her chair and folding
her arms, in an exaggerated listening pose. "I'm all ears."

Akiko frowned. "What does that mean, Mrs. M? You
seem to have only two, like all of us?"

"Get on with it, boy, do," said Gran to Jamie. "I've got
work to do."

Jamie's revelations did not come as much of a surprise
to Lois. "We could have guessed that Parsons would have
form," she said. "I suppose it could be useful to know where
and when. Was that all she had to say?"

"Only that Akiko's father would be here on Monday,
she hoped. I think she would like to have a chat with you,"
he added, turning to Akiko. "She wants to make sure that
she has everything your father is likely to need. She's very
capable, but there will be personal things, I expect."

"How did she find out about Parsons's previous crime?"
said Akiko. "He has been with my father for years and years."

"It was a really professional enquiry job Robert did," he
answered, and explained about legal records. "She said it
was from a very long time ago, when he was just a teenager.
Already off the straight and narrow, apparently. Then she

asked me some questions. She's really on the ball, Mum. No senility there!"

"Well," said Gran sarcastically, "if Mrs. Tollervey-Jones says so, it must be correct, don't you think, Lois?"

"Drop it, Mother," said Lois shortly. "I reckon Mrs. T-J and Jamie have done a really good job. When I next see Inspector Cowgill, I shall have more to tell him."

"But before you do that, Mum, shouldn't we decide on how to trap Parsons into approaching Akiko?" Akiko said nothing, and Lois replied virtuously, "I'm afraid I'm not in the business of concealing information from the police."

"Huh!" said Gran. Time to change the subject, she decided. "So, Akiko, how did you like our countryside? Waltonby is a lovely village, isn't it. I used to cycle over there when I was young, to see a friend whose dad was a farmer. Came back with eggs in my bike basket and never broke a single one."

"Ah, a love gift! That was very clever," said Akiko, responding warmly. "I, too, thought Waltonby a beautiful village. But I did not like the look of that house behind the dark trees. The little tower on the roof with a bell inside reminded me of a prison I have seen. Or a watchtower, like they had in those war films."

It was as though a frost had suddenly hit the warm kitchen.

"Oh Lor," Gran said. "Somebody just walked over my grave."

Akiko looked puzzled, and Jamie could see this whole conversation getting out of hand. "Now, Gran, anything we can do to help? Tomorrow morning, I thought Akiko and I might take Jeems for a walk up in the hall spinney. I'm sure the Norringtons wouldn't mind, would they?"

*   *   *

After lunch, Akiko asked Jamie if he would go with her down to Stone House, and if he did not wish to stay, she would be perfectly safe. She was keen to make plans for her father, and needed to express her gratitude to Mrs. T-J for her kindness. She was just the kind of person to persuade her father to be sensible and not try to get back to business too soon. Mrs. T-J was aristocratic, proud of her considerable abilities and experience as a magistrate and firm enough to quell the most rebellious character.

But Papa was no pushover. What a strong influence he had had on her life! She knew he loved her twice as much as usual in a family, because of losing his lovely wife so soon. Akiko had been told that she looked exactly like her mother, and she had seen this for herself in family photographs. A good thought struck her. Perhaps Papa would like some photographs around him in his convalescence? She would ask Mrs. T-J if Robert could collect some from the convent. It could be arranged, she was sure, and then they could be posted to Farnden. Father would be so pleased!

They set off for Stone House, with Akiko bubbly and cheerful, delighted with her new idea, which Jamie had approved. Everything was going to be all right. She skipped along, humming a happy tune.

THIRTY-EIGHT

❧

DEREK HAD BEEN BROUGHT UP TO DATE BY LOIS, WHO HAD chosen a sleepy moment last evening, when he was full of food and drink and settled in front of the television. She had given him a short account of the latest on Ezekiel Parsons and Nakamasa and was happy to note that he answered in monosyllables, patted her hand and said wasn't that the actor who had played in the last James Bond movie?

Now, with a quick breakfast inside him, he departed for a meeting with a pal, waving cheerily. "Shan't be in for lunch, Gran!" he shouted from his van halfway down the drive.

So that's okay, thought Lois, checking her phone messages. There wasn't much admin to do this morning, and she took a large sheet of clean paper and began to jot down notes on how to trap Ezekiel Parsons in the safest possible way for everyone. After checking with Cowgill, of course.

First, they had to find out where Parsons was now. Last seen in London by Jamie and Akiko in the convent. So only they would be able to recognise him. If he meant to approach Akiko again, he would expect them to have stayed together, at least for a while. He had probably tried Jamie's flat in London again and found it empty. Then the next most likely place would be Long Farnden, where Jamie's family lived. He probably already knew where that was, from shadowing Akiko when she came to Josie's wedding.

From what Akiko had said about him, he would be staying at Last Resort House. Or would he? His long association with the community would perhaps be too well known by the police for him to go there. Would he be thinking Nakamasa must be dead, or was he planning on the possibility that he was still alive? A tricky one.

Lois got up and went to the window. The street was empty, and a light rain had begun to fall. She tried to put herself in Parsons's shoes. What would he be thinking? Worried, probably, about Nakamasa's state of health. If the old man had died, then he would need to be as far away from the law as possible. Out of the country, preferably. Or, in the event of Nakamasa being still alive, he would reckon on worming his way back into favour and going on as before.

But even supposing he was around here already, they could not assume that he had seen Akiko. But he would certainly be looking for her. So they had to arrange that he *would* see her, but not be able to approach her because she would be with someone. Even more important now, then, to make sure she was never alone whenever she left the house.

Then set the trap. They would tempt him out into the open with a message that Akiko would be in a certain place at a certain time, and alone. How would they do that and at the same time make sure she was strongly protected? One for the discussing with the others.

So, Parsons finds Akiko alone, and she keeps him talk-ing, when out of the bushes and round corners of buildings would appear a crack team of armed policemen led by Inspec-tor Hunter Cowgill, shouting war cries as they came, to arrest and carry away Ezekiel Parsons?

She laughed loudly. Rubbish! She could just imagine what Cowgill would say to that.

"Mum?" said Jamie, putting his head round the door. "Are we having a planning meeting today?"

"Yes, sometime. I thought you and Akiko were taking Jeems up to the hall spinney this morning?"

"Yep, that's right. Akiko had a long talk with Mrs. T-J yesterday, but mostly about taking care of her father. The old thing is keen, and might want to join us this afternoon. Say about half two? I'll let her know, if you like."

Lois took a deep breath. "Fine," she said. "But if she's not free, we'll go ahead anyway. I've made some notes, and I don't want to waste time fixing another date."

"Yes, ma'am," said Jamie, grinning. "Why don't you come with us now? The extending dog lead seems to be missing, but we can let her off the short one where it looks safe. And she's more likely to return, if she knows you're with us."

KNOWING FOR CERTAIN THAT THE HUNT FOR HIM WOULD BE ON, Ezekiel Parsons kept to the shadows, as would have to be his habit from now on. He had been avoiding Foster after their noisy argument, but he still needed the man to help him. He planned to find him and eat humble pie, so their friendly relationship could be restored.

He was playing truant from Last Resort House upon

learning that Solomon Grundy intended to set him on the worst job in the community—cleaning out the pigs. For a start, he would have to move them out into the field while he scraped, brushed and hosed down their concrete sties, and he was scared of pigs. He knew they could be powerful, angry beasts when roused. And then there was the smell! He would not be able to stop vomiting, and so had decided to skip out while someone else was volunteered.

"Foster! Wait for me!" Ezekiel had seen him through Last Resort trees, wearing a symphony in brown and green, and looking for all the world like the country gentleman. What a twit the man had become! Still, that shouldn't get in the way of him giving help to an old friend.

"What is it, Ez? I'm not sure I'm speaking to you."

"Oh, c'mon, boy. All forgotten and forgiven. Let's shake hands and start again."

Foster looked at Ezekiel's muddy hands and declined. "No thanks," he said. "But what did you want, anyway?"

"Why don't we go along to the park, and talk about it at our leisure? Kids and their parents don't get down there until later."

"What's the job, then?"

"Well, there's a girl I'm keen on, and she won't have anything to do with me."

"Surprise, surprise!"

"Okay, okay. But I clean up pretty good, and if I can just open a conversation, I know she'll listen. She's a nice girl, but just a bit timid. You know the sort."

"Not these days," said Foster. "But what would I have to do?"

"Loiter, my friend. Loiter outside Meade House in the

high street. I can give you likely times. There's a snappy white terrier they take for walks, and just once or twice I've seen my girl by herself with it in the spinney by the hall."

"I am certainly not approaching strange girls! Maybe you can do that in town, but in villages they put you in the stocks."

"No, you don't have to approach her. All you have to do is ring me on your mobile and tell me she's on her way. It's not that far, and I can borrow a bike from Grundy."

"And then what?"

"That's my business. Your part is over. I'll slip you a fiver if it works."

"Payment in advance, or else I don't do it. I'm skint."

"So am I, but I can find a fiver."

"How shall I know it's her?"

"Easy," said Ezekiel, "she's Japanese."

As Foster walked away, choosing a narrow road to Farnden and dodging onto verges when farm traffic came along, he thought hard. Was Parsons losing his marbles? His ridiculous idea was totally unworkable. He had agreed to it in principle, but only to get away from him. What is more, he did not believe a word of it. Parsons in love? If it was true, there was no chance a nice girl would look at his scruffy, unsavoury person twice! No, he would loiter for a short while, and that would be that.

He walked on in the direction of Farnden Hall and the spinney, where he planned to look around, just in case Ez insisted in some horrible way on his cooperation. If Norrington was not there, he would be safe enough. Sunday mornings, Melanie was usually early in the shop. Sunday was their busiest day, with trippers and shoppers with nothing else to do. But that would be later. He quite fancied her, but knew she didn't like him. He could avoid her if necessary. A diversionary tactic might be required.

IT HAD BEEN A BORING MORNING FOR MELANIE IN THE SHOP so far. Not a single customer. It was still early, of course. There had been a cool breeze in the park this morning, but now it was warming up, and the shop was stuffy.

She opened the door and stood outside for a minute, breathing deeply. Then she heard their new guard dog, Bonzo, barking his head off, real angry barking at the back of the house. That meant only one thing. Someone was in the stable yard, someone he didn't like. Without thinking, she ran as fast as she could to see who was there.

Foster, watching from the shadows, smiled triumphantly. Plan B: help himself to petty cash from the shop. Call it wages owing. He made his way swiftly and in no time had the contents of the till in his pocket. Then he turned to leave.

"Oh, it's you! What are you doing here?" said Lois, standing front of him, blocking the exit. Akiko was lagging behind, but now watched as Foster edged towards the door.

"Fancy seeing you, Lady C!" said Foster, ignoring her question. "And is that your man-eating dog?" Lois turned to look where she had tied Jeems to a post. It was all Foster needed to distract her, and "Must go!" he shouted, pushing past her. He nodded at Akiko and Jamie, and then sprinted away until he was sure he was not being followed.

THIRTY-NINE

❧

"WHO ON EARTH WAS THAT?" SAID AKIKO, WATCHING AS Lois chased across the grass in pursuit of the ex-gamekeeper. The three of them had reached the shop on their way to the spinney, and Lois had said she would just nip in for a word with Mrs. Norrington.

"One of Mum's lost causes, I suppose. It wasn't Parsons, anyway. I'd know him again anywhere," said Jamie. "Presumably Mum knows who it is. She must have a good reason to be on his tail so enthusiastically."

Lois came back to join them, puffing a little, and furious that he had got away.

"And what were you going to do with him, if you'd caught him, Mother? Who was he, anyway, and why the chase?"

"It was that nasty character who was briefly a gamekeeper here. Given the push twice by Mr. Norrington. He was coming out of the shop, and I'll bet you five pounds to a penny the till is empty."

"Where's Mrs. Norrington, then?"

"Just coming," said Lois. "We'll give her the bad news."

"Don't tell me," Melanie said, as she approached. "He's taken the cash."

"Ah, so you've worked that out already," said Lois. "Did you see who it was?"

Melanie shook her head. "Not close enough, but a cast-iron guess would be Foster, our ex-gamekeeper. I hope he didn't hurt you, Mrs. Meade? I never trusted him and wouldn't put it past him to be violent. Geoff says I'm imagining things, but he looked a bit mad sometimes. D'you know what I mean?"

"SO I WASN'T EXACTLY HEROINE OF THE HOUR." LOIS LOOKED across the lunch table at Gran. "If Jamie hadn't called out to stop me running after him, I might have caught him. But he was right. What would I have done with the rotten sod, if I'd got him? At least it might be useful to know he's still around, and almost certainly up to no good."

Gran had been biding her time, and now she said sternly, "It is just as well your husband isn't here, Lois Meade. He would be so angry with you, you silly woman, he'd never let you stir from this house again! It's no use telling you to behave like a normal person. You'll just have to go your own way, but don't blame me if one day you end up in big trouble."

A small silence followed this heartfelt attack, and even Lois was for a moment without a sharp reply. Then she sighed, and said that she was sure her mother was right. She would do everything she could to mend her ways and be like a normal person.

Then she turned to Jamie and Akiko and said, "Mrs.

T-J rang, Mum says, and invited us all to go to her house for the meeting. You will be pleased to hear your gran accepted politely for us, just like a normal person."

"Well done, Gran," said Jamie, frowning at his mother. "So, two o'clock at Stone House?" He looked at the kitchen clock. "Nearly time to go. Shall we all go together?"

"So am I included in this planning meeting?" Gran said.

"Of course not, Mother," said Lois impatiently. "You know perfectly well this whole business is best left to as few people as possible."

"But thanks for offering," said Jamie placatingly. "We need you to stay and take any messages that come through for us. Particularly any that claim to be for Akiko Nakamasa."

Mrs. T-J was waiting at the door for them, and ushered them into her drawing room. She had set out small tables, with notepads and pens, and Lois was touched by her efforts to seem businesslike.

"It is very kind of you to have the meeting here," she said. "Shall I begin? I've made some notes which might be useful for a start."

"Blimey! This whole place stinks of pig shit," Ezekiel said under his breath. He was sitting next to Foster in the big dining room at Last Resort House, and Foster had to agree that the entire estate was bathed in the odour of pig.

"A good breeze will blow it away," Foster said, and Solomon Grundy frowned. Not for the first time, he wished he could think of a way of getting rid of the pair of them. But he had used both in the past, returning faked musical instruments to the unsuspecting owners of the originals and collecting dues. The cello they had successfully lifted from Meade House was now somewhere in Europe with a rich collector, and his skilled resident was taking time off from Noah's Arks to put the final convincing touches to the replacement.

No, Parsons and Foster knew too much. It was stalemate, he reflected sadly. He knew too much about them, and they about him. Parsons was in trouble, he knew that. The police had already been round, and he had lied convincingly, as usual. He would make no effort to conceal him, nor would he shop him to the fuzz.

"But hey, Ez, listen to this," said Foster. "I was innocently spying out the lie of the land around Farnden Hall this morning. In your interests, of course. There was a small altercation in the chapel gift shop there, when some cheeky bloke had helped himself to the cash. Three people appeared inconveniently. The first was Mrs. Lois Meade, of Meade House, known to us to be an interfering busybody; the second, a young man who is obviously her son; and third—wait for it—a very attractive girl who was without doubt Japanese! How's that for a good morning's work?"

"I thought as much," Parsons muttered. He was aware that Grundy was still staring at them, and half-whispered, "Keep it quiet. Himself is watching our every move. But thanks a lot. Ready for stage two?"

Foster shook his head. "Sorry, old lad. Think of some other plan. And if you're on the run, as seems likely from your reluctance to do your own romancing, I'm out of it. *And* you owe me a fiver."

*   *   *

THE MEETING AT STONE HOUSE HAD NOT BEEN A SUCCESS. FOR A start, Lois let it be known she had come to the conclusion that, in the inspector's words, Jamie's scheme was amateurish and dangerous. They would have to think again, she had said, and the response was chilly. Mrs. T-J tried hard to put things right by saying she was sure that with some extra safeguards put in place, it stood a good chance of success. What did they have to lose? But Lois had not agreed. She was sure that they had to wait for a sighting of Parsons, and then do what a normal person would do—call the police.

Jamie and Akiko had been suspiciously quiet. Lois had expected them to protest and accuse her of chickening out, but no, they maintained mutinous expressions and said nothing. This was worrying, Lois decided. Were they contemplating acting on their own?

Then, sensing defeat, Mrs. T-J had changed the subject to the arrival of Mr. Nakamasa. He was being brought to Farnden on the following day, and everything was ready. She had asked them if they would kindly go through her list with her, just to be absolutely sure.

Lois had excused herself, leaving Jamie and Akiko to do the checking, while she returned home to make her peace with Gran.

FORTY

~

Lois had much to think about, and after she had returned home, she apologised to Gran, who wiped her eyes and said nobody knew how much she had to put up with.

Lois had told the others to start again from scratch, and now she intended to do just that herself. The new and possibly most important factor in the whole thing was the arrival of Nakamasa and the likelihood of being able to talk to him.

This would obviously not be possible the day he arrived at Stone House, but quite soon he might be pleased to meet Akiko's friends. Or would he? Perhaps he had had no change of heart and still regarded the English collectively as undesirable. But in that case, why would he have agreed to Mrs. Tollervey-Jones's offer of convalescence? Then again, English policemen had rescued him from not only a severe heart attack but disabling handcuffs as well. This might well have led him to reconsider.

Time to report to Hunter Cowgill. She dialled his direct number and he answered immediately. "Lois? Can I come and see you? I know it is Sunday, but I was just about to ring you."

"Why? What has happened?"

"I'll tell you when I see you. I shall be with you in about half an hour."

"Yes, all right. I'll be in my office, so you can go through the ordeal of Gran answering the door. Derek is going to be late home, but Jamie and Akiko should be back soon, if you want to speak to them."

"Shouldn't be necessary at the moment," he said.

TRUE TO HIS WORD, HALF AN HOUR LATER INSPECTOR COWGILL lifted the heavy knocker on Meade House front door, and in seconds he heard Gran's footsteps approaching. He squared his shoulders and fixed a stern, official look on his face.

"Ah, Inspector Cowgill," said Gran. "How can I help you?"

"Your daughter is expecting me, Mrs. Weedon," he said, and moved towards her. But Gran was too quick for him. She stood firm in the open doorway and asked was it about the awful thing that had happened to Akiko's father? They were all very upset, she said, and if anything new had come up, they would *all* be very keen to hear what he had to say.

Lois finally took pity on him, and came out of her office. "Thanks, Mum. I'll take the inspector into my office now. I'm sure he'd appreciate a cup of coffee?"

Cowgill nodded and followed Lois, breathing a sigh of relief. "Your mother is better than a guard dog," he said, sitting down opposite her.

"Not really. But what with my new assistant ferreter and my strong-minded mother, I'm up to here with old ladies. So, you first?"

"Right. We have been pursuing what has emerged about the man who is the most likely suspect for abandoning Nakamasa to what could well have been his death. According to the team who found the old boy, he had not many hours to go. Now, Lois, this Parsons is dangerous. He is acting on his own, so far as we know. I must insist that if Jamie or Akiko spots him, they are on no account to approach him."

"Right," said Lois. "Then you will be relieved to know that I have cancelled Jamie's scheme. He is not pleased, and he and Akiko have gone quiet. Nothing more I can do at the moment. That is, until Mr. Nakamasa arrives at Stone House tomorrow."

"Then I hope you have more success with him than we had. Mind you, they wouldn't allow us more than five minutes to question him. I am on my way to see Mrs. Tollervey-Jones to make sure she does not admit any strange men claiming to be Nakamasa's friend. If anyone does turn up, I shall ask her to let me know at once."

"I should think so!" said Lois. "He is a very old man, isn't he? They wouldn't even let Akiko see him at first."

"It may prove to be a stroke of genius to get him brought to Long Farnden," admitted Cowgill. "He'll do much better with his daughter beside him."

"Mrs. T-J's idea," Lois said. "My new assistant, groan, groan."

"Oh, Lois, my Lois," said Cowgill. "I am never quite sure whether you are friend or adversary!"

"I'd tell you, if I knew what that meant," Lois said with a grin. "So, nothing more to be said or done at the moment.

Except that I'm very sure Parsons will turn up in Farnden before very long. He'll be keeping out of sight, but I reckon he'll really need to know whether Nakamasa is alive or dead."

"We're watching out for him, my dear. I advise you all to do the same, but not to approach him. Get a message to me at once."

FORTY-ONE

❧

AKIKO HAD SLIPPED OUT OF MEADE HOUSE, TAKING JEEMS on her lead, hoping she had not been seen by anyone. She needed to think. Her father was due to arrive at Stone House around two o'clock this afternoon, and she knew he would be warmly welcomed. She had agreed to be down there to greet him, and now felt she needed fresh air before the big event.

Although Lois had backed out of Jamie's scheme, she had said that Akiko must continue to be closely monitored. Cowgill had agreed with her on this. She should certainly not be out on her own, dog or no dog, and on no account must Parsons be approached.

There had been no shouts from Meade House as Akiko left, so she trusted that no one had seen her. Derek had gone to work earlier, Mrs. M was in her office, and Gran was forcing food into a reluctant Jamie in the kitchen. He had been in a very strange mood since his mother had turned against his plan, and the atmosphere generally in the house was claustrophic. She was pleased to be out and away from it all.

She met several cars on their way to visit the hall grounds, but she continued walking down the small lane until it wound around the edge of the estate and entered the spinney behind the house. She knew Mrs. M had permission to take Jeems walking in there, and she followed the narrow path leading to where the trees were young and well spaced out, and where a low level of thicket, brambles and ferns grew in profusion. An occasional shaft of sunlight picked out summer yellows and greens, and Akiko smiled with pleasure.

"Oh, poor Jeems!" she said, as the long lead became entangled in the underbrush. She made an effort to free the cord, but it was hopeless. In the end, she told Jeems to stand still while she untangled the lead, unhooking her for a moment. "Then you can find your way out, but must go again on the lead, as Mrs. M ordered," she said.

Jeems obediently halted, but at that moment, only a few feet ahead of them, a rabbit started up from the thick tangle of ferns. This was too much for the feisty terrier, and she shot off after it, soon becoming lost from sight.

"Jeems! Jemima! Please come back!" shouted Akiko. The sky had darkened, and drops of rain fell heavily on the leaves. She felt a sudden quiver of fear. If she left the footpath in order to hunt for the little dog, and Ezekiel *was* around, as they had originally hoped, he might feel safe enough to do more than approach her. He could abduct her! He had done it twice and could do it again.

Akiko remembered suddenly that once, when Jeems had run off across the playing field, Jamie had told her not to worry. The dog would come back to them, he said. She was very clever, he had assured her, and had a good nose for picking up the scent of people and things. He had been right, of course. Although she had now disappeared, it was not long before she was back, wagging her tail.

Akiko continued along the footpath until she could see clear daylight ahead. She knew she would soon be out on an estate road where visitors would be strolling. She was thirsty and tired, and thought of the coffee machine inside the chapel shop. Melanie would be on duty, and with returning confidence she tied Jeems to a sapling growing outside and joined a small crowd looking at the souvenirs.

"Good morning, Akiko!" said Melanie. "A bit wet for walking? And how's young Jamie? You must soon be returning to concerts and things in London?"

"Oh yes, I hope so," Akiko replied. "But my father is coming to rest at Stone House for a while, and so I shall be staying on here. Oh, and I was wondering," she added, "if you knew anyone who would lend me a cello for me to practise on? I would, of course, pay a fee. I have left my hired one in London, and should be keeping in practice every day."

Melanie thought, but shook her head. "Can't say I do," she said, "unless you try the music shop in Tresham."

But then a tall girl, about Akiko's age, came forward and said that she was staying locally and might be able to help. "I am temporarily at Last Resort House, and there is a man there who is very clever with musical instruments," she added. "I have seen him at work."

Akiko beamed. "I wonder if he could at least point me in the right direction. Isn't that what you say? My English is not good, I'm afraid. If you could ask him for me, that would be very kind," she said. "I am staying at Meade House in the main street. You could ask anyone. They all seem to know where the Meades live! I would take great care of it. Where is

Last Resort House exactly? I think I saw it from a distance once."

"It is a big old farmhouse in Waltonby. I am there with a friend. It is a community, you see. I don't really know much about it, and I don't expect to be there long. But I could ask and let you know?"

Akiko nodded, remembering what Lois had told her. She thanked the girl again, and decided to go straight back to ask for advice. The thought of playing a cello again was overwhelmingly good news for Akiko.

"HI, DIANA," SOLOMON SAID, AS HE GREETED HER BACK FROM her walk. He was quite attracted to this new visitor to their community. She was tall, blonde and slender, and had a warm smile. Arriving with Foster, she had been introduced by him as his sister's friend. Solomon had taken that with a pinch of salt, and guessed that she had been cohabiting with Foster in the gamekeeper's cottage until they were turned out.

He had not yet had time to discover all he needed to know about her. Foster had said that she was in shock after the death of her parents in a sailing accident, but Solomon had heard many variations of that over the years and re-served judgement. She was probably not full-time Resort material, though she had every appearance of being wealthy. Meanwhile, she was very fanciable and he liked having her around.

"Been for a walk?" he continued. No one had yet told her that solitary walking outside the bounds of the community was not allowed. For residents' own protection, of course, he would stress.

"Yes, I thumbed a lift to Farnden to pay a visit to the

hall. It is open to the public, and until it started to rain, it was a beautiful walk back. There is a gift shop there, with souvenirs. Look, I bought some postcards with views of the hall."

"Very nice," said Solomon. "Now, I think it is time for us to have a little talk about how we expect people to make the most of life in our community. Perhaps you would like to come to my office and have a coffee? Shouldn't take long," he added, with a beaming smile.

"Right, of course," she said. But a small seed of suspicion took root, and she decided not to mention that she planned to go over to Farnden again this afternoon with advice for the Japanese girl. As for a cello, it did not seem an appropriate time to mention it. Everyone here had been very kind. But something about this smooth-talking man jarred, and he never looked her straight in the eye.

Never mind, she told herself, if I don't like it here after all, I can always go back home. But where was home? Perhaps she should try a little harder to settle here, but she had no wish to be a prisoner, even for a while.

FORTY-TWO

ᔬ

L OIS WAS WORKING IN HER OFFICE WHEN SHE SAW AKIKO and Jeems walking briskly back to the house. She went to the front door, ready to deliver a rocket about leaving the house without telling anyone. Surely Akiko knew by now that she must not be out alone?

"But I had Jeems with me!" she protested. "I had a lovely time and nobody stopped me or tried to molest me."

"I should think not, indeed. Jeems wouldn't be much use against a weapon, anyway. She can be fierce, but she's very small!"

They walked through to the kitchen, and Akiko dried the dog's paws gently with an old towel. Behind her back, Lois shook her head at Jamie, who looked as if he was about to follow up with a stern lecture.

"Right, well, I'll say no more," he said. "But do be sensible, Akiko. We're not playing games here. Now, it'll soon be lunchtime. Dad's out and Gran's gone to see her friend.

But she's left food in the oven. Why don't you tell us how you got on?"

"Well, I was glad that there was no sign of Ezekiel Parsons. I have decided that we are wrong about his likely movements, so I did not expect to see him. He is probably very far away now. I shall be happy if I never see him again. I walked through the spinney, and even when Jeems got lost, I did not stray from the footpath. She came back and I put her on the lead again. But I did not meet anyone in the spinney. Not a single person. I am now sure he is not around."

"We're not so sure, not by any means!" Jamie said. "I was getting worried about you. You didn't say you were going. Never mind. You're safe home now, but *please* don't venture out on your own without telling me. He may be around tomorrow morning. Probably more likely then, anyway. He'll be on the run, but may get desperate to find you."

Lois cleared her throat. "I suppose it is no good my saying again that this plan of yours is dangerous and amateurish?" she said. "Really, Jamie, I am surprised at you being so blockheaded. If Parsons turns up, and we see him, fair enough. We report to Cowgill. But no traps! And I'm sure Akiko thinks the same."

"I don't think he is around here anywhere," Akiko repeated stubbornly. "Anyway, I have not finished telling you about my nice morning. I did not come straight home, but was thirsty, and as I had seen a coffee machine in the chapel shop, I went to get a drink. I tied Jemima to a tree outside, as you do, and went in. Mrs. Norrington was there and greeted me nicely. Then I remembered that I was going to ask her if she knew of a cello I could hire or borrow. I told her that I should be practising and miss my cello very much."

"So you asked around the people in the shop?" Lois was not sure why, but this seemed a dangerous thing to do.

"Oh, not everybody! Just Mrs. Norrington. But this girl must have heard me, and offered to ask around. She said she knew of a possible source. But this is the strange thing, Mrs. M, and I need your advice. She said she would be in touch and I told her where to come. And then I asked her politely where she lived, and she said at the moment in Waltonby at Last Resort House!"

There was a stunned silence. "Oh dear," said Lois finally. "Not that place! I have nothing against it except rumour, but I don't want us mixed up with that lot."

"But, Mum," Jamie said, "it would be so nice for Akiko to be able to play. We could do some practising together. I know how much she wants to."

Blimey, thought Lois, whose only brush with performing had been as a child, when she had three guitar lessons and then gave up. "Oh well," she said reluctantly. "I suppose there's no harm in it. She may not turn up."

"Now I must go quickly down to Stone House to welcome my father," Akiko said, brushing aside the fact that she had had no lunch. "I am sure Mrs. T-J will have been baking," she said.

"And I'm coming with you," said Jamie. "I shall not stay, but you must ring me when you are ready to come home."

FORTY-THREE

~

Mrs. T-J could not relax. She ran from room to room with excitement, and kissed Akiko on the cheek when she arrived. "They will soon be here," she said. "I telephoned the hospital to make sure, and they are on their way. Oh, I do hope he will like it here, my dear. I know he is used to luxurious living, but I have some good old things, and Robert is ready and willing to go to the convent again to find anything he needs."

"Did you manage to put the photographs in an album, as you kindly suggested?" said Akiko.

"No, I haven't done that. I thought it would be nice for him to sort them out. I have an empty album ready for him, and he'll be able to tell us who all the people are in the photos."

"How kind," said Akiko, "he will be so grateful."

A shadow passed the window, and Mrs. T-J rushed to the door. "There's the ambulance! He's here!" she shouted. "Come quickly, Akiko."

The paramedics opened the rear doors of the ambulance, and a wheelchair was gently lowered down the ramp.

"Papa!"

"Akiko, my darling!"

Mrs. T-J stood back, fumbling for a handkerchief to mop sudden tears. It would be all right. It *would* be all right.

THE REST OF THE AFTERNOON WAS SPENT SHOWING NAKAMASA around, especially where Mrs. T-J had converted a ground-floor study into a pleasant bedroom, with all mod cons and a French window leading out into the garden.

Finally they all settled in the drawing room for tea—Japanese green tea thoughtfully provided—and a catch-up conversation between father and daughter. Mrs. T-J listened carefully, and observed the fragile old man's obvious devotion to his daughter. She made no attempt to join in, realising just how anxious Akiko had been. There was clearly a very strong bond between the two. When they began to talk about the old days and Akiko's mother, she thought it tactful to withdraw, and said she would be in the kitchen seeing about the evening meal.

"What a very nice woman," Nakamasa said, after she had disappeared. "She must be very fond of you, my dear, to take so much trouble over a sick old man."

"But you are not so sick now, Papa. You will be stronger, of course, but with the magic machine inside, you will be a new man. Everyone who has a pacemaker says the same. I agree that Mrs. Tollervey-Jones is a special person. And she is very English, you know. I shall say no more, but perhaps you will reconsider some of your views."

"We will not talk about that, Akiko," he said firmly. "I

am alive, no thanks to Parsons, and that is enough for the present."

"Now you know what kind of man Parsons really is! I do have some questions to ask when you are feeling strong enough to look back. Meanwhile, let me give you a surprise."

She walked over to a small table, where Mrs. T-J had put the photographs and album.

"Look, at these, Papa. Mrs. T-J's son collected them from the convent. I told him where to look, and he found them. You can sort them out and put them in this album."

Nakamasa took the packet from her and opened it. He pulled out a faded photograph of a young woman and a proud, upright, middle-aged man. The woman held a small baby, swathed in shawls, the tiny face barely visible.

"Oh, Akiko," he said, and his face crumpled. "How thoughtful you have been, you and your kind friends," he whispered, and took her hand. "We will talk about everything, I promise. But later, my dear. Later."

FORTY-FOUR

❦

THE NEXT DAY PASSED PEACEFULLY, WITH DEREK BACK TO work after lunch, Lois out in the garden weeding, and Jamie and Akiko walking down to Stone House to see Mr. Nakamasa and Mrs. T-J. Akiko had insisted on Jamie going with her, saying if he did not wish to meet her father, he could stay in the kitchen and talk to Mrs. T-J.

"He's surely not going to lurk in the servants' quarters, is he?" said Gran, affronted. "Our Jamie's good enough to meet anybody, and better than most."

Akiko blushed. "I did not mean that, Mrs. Weedon. It is just that, well, my father is still weak, and one visitor at a time is enough for him, I think."

"Don't worry, Gran. I know what Akiko meant. I shall be glad to talk to Mrs. T-J. I have things to discuss with her."

"Not going to talk about your plan, I hope," said Lois, as

they made their way down the drive. "Just keep your eyes peeled. You never know, he might be hanging about, but do not approach him on any account! If he is around, we can set the police on to him and forget the whole business."

Akiko changed the subject tactfully. "If you see the girl from Last Resort House, could you explain to her that I will be back shortly? I know my father will not want to be disturbed for too long. Thank you, Mrs. M."

"How shall I know it's her?"

"She is tall, blonde and has a very nice smile. She will probably come to the house."

"Fine. We'll keep a watch. Give my regards to your father, and say I hope to meet him very soon."

Lois watched them walk slowly along the high street, and then returned to her weeds.

AT LAST RESORT HOUSE, FOSTER AND PARSONS WERE HAVING an argument. Foster ended by saying he had no intention of spending any more time spotting Japanese girls. "Not my type," he said.

As to Parsons's second request, which was an unexplained and sudden need to get as far away as possible, preferably away from this country, he again refused to have anything to do with it.

"If you won't tell me why you're on the run, then I'd be a right fool to help you. Accessory after the fact, an' all that. If it's all legal and aboveboard, and you just want a holiday break, then I can probably help. But since when did you take a holiday break, Ez? No, nothing doing, I'm afraid."

Parsons drifted away, down to the summerhouse at the

bottom of the garden. This usually had two or three people sitting there, but this morning he had it to himself. He needed to work out just exactly how he could discover the fate of Nakamasa, and once he knew for sure, he could then get out of the country and find a suitable place to retire, never to return. Other famous villains had managed it. Train robbers, bullion thieves, they'd all gone abroad and lived the life of Riley.

But he was not a famous villain. He was an unsuccessful blackmailer, kidnapper and possibly murderer into the bargain. It couldn't get much worse! He had to do something. The last thing he intended was to be arrested by local cops and sent to prison for life.

"Excuse me? Do you mind if I come and sit here for a bit?" A tall, blonde girl with a lovely smile addressed him, and he nodded. It really didn't matter much to him one way or the other. Perhaps he should confess all, throw himself on her mercy and beg for help? What rubbish! If she knew what he had done, she would run screaming for Solomon Grundy.

"It is a lovely day," she said. "Please tell me if you don't want to talk. I know some of the residents here are very troubled and frightened of strangers. I am good at being quiet."

"No, dear. I can't imagine anyone being frightened of you. Talk away, if you like. Are you staying here?"

"Not for long," she said with a grimace. "Not my kind of holiday resort!"

"Ah, yes. You're a friend of my friend Foster, aren't you? He told me a bit about you. I'm sorry about your mum and dad being drowned. That must have been grim." Perhaps I should drown myself and end it all, he thought glumly. It'd be an easy way out. Nobody would grieve for me.

She nodded. "Thanks. It's not that long ago, and I'm still a bit confused. It's like being in a bubble, where you're inside and everybody else is outside getting on with their lives. Detached, I suppose, would be the word."

"Time heals, so they say. Anyway, I'll leave you in peace," he said, getting up to go. "Best of luck, dearie."

"Same to you. And thanks. Oh, and just before you go, you don't know anyone who could lend a cello, do you? I was talking to a girl who needs one to practice on. She's a professional, and her own instrument was stolen."

"Ah," said Parsons. "I might be able to help."

AT STONE HOUSE, THINGS WERE GOING WELL. AKIKO WAS pleased to see her father looking much better already, and even taking a few steps out into the garden. Then Mrs. Tollervey-Jones appeared with tea, followed by Jamie with a plate of freshly baked scones.

Jamie was holding his breath as he approached Nakamasa. "Good morning, sir," he said politely.

"Good morning, young man. You must be my daughter's accompanist. I have heard so much about you. Please come and sit with us. Jamie, isn't it?"

"We might as well sit out in the sun," said Mrs. T-J, and she and Jamie fetched chairs and parasols and soon they were chatting amiably about nothing very much.

Then Nakamasa said, "I must apologise, Jamie, for my villainous assistant imprisoning you in the convent. If I had thought calmly, I would have searched every nook and cranny.

But I was so sure Akiko would have fled to join you. An old man's folly, I am afraid. But here you both are, and I am very pleased to see you."

Akiko could not believe her ears. Was this really her father speaking? She smiled broadly at him, and said, "I am sure we have forgiven you for not looking for us, but we will never forgive Parsons. The police are on his tail, as we say, and I know he will make a mistake and show himself very soon. Now, how are you getting on with the photographs?"

"I'll fetch the album," said Mrs. T-J. "You will see how well he is doing! And I have been introduced to all your relations, Akiko."

Jamie got up to help, and followed her inside. The old thing was quite girlish! Could it possibly be love at first sight? He chuckled. That would put the cat among the Japanese pigeons!

They returned, bearing fresh tea and a large leather-bound photograph album. "Me first!" said Akiko. "I want to show Jamie my family. Come, Jamie, sit by me."

Jamie began to turn over pages, with Akiko excitedly identifying her mother and grandparents, and then, "Here is Papa, a proud soldier," she said.

A chilly silence descended on the little group. Jamie felt sick as he looked at the familiar image of a Japanese soldier, helmeted, heavily armed and holding a curved knife.

"Are you all right, Jamie? You look so pale. Does this photograph bother you?" Akiko looked anxiously into his face.

He shook his head dumbly, but Nakamasa answered. "Of course it does, daughter," he said. "Just as the sight of an English soldier in uniform, bristling with weapons, would bother me. Please close the album, Jamie. We will talk of happier times."

"Don't worry, sir," said Jamie. "You looked so young. Only a boy, I guess?"

"More scones, anyone," said Mrs. T-J firmly. "Lots more in the kitchen."

FORTY-FIVE

❧

BY THE TIME AKIKO AND JAMIE RETURNED TO MEADE House, the rest of the family were sitting in the best room, conducting a halting conversation with the girl from Last Resort House. "My name is Diana. I have come to see Akiko," she had said, when she found Lois gardening by the front gate.

Lois had felt obliged to invite her in for a cup of tea, and the conversation had soon dried up. She jumped to her feet with relief when the others arrived, and handed over to Akiko. "We have had a nice talk with Diana," she said. "She has some good news for you."

"It is so kind of you to come, Diana," Akiko said. "Did you have any luck with the musical instrument man?"

"Yes, I did!" she said, and got up to look behind the sofa. "How about this one? Would it be any good to you?"

"How clever of you!" said Akiko. "It looks brand-new.

Very much how my own lost cello must have looked when it was new! Oh, I must just try out a few bars."

She settled carefully on an upright chair, set the cello up and tried tuning a few strings. Then she played a short scrap of music.

"Sounds good to me," Jamie said, smiling at Diana. "How did you work the miracle?"

"It was a funny little man I met in the summerhouse. He took me along to the craft workshops, but the instrument maker was not there. I spotted the cello, and he said he was sure the maker would be pleased to lend it to a professional cellist. He put it into its case, and told me to take it, and he would explain to the maker. So that's it!"

"This is marvellous," said Akiko. "And of course I shall pay him well when we return it. He must be an extremely clever craftsman?"

"Never met him," said Diana, with a shrug. "But I did see some half-made Noah's Ark animals on the bench. I suppose those are a money-making line. I do hope he won't be cross!"

"Please tell him I will take great care of it, and if he wants it back straightaway, I will bring it personally," said Akiko. "It may be a commission for a client."

WHEN LOIS AND GRAN RETURNED TO THE ROOM, THEY WERE followed by Derek, carrying a tray with glasses and a wine bottle.

"A small snifter to celebrate?" he said.

"Wow!" said Diana. "It's only a glorified banjo to me. No problem! But I never say no to a glass of wine. It's really nice of you."

"It is very important to me, Diana. So thank you again," repeated Akiko, smiling broadly. Then she looked at Gran and said wouldn't it be a lovely thing if Diana could stay for supper? "Mrs. Weedon is an excellent cook," she added.

What a difference a cello makes, thought Lois, seeing a new Akiko in front of her. The girl looks as if she has been part of the Meade family for years, talking about supper and super-cook Gran. Of course, she had been to see her father and was pleased with his progress, so that must count. This thought, as always, gave her a moment's pause.

SOLOMON WAS CONCERNED ONLY WITH A MISSING GIRL, DIANA Smith. As yet, the cello had not been reported removed.

"Where the hell is she, then?" he asked around. But nobody had seen her. They must all have been at the prayer meeting in the big hall, they said.

He thought one or two were looking furtive. But then, some of them looked furtive all the time, poor sods. "Diana Smith is not allowed to go wandering off on her own!" he shouted. "I already explained that to her not three hours ago! She said not a word about going out again, and now she's nowhere to be found."

He looked around for a scapegoat and picked on a likely looking woman. "You were the last to talk to her, so you'd better smarten yourself up and go and find her. I want her back in my office before seven thirty this evening. Or else."

The woman shook, knowing what would happen if Diana was not back. She rushed away to ask friends when they had last seen her, and Solomon returned to his study, banging the door with a crash behind him.

When he had calmed down, he decided to search Diana

Smith's room to see what he could find. He regularly did the rounds of his residents' rooms. Amazing what people left lying around! Personal papers, letters, all kinds of things. She seemed a nice girl, but there was something decidedly shifty about her. On his way to the stairs, old Herbert came rushing up to him, stammering even more than usual.

"What are you trying to say? Spit it out, man!" Solomon turned to go upstairs, when Herbert finally said, "My cello! It's gone, Mr. Grundy. My unfinished cello!"

"Don't be ridiculous, Bert, it can't have gone. You must have put it somewhere safe and forgotten where you put it. You are about to age it, aren't you? Have another look. I'll be down in a few minutes." What an old fool! For two pins he'd give him the push. But he'd never find anyone as skilled as Bert.

He charged up the stairs two at a time, and in Diana's room, his temper rising, he opened every drawer, shaking out the contents on to the floor. Books, neatly arranged on a shelf, were thrown higgledy-piggledy around the room. A vase of flowers picked from the garden was knocked over, spilling water over everything, including pages of beautifully illustrated books.

Nothing of interest to Solomon emerged, and he left the room without locking the door or attempting to clear up the mess.

House policy, he reminded himself as he went downstairs. Every so often at Resort House they encountered a rebel, and now here was another one. He had forgotten to tell the unfortunate woman who would be looking for Diana Smith that she could go beyond the usual boundary, but when he asked the others, they said she had already left in search of the truant.

Solomon sighed. It was definitely one of those days. He supposed he should go to the workshop and see if Herbert had found his cello. It had better be found! It was due for collection next week. He opened the door to the craft area, and saw Herbert on the floor beside his bench.

"Bert? What on earth are you doing?" No reply. "Bert? Speak up, do!"

A mumble reached his ears, and he went closer. Bert buried his face in his hands. He mumbled again, and Solomon heard only the word "gone."

It was growing dark now, and Ezekiel had been loping about in the wood, keeping out of sight. Like a rabbit, he told himself. He was used to alfresco sleeping, but he had decided to keep himself awake at all costs. Old Bert's cello had been a neat trick! He grinned. Diana Smith would deliver it to Akiko, and Solomon would be desperate, but never connect it with him. A small revenge on Grundy, but not nearly enough to pay him back for past humiliations. Grundy would talk to the blonde later, find out where the cello had gone and make sure he retrieved it.

Parsons sighed. He had left Resort House long before Diana was likely to return, vanishing with his meagre belongings before anyone had seen him. The Resorters were all on their knees in the hall, so it was perfect timing. On his way out, he had said a few short prayers himself, but doubted if anyone was listening.

Now he crouched down uncomfortably in the woods, his back against a tree. He was deliberately uncomfortable, so that he would not fall asleep for more than a few minutes. He would have to take some risks tomorrow, his last chance

to find Akiko alone. He would just ask her a quick question—
was Nakky dead or alive—and then scarper on his way. He
would know then whether he was a clumsy villain or a murderer. It was important to him to know. Whichever, he had
decided to head for the coast and see if he could get a job on
one of the boats. It wouldn't matter where it was going, as
long as it was a long way away from merrie England.

PEACE REIGNED IN MEADE HOUSE. LOIS AND DEREK HAD
discussed with the others the afternoon's events, and Gran
had excelled herself with a show-stopping supper. They had
all sat round watching an antiques valuation programme on
television, Lois's favourite, and conversation had declined to
the odd grunt from a sleeping Derek and some hoots of
derision from Lois when hideous ornaments proved to be
worth thousands.

Finally, Diana Smith stirred and said she really must be
getting back. "There is a kind of curfew, which is long past,"
she said, looking at her watch. "I expect I shall be locked out,
or maybe drenched in boiling oil as I go across the draw-
bridge."

"What!" said Akiko. "Then you cannot go! Mrs. M! She
cannot go back and be covered in boiling oil!"

Lois laughed. "A joke, Akiko. Just a joke." Then she turned
to Diana, and said that perhaps it had not been that much of
a joke? Was she actually afraid to go back to Resort House?
"I don't know much about the place, but I've never heard any
good of it," she added.

"Stay here, if you're frit," said Gran. She had taken to the
pleasantly spoken girl, and felt kindly towards her when she
heard of her parents' accident. "She can have Douglas's old

room. Not very jolly, I'm afraid, but probably better than boiling oil. You'd be very welcome, wouldn't she, Lois?"

Lois thought rapidly, and answered that yes, of course, that would be fine. Diana said that she was not exactly frightened, but would really appreciate a break from the community.

LONG AFTER HER MOTHER HAD GONE TO BED, LOIS SAT ON IN THE quiet sitting room, winding down from the excitement and revelations of the evening. Derek had woken refreshed and demanding to be filled in with what had happened whilst he was asleep, and Lois was happy to oblige.

"Now then, let me get this straight," Derek said. "You've got this plan to trap Ezekiel Parsons, using Akiko as bait. Right?"

"No," said Lois.

"Sort of," said Jamie.

"Right. Well," said Derek, "I can see you're in full agreement. So who's the boss?"

"Me," said Lois.

"Me, sort of," said Jamie.

"Well, pardon me if I'm wrong, son James, but I think this is a pretty loony plan. I'm with your mother on this one."

"What does Akiko think?" said Lois, curling up on the sofa beside Derek.

"Akiko?" said Derek.

Akiko hesitated, looked sideways at Jamie, and said, "I'm a little worried. My instructions are to run like hell, and Jamie will be right behind me. This could easily go wrong. Parsons will be a desperate man by now, and I suppose I must accept that he is likely to be in this locality."

"Akiko!" said Jamie. "I thought you were happy with the plan?"

"Not now. I'm sorry, Jamie, but I know him too well."

Lois stood up, hands on her hips. "That's that, then, Jamie. Plan cancelled, thank goodness. Parsons is bound to show up sooner or later, and then we'll act."

"So what next?" said Derek, also getting to his feet.

"Easy," said Lois, stroking his stubbly cheek. "Bed. Right?"

"Right!" said Derek.

FORTY-SIX

"CAN YOU HEAR SOMETHING?" LOIS SAT UP IN BED AND nudged a still sleeping Derek.

"Huh? What? Is it morning?"

"Yes, it is. Early morning, I'm afraid. But I just woke up and heard this noise. There it is again! Is it music or what?"

Derek groaned. "If you call it music, yes, I suppose it is."

Lois collapsed back on to the pillows. "Oh my God, I think it's Akiko playing her borrowed cello. Where's my earplugs? Ah, that's better. Now, since we're awake, shall we get up?"

"No," said Derek, now wide-awake. "Let's dance to the music, Mrs. M."

"What did you say?" Lois said loudly.

Derek put his arms around her. "I said, let's dance to the music," he repeated poetically, "while we've got the chance."

*   *   *

Gran, meanwhile, was up already and clattering about with frying pan and eggbeater. She did not hear Diana's silent approach, and started as she looked round. "You made me jump, gel!" she said. "Here, sit you down and have a cup of tea while I get the breakfast. I suppose you couldn't sleep?" Poor thing looks quite worn out, Gran thought. We'd better look after her for a day or two.

"Thank you, Mrs. Weedon," Diana said, and her chin wobbled. "It's all been a bit much lately, what with Mum and Dad, and that awful place . . ." Her tears plopped into the tea placed in front of her, and she scrubbed at her eyes with a tissue. "Sorry," she said in a muffled voice. "I reckon you've got enough on your plate as it is. Am I right?"

"You've said it! I reckon my Lois is going mad, rushing about after imaginary criminals and stirring up that old fool, Mrs. Tollervey-Jones, when the silly woman ought to be settling down with her knitting at her age. I don't know what her son, Robert, is thinking of, letting her loose in her dotage! Now she's turned Stone House into a convalescent home for sick Japanese gentlemen. Then there's my grandson Jamie and his friend—her with the cello—getting into all kinds of trouble up London! I don't know, I'm sure," she added, placing a plate of curly, crisp bacon and a mound of buttery scrambled eggs in front of Diana. "Get that inside you and you'll feel a whole lot better."

At this point, the door opened and Akiko appeared, a smile stretching from ear to ear.

"Good morning, Gran, and Diana," she said. "I have been having a lovely time playing again. It is such a beautiful instrument, even though it is new. I do hope I did not disturb anyone?" she asked, looking anxious.

"Oh no," said Gran, "not at all. It sounded lovely." She crossed her fingers behind her back, and thought privately that it was just like a load of howling monkeys. She supposed she would have to get used to it, if Akiko was going to be a frequent visitor to the family. "And, as my dear hubby used to say, you can get used to anything," she could not resist adding.

Akiko sat at the table next to Diana and asked her warmly if she had had a good sleep.

"Oh yes, the first good night I've had since I came to these parts," she replied. "Nighttime in Last Resort House was full of eerie footsteps and creaking stairs. And sometimes, the footsteps stopped outside my door, and I was terrified."

"So you don't mind our Douglas's bed? He'd broken practically all the springs by the time he left home. Used it as a trampoline," said Gran. "You've not much time for Last Resort House, then? I think it would be best, my dear, if you collected your things from there, and we'll find you a place to stay in the village. Mrs. Tollervey-Jones might fit you in, even though you're not Japanese."

"My father will not be there long," Akiko said. "He is a very active person usually, and as soon as he feels stronger, I am sure he will want to go back to Japan. And then I shall be faced with a decision to make," she added, almost as if talking to herself.

Diana was still unsure about the relationship between Akiko and Jamie, and did not like to ask. Once or twice she had caught Jamie's eye last evening, and that old familiar frisson of interest had sparked up between them. Not for the world would she come between Akiko and him, but it was possible that theirs was only a professional partnership. Give it time, Diana, she could hear her mother saying.

"What decision is that, if you don't mind my asking?" she said now to Akiko. "Any help needed?"

Akiko shook her head. "No, only I can make this decision. I have spent more time with my father since he has been here than for a very long while. He was always so busy, and I had music commitments to fulfil."

"And nonmusical ones?" Diana risked a pointed question.

Akiko laughed. "Those ones are private, Diana. And you? You were living with the gamekeeper at the hall, weren't you? I hope that is not an impertinent question. I do not always get the right words. Please forgive me."

Diana was quiet for a moment, and then sighed. "Yeah, you're right. I was living with Foster. He took advantage of my being in mourning for my parents and not thinking straight. But now I am thinking very straight and shall have no more to do with him."

"So will you fetch your things?" said Gran. "Lois will ring Mrs. T-J for you, and then you can go down to see her."

"Tell me about her," replied Diana. "She sounds an interesting person. Has she lived here long?"

"Generations, that family," said Gran, and embarked on a long and much-embellished history of the Tollervey-Joneses.

This lasted until the kitchen door opened once more and Derek and Lois appeared, smiling. "Morning, everyone," said Lois.

"And this is a fine time to come down to breakfast! These two girls are finished and on their last cups of coffee," said Gran in a stern voice. But Lois could see a twinkle in her mother's eye, and asked if there was anything she could do to help.

"You can give your son a shout. I can't keep this bacon hot much longer. It'll be like dried leather. And I'm intending to go to midweek matins this morning in church. That new bishop is visiting, and I want to give him the once-over."

On cue, Jamie came smiling into the kitchen. "Morning, everyone," he said. "Morning, Diana! Glad to see you're still here."

"Help yourself, Jamie," Gran said. "I must wash the smells of cooking off me hands."

"You go, Mum, and get ready," Lois said. "I'll finish breakfast. Now, did everybody sleep well? Hope so. You and Jamie are off for a walk this morning, Akiko, aren't you?"

"Oh yes, I am ready for anything today," she replied. "But we do not go to the spinney, Jamie. This I insist on." Her face was unsmiling, and he did not answer.

"Something else, before I go," said Gran. "Diana's been talking about that place at Waltonby, and doesn't want to go back to stay. I've said you'll ask Mrs. T-J about putting her up for a while. Can you do that today?"

"Certainly," said Lois, smiling kindly at Diana. "Are you all right for collecting your possessions, or do you want Derek to go over to Waltonby for you?"

Diana hesitated. "I would love that," she said. "But I think I have to go and sign off. There are some things I need to say to Grundy. Then again, I might leave a few presents for the poor souls who were nice to me. But thanks, Derek."

"No problem, gel," he said. "You do what you think best."

EZEKIEL WAS TIRED AFTER KEEPING HIMSELF AWAKE THROUGH the night. He thought he had heard sounds of searching, but had managed to avoid them. Now he was hungry, and decided that he would sneak into the hall kitchen when the coast was clear and snitch something to eat.

The Norringtons were both off to the supermarket this morning. The chapel shop would be open and Dot Nimmo had agreed to deal with customers until they returned home. She had no New Brooms tasks this morning, and fancied herself as an upmarket shop assistant.

"Who is that over there, Mel, by the stables?" Geoff asked, as he and Melanie walked to where their four-by-four was parked. Melanie shrugged. "Don't know," she said. "It's not our ex-gamekeeper. I'm sure of that. We get so many people here now, it is difficult to remember them all." She looked at her watch. "Come on, hurry up," she said. "We want to miss the rush."

Ezekiel Parsons watched from a place of shadows in the stable yard as they climbed into the car and drove off at speed. What an idiot, he thought to himself. Old Norrington was putting on weight, and it'd do him a power of good to have a good walk occasionally. "Still, it's his choice," he said, as he quickly opened the kitchen door and tucked bread, butter and cheese into his knapsack. He fled at top speed, glad of his own lean and hungry frame.

As Akiko and Jamie set off with Jemima on her lead, she began to think about what their future together might be. "I shall miss these walks with Jeems," she said, taking Jamie's hand. "When we go back to London, perhaps I will buy a very small dog that I can carry about with me. Would that be possible? We could walk it in the park, and buy it a little bed with a cushion."

"Don't know," Jamie said. The plural "we" was beginning

to alarm him. He had no serious intentions of making a more permanent duo than they had now. They were from different cultures. He had seen that very clearly when Akiko was with her father.

He could not help noticing that she was starting to be possessive with him, and thought that quite soon he would have to have a talk with her. She was so alone in this country, and once her father went away again, she would rely on her musical partner more and more. He knew now that this was not a good idea, but Akiko was stubborn. It would not be easy to get her to change her mind. She had only recently said to him, admittedly in the abstract, that she believed in the soothing power of love, and discounted any differences in race or colour.

Then there was her father. He seemed to have had a change of heart, but that might fade once he was completely recovered. With any luck, Jamie thought, feeling slightly ashamed, Nakamasa might persuade her to give up any idea of marrying a foreigner.

"You are very quiet, Jamie," Akiko said now. "A penny for them. Isn't that what you say?"

"Not worth having," he said quickly. "Come on, let's step out."

They were out of the village now and walking through a field belonging to John Thornbull, the husband of one of Lois's team. Jamie released Jeems, and she shot off across the long grass towards a high hedge.

"Rabbits," said Jamie. "There's a warren under the hedge over there. I expect I shall have to pull her out by her tail. Come on, follow me, Akiko!" He ran off, quickly gaining ground.

And then she saw Parsons. A motionless figure standing

by a gap in the hedge on the far side of the field. For a moment she was not sure, but as she looked again she saw that it was the man she hated most. It *was* Parsons, she was sure, and she stopped, frozen to the spot.

"Jamie!" she yelled. "Come back!" He had nearly reached the far side of the field, and when she looked back, the figure by the gap had melted away.

"Jamie! Look over there! It was Parsons!"

But Jeems was barking furiously now, hot on the scent and halfway down a burrow, and Jamie did not hear.

FORTY-SEVEN

W HEN AKIKO CAUGHT UP WITH JAMIE, SHE WAS BREATH-
less and said in a hoarse voice, "Did you see him?"

"Who?" Jamie looked at her curiously. "I didn't see anyone. I was too busy extracting this small dog from a rabbit
burrow. Did you see someone?"

Akiko nodded. "Yes, I did. I saw Parsons! I yelled to you,
but Jeems was barking and you did not hear. He disappeared
very quickly from the gap in the hedge. I think he might
have been watching us."

"Are you sure it was him?"

"Absolutely certain. Don't forget the many years I have
known him."

"Of course. I'm so sorry, Akiko. I should have chased after
him."

"No, Jamie, do not ever do that. Remember what your
mother told us. And don't forget that he stole my father's

gun from his pocket. Papa told me it was the last thing he did before he abandoned him to his fate."

"Do you think he would use it? In the middle of a field in broad daylight?"

Akiko nodded vigorously. "I think he must be desperate by now. He would do better to go as far away as possible. But I think he needs to know if Papa is still alive."

"Because he feels remorse? Doesn't sound like the Parsons I have encountered. More likely he wants to have another go at him."

Akiko frowned. "Jamie, please! It is possible, but I don't think he would attack Papa at Stone House, as it would be too dangerous. And he has no real reason to kill him. Papa always treated him fairly. It may be remorse, but if I were in his shoes, I could not rest until I knew for sure that I was not a murderer. This is not quite the same as remorse, no? But I think that is why he is still around. And why perhaps he does not need to see Papa, just to know that he is alive."

"Well, whatever," said Jamie. "If you are right, he'll still be hanging around until he's found out. It'll be difficult for him, because the police are going to be everywhere, once Cowgill's been told you've seen him. Like a fool, I didn't bring my mobile."

"Nor I," said Akiko. "You do not expect to need a mobile when you are walking a dog."

"Don't worry. It's probably better coming from Mum, anyway. Parsons will still be around, looking for another opportunity to find you alone. He nearly made it this morning! Then he can get his answer and scram."

"Perhaps, Jamie. But I am not willing to try out your theory! I do not forget the gun. He is not fond of me, though he may possibly have some good feeling for Papa. After all, Papa has supported him all this time. But he knows I want him got rid of. And so he wants to be rid of me!"

Jamie smiled at her. "Then I shall stick to you like glue, Akiko. You are never to be out of my sight until we catch him. The one good thing about a desperate man is that he's bound to make a mistake. Then we've got him. Come on, now. Cheer up! Lets go home, tell Mum all about it and see what Gran has made for lunch. Our new friend Diana should be around, and we can give her a recital this afternoon, if she's musically inclined."

She took his hand, and he thought again how small and defenceless she would be, if she had to face an armed and desperate Parsons. It was urgent now to tell Mum they had seen him, and let her alert her chums.

EZEKIEL PARSONS HAD MADE IT BACK TO THE PLAYING FIELD AND was out of sight in the piece of rough ground beyond. He considered what he had seen. It was Akiko all right! And, of course, lover boy. Perhaps he should have approached them, but he had been reluctant. He was still convinced he would find Akiko alone soon, and ask her the one important question. The presence of Meade would have made things difficult. Lover boy was an athletic sort of idiot, and could probably floor a weed like himself. He was almost certain they had not seen him. Meade was too far away, peering down rabbit holes, and Akiko had not caught up. Before they turned back, he would have gone.

He had eaten most of the Norrington supplies, and needed to keep up his strength for a long retreat. Perhaps he could choose his moment and lurk in the small access road that led out of the playing field straight up to the shop. Then, when the coast was clear, he could slip in quietly and grab enough stuff to last him for a while, and beat it, fast. If Meade and Miss Akiko showed up, he would have to think again.

It was the best of a bad choice, but at least he could disguise himself with the old woollen hat he always kept handy in his knapsack.

JOSIE HAD HAD A BUSY MORNING. AFTER THE WEEKEND, THERE were always those who had run out of essentials, and they would make their one weekly visit to the village shop to buy goods in small amounts. It annoyed her sometimes, when she saw them returning from town with overflowing supermarket bags. But there was no point in grumbling. All business was good business, and there were still a few customers who ordered all their weekly needs from her. After the shop closed on Friday afternoons, she delivered boxes to outlying farms, and was always welcomed with a cup of tea and a gossip. She felt that in a small way she was keeping the village traditions going.

Now she looked at her watch. She had a new regime. Few shoppers came in at lunchtime, and so she retreated to the stockroom at the back and made a coffee and a sandwich. Nine times out of ten, she would not be interrupted. Perhaps she would give her mother a call now, and catch up on the news. Things at Meade House seemed to be changing hourly, what with Jamie's girlfriend disappearing and reappearing, and the new girl, Diana Smith from Last Resort House. Poor old Gran! But Gran seemed to thrive on it! She was a towny at heart, and loved having lots of people around.

She left the front of the shop with the door ajar, and

settled down for a chat. Lois was at home, and pleased to hear from her, and Josie was unaware that a prowler was outside, peering in through the shop window. She heard the door bell, and looked through but could see no one. "Didn't shut the shop door properly," she said, and had a quick look round. Parsons had just managed to slip in like a snake and was hiding behind a long line of shelving. He waited until he heard her voice once more coming from the stockroom. This might be interesting, and he decided to stay stock-still and listen.

"No, it's okay, Mum," said Josie. "Nobody there. I think the wind must have shut the door and made the bell ring. Now, where were we? Oh yes, Akiko and Jamie. So you really think there's nothing more than friendship there? When are they returning to work? It's a bit much of Jamie to sponge on you and Dad. What? Akiko's father, did you say? What about him? Oh, he's arrived, has he. Well, I never thought Mrs. T-J would turn her house into a convalescent home!"

The bell rang again, and once more she looked through to the shop. It was empty.

"You still there, Mum? I think we've got a poltergeist. Nobody there! I might as well have another sandwich. So, see you later. Bye!"

Parsons, safely out and walking head down to the scrubby field, could hardly keep from laughing aloud. The old Nip was alive! And here in Farnden. He was a jammy bugger. Always fell on his feet, right from when he was a child soldier being nasty to prisoners of war.

He unwrapped a bar of chocolate, and made short work of it. Then, feeling better, he considered what he had to do next. Fancy old Nakky being in Farnden! He wondered briefly whether he should pay him a farewell visit. The old boy could have treated him a lot worse over the years. He had probably deserved much worse. But no time for that now. He had to get away, and he could do that at last with a reasonably clear conscience.

He found his way to the Waltonby road and began a quick run back over the fields. Then he halted. The idea of a last goodbye nagged at him. Maybe out in the garden at Stone House? You bet they'd have him out there taking the air for the good of his health.

"Then he and me could wrap it all up and say goodbye with no hard feelings," he muttered, knowing as he said it that it was a really stupid idea. But it wouldn't leave him. He considered how rotten he'd been to the old chap, leaving him in the car to die. But he hadn't died! Perhaps a quick in and out of the garden, say sorry and vanish for good.

DEREK HAD SPENT THE MORNING ON THE ALLOTMENT, AND NOW turned up in Gran's kitchen bearing a trug full of vegetables. He handed them to her, and she nodded absently.

"Thanks for the welcome!" he said. "What's eating you, Gran? I was feeling rather pleased with myself, bringing you produce from the allotment, but perhaps I'll just put it in the bin."

"Sorry!" Gran replied, blowing him a kiss. "That all looks great. Nice to have something wholesome to talk about, instead of Lois's basket of troubles. Or maybe I should say Akiko's. She and Jamie are back from a walk, saying they want to know the minute Lois gets back."

"Where is Lois, then?"

"I think she went round to have a quick word with Floss. She was talking to Josie for quite a while on the phone. She's only just gone. I think one of her cleaners has gone off sick.

She called out she'd only be a few minutes. She'll be back shortly, I expect."

Derek cupped his hand around his ear. "The duo is at it again, I hear," he said. "Perhaps I'll go and offer them a pre-lunch drink to wet their whistles. And while I've been gardening, Gran, I have come to a decision. This ridiculous case of the missing cello thing is going to be Lois's last ferretin' case."

"Oh yeah? My money's on Lois, I'm afraid. I've known her longer than you have. She is just like her father, and he never gave up."

"Well, he must have, eventually, else you'd not be the Widow Weedon, would you?"

"Derek! Don't be flippant about losing a loved one! Ah, there's Lois back. Now go and get those drinks, and I'll have a large gin and tonic. Please."

FORTY-EIGHT

❧

"Now then, Mr. Nakamasa," said Mrs. Tollervey-Jones. "It is a lovely day, but the weatherman forecasts rain this afternoon. Why don't you let me set you up with some delicious homemade lemonade and the *Times* newspaper, under the shady apple tree in the garden? Doesn't that sound a good idea?"

Nakamasa smiled at her. "You are so kind to me, Mrs. Tollervey-Jones. That does indeed sound a very pleasant way of spending an hour or two. Perhaps you might join me for an hour or so? Thank you, my dear."

Mrs. T-J flushed. She could not remember the last time anyone had called her "my dear," and she hurried off to set out garden chairs and a tray of drinks.

After she had settled Nakamasa comfortably with the *Times* and a crystal glass of clinking ice cubes in lemonade,

Mrs. T-J said that she was nipping up to the shop for bread, and would be back very shortly. Would he be all right?

"Of course," he had answered. "Don't hurry, please. I might even have a doze while you are away."

He closed his eyes, and thought about Akiko. Now that he was feeling so much better, he began to plan his return to Japan. The heart attack had given him a big scare, and he was now quite determined to retire permanently, full time. It would be necessary to go back soon to his principal offices and make all the necessary arrangements. His deputy was a distant relation, and a much younger man, efficient and practical, and could safely be trusted to continue the House of Nakamasa. Akiko's financial position had been sewn up years ago and would be secure. She would be a very wealthy woman one day.

A blackbird landed on a branch above his head, and he remained perfectly still, listening to its heavenly song. If only Akiko would accompany him back to Japan, just for the few years he had left, he would be perfectly happy. Jamie Meade could visit as often as she liked, and he was suddenly struck with the most attractive thought that Mrs. T-J, too, might like to spend a holiday with them!

The blackbird flew off, and instead of its fruity song, Nakamasa heard an odd sound.

"Pssst! Mr. Nakamasa!"

He looked round to where the voice came from, but could see nobody. His heart quickened.

"Who is it? What are you doing here? This is private property. Please go away at once!"

"It's me. Ez Parsons. I just want a quick word."

Nakamasa's head began to swim. "No, no! Go away, or I shall call the police!"

"Just wanted to say I'm sorry about the heart attack. I should never have left you, I know that now. Anyway, I'll be going out of your life forever. Best of luck, sir."

Nakamasa steadied himself. He peered into the shrubbery, but could see nothing. "Are you still there, Ez?" he said.

"Yeah, but I must go now."

"Right. These are my last words to you. I shall give you thirty minutes to get away, and then I shall telephone the police. Now go."

There was a soft rustle in the shrubbery and then silence. Not even the song of a bird to brighten the day. When Mrs. T-J returned, a puzzling sight awaited her. As she approached Nakamasa in the garden, she halted, not sure what to do. He was still sitting where she had left him, but now his eyes were closed and his face was wet with tears.

As soon as Akiko heard Lois's voice, she rushed to find her and tell her that they had seen Parsons. Lois wasted no time, but immediately telephoned Cowgill.

"Lois? Hello, my favourite sleuth. How are you this fine morning?"

"Cut it, Cowgill. This is very important. Akiko and Jamie have just seen Parsons in a field not far from the village. Well, Akiko saw him, but he'd run off before Jamie could give chase. It was Jeems, you see, down a rabbit hole, barking her head off, and Jamie didn't hear Akiko shouting at him that she'd seen Parsons through a gap in the hedge, and it was too late by the time she reached Jamie to tell him."

"Um, Lois, dear, would you mind taking a deep breath and starting again, slowly? It was a tiny bit scrambled for my old ears."

"Don't mess about, Cowgill! There's no time to be lost. He'll be far away from here, now he knows he's been seen. Get the troops out at once! I'll be in touch later."

Lois cut off the call and thought angrily about Cowgill. "A tiny bit scrambled" indeed! The man didn't deserve to have people ferretin' for him for free. Still, he'd never ignored her reports in the past, and she was hopeful he would have men into the village in no time.

It would have been better if she hadn't been round at Floss's. Some time had been lost. She had come home as soon as Jamie rang, but even so, Parsons was unlikely to be still in Farnden. There was nothing more to be done now. Derek should be pleased, she thought wryly. She had handed over to Cowgill, and trusted in him.

Down at Stone House, Mrs. T-J's first priority had been to insist that Nakamasa should come back into the house and stretch out on his bed to recover. He had a heart puffer for emergencies and had meekly employed it. "Orders!" Mrs. T-J had said.

Now he was sleeping peacefully, and she tiptoed out of his room and into her kitchen. There she made herself a cup of strong tea and sat down to think. He had been having difficulty speaking, so she had not insisted. But she had caught the words, "Nothing serious," as she brought him indoors. She would have to wait to question him more closely.

What on earth could have happened? She had been in the shop for such a short time, and had not stayed to chat with anyone on the way back. The album was on the table, where he had sat earlier, putting in the last few photographs. He had begun to talk about returning to Japan, and Mrs. T-J wondered if he had fixed a date. Several times she had heard him on his mobile talking in what she assumed was Japanese.

They had chatted a lot recently, he and she, sitting comfortably in her pleasant drawing room, and he had been quite firm about retiring at once. He had said there would be much to do to organise everything, but once he had set it in motion, he could sit back and relax. Perhaps even return to England, she had suggested tentatively.

She pulled the album towards her and began idly turning over the pages. There he was, in full soldier kit, staring solemnly at the camera. It was an image so closely associated with wartime and all its horrors that she found it hard to resist the temptation to rip it out and destroy it forever. It was all so long ago, and seemed to have little to do with the courageous man asleep in her study.

Closing the album, she decided to forget it, if she could. But it was all very well for an elderly, wealthy widow, cushioned from the world by money and privilege, to forget it. Not so good for prisoners who had suffered extreme hardships, some of them still alive and with cruelly clear memories.

"Mildred, dear!"

Her heart leapt. It was Nakamasa, calling her, and using her name. How had he discovered it? She was always reluctant to admit to such an old-fashioned name, and tried to use Elizabeth, one of her others. Still, the way he'd said it, she didn't mind at all.

She rushed into his bedroom, and was relieved to see him sitting up and smiling at her. "How do you feel now?" she asked. "Would you like me to send for an ambulance to check you in the hospital?"

"Goodness no, thank you. I am perfectly well, and my little machine is beating away with reassuring regularity! I would like to return to the garden now, if you would give me your arm."

They walked out of the French window and across the lawn to the apple tree. Lois, coming round the corner of the house and seeing them arm in arm, was touched. How sweet! Could there possibly be a late romance for these two?

"Hello!" she called. "Can I have a word, Mrs. T-J?"

"SO HE WAS HERE IN THE VILLAGE?" MRS. T-J LOOKED ANXIOUSLY at Lois. The sighting of Parsons by Akiko had alarmed her, and she added sharply, "You've called the police, of course!"

Lois nodded. "Straightaway, natch. They will be on to him by now, I shouldn't wonder. Inspector Cowgill may be semiretired, but he's still the best cop in the county, so my son-in-law says. He'll call me as soon as they've got him."

"So no need for me . . ." Nakamasa muttered.

"What did you say, my dear?" asked Mrs. T-J.

"Nothing, nothing. Just an old man wandering," he replied. "Now, Mrs. Meade, when is my daughter coming down to see me?"

FORTY-NINE

❧

IN SOLOMON GRUNDY'S OFFICE, DIANA STOOD DEFIANTLY clutching her packed bags and refusing to sit down as told.

"I'm off now," she said. "Tell me how much I owe you, and I'll settle up. Then there'll be no need for me to come back."

Solomon smiled. "Why the hurry, my dear?" he said. "I hate to think you have been so unhappy here that you cannot bear to stay at least an hour or so to have a farewell lunch with us. Please put down your bags."

Diana shook her head. "No, thanks," she said, and continued, "and if you haven't got my bill ready, I'll let you have an address where you can send it. I think you can trust me to settle up."

"Trust?" said Solomon. "I'm not so sure about that. I thought you would be trustworthy enough to consult me before you took a valuable musical instrument and gave it to a total stranger."

"How do you know it was me?" she replied shortly.

"You were seen. It is my job to make sure nobody leaves here without being monitored. For their own safety, of course. Anyway, no harm done. Perhaps you will tell me now where it has gone, and I can retrieve it."

"It is in the safe hands of a professional cellist. I am perfectly willing to stand surety for her."

"But it is a commission, and now it is almost finished, it must be delivered soon to my client. Name, please, and address."

"I don't believe your client would mind if this person borrowed it for a few days. She is a well-known concert performer, but likes to keep her private life private." Diana knew she was being unreasonable, but was suddenly fearful of this man, and had no intention of putting Akiko Nakamasa in danger. Danger? Did she really think he was dangerous? Maybe not, but she was unwilling to risk it.

Saying that she was sorry and could see his problem, she said she would go right now and retrieve it for him. She turned and made for the door. But when she tried to open it, she found it would not open.

"Oh, for God's sake!" she shouted, suddenly afraid. "Cut the dramatics! Let me out at once!"

Solomon Grundy merely smiled. "Don't worry, my dear. I have a messenger on hand who will fetch the cello for me," he said. "Name and address?"

GRAN LOOKED UP FROM THE RAYBURN AS LOIS WALKED INTO the kitchen. "I don't know what's happened to your latest lame duck, Lois," she said. "Didn't she say she would be back for lunch?"

Derek was sitting at the table reading the sports pages. "I don't know about you, gel," he said. "I'm due to see old Bill in Tresham this afternoon. Promised him a couple o' rabbits. We'd better start very soon. You can always keep a plate hot on the stove, can't you?"

Lois frowned. She had had a brief word with Cowgill, and was aware that a police car had cruised through the village already. "But what can have happened to her?" she said. "I know she intended to spend no more than half an hour signing off at that place."

"Can I make a suggestion?" Jamie had been sitting quietly in the corner with Jeems sleeping sweetly on his lap.

"Go on, then," said Gran impatiently. "I know what *I'm* doing this afternoon. I'm going round to Nancy's for a nice quiet cup of tea and a gossip." She made a great production of turning down the Rayburn and moving the joint of beef to the warming oven.

"Why don't we eat now," Jamie suggested, "and then drive over to Waltonby this afternoon. It would take Akiko's mind off seeing Parsons this morning. We could take Jeems round the cricket pitch and across the field. There's a footpath there, and it backs on to Last Resort House."

"You're not suggesting storming the place if Diana has not come back, I hope?" Derek looked at his watch. "But anyway, I agree that we should eat."

"What has happened to Diana?" Akiko had come into the kitchen as Derek was speaking, and looked around, puzzled at their solemn faces.

"Nothing, probably," said Jamie. "Come and sit down.

We are about to eat. Then after lunch we are going over to Waltonby, taking Jeems for a walk."

But Akiko's face fell. She said that she had really had enough walking with Jeems for one day, and would it be all right if she stayed behind and practised her cello. "And maybe have a little nap?" she added. "I will lock up everything and be quite safe."

BACK IN THE SPINNEY, HIS WORLDLY GOODS ON HIS BACK LIKE A snail, Ezekiel had decided to keep on the move until dark. He had weighed instant flight in daylight against the safer cover of night and decided on the latter. Nakky would have the village crawling with policemen by now. A good thing he had had plenty of practice in dodging from place to place out of sight.

A cough caused him to freeze. Then he heard footsteps crackling through the underbrush. He vanished, but only a few yards away, waiting to locate the steps' direction. A voice suddenly said his name, sharply and with authority. His heart sank. Grundy! Should he run, or might his old adversary be prepared to help?

"Ah, I thought so," said Grundy, appearing with a satis-fied smile. "Now, among other things, we have to talk about a certain valuable cello. It has gone from Bert's bench, and you are responsible for it. Get it back. I could send the Diana girl, but don't trust her. I don't have to trust you. You know what's good for you, Ez. I shall need to have it back in my office within the next two hours, or sooner. I have a buyer, and like me, he does not suffer fools gladly. Oh, and keep your eyes open for cops. We've already had one visitor looking for you."

*   *   *

LOIS CLIMBED INTO THE NEW BROOMS VAN, WITH JEMIMA sitting neatly by her side. She set off for Waltonby in silence, until she turned a corner and in front of them could see the tall chimneys of Last Resort House.

"D'you think Diana's still in there?" Lois looked at the little dog. "If only you could talk," she said. It was a pity Jamie had decided to stay with Akiko. She could have done with some company in the van, but he was probably right. At this late stage it would be disastrous if Parsons was still on the run and something dreadful happened.

She passed the tall iron gates to Resort House, but could see nothing but massive trees and high fences. The footpath ran behind the property and was not part of it. Lois parked, and released Jemima. They set off along the path, and Lois looked up at the darkening sky. "Better not be too long, Jemima," she said. "Looks like rain."

AFTER AN HOUR OR SO TRYING TO SLEEP, AKIKO GOT UP AND went downstairs. Jamie had insisted on staying behind with her, and she found him dozing in the sitting room. Poor Jamie. She had brought him nothing but trouble, but one day she would make it up to him. "Jamie," she said softly, and kissed his cheek.

He woke with a start. "Something wrong?" he said quickly.

She shook her head. "No, nothing. I just cannot sleep. Shall we set out and meet your mother coming back from Waltonby? The walk would do us both good, I think."

Jamie was not sure. He felt safer in the house. But he saw Akiko's pale face, and reluctantly agreed. Akiko's shoes were not really suitable for a long walk, and all the Meade boots were too big for her. Still, the road was well made, and in the absence of pavements, she walked close to the edge, jumping on to the verge when heavy farm traffic passed them.

About a mile along the way, a car pulled up behind them. Then a familiar voice called out, and they looked round.

"Akiko! Jamie! Where are you going? Can I give you a lift?" It was Mrs. Tollervey-Jones, smiling broadly and coming up to be level with them.

"Oh, good afternoon," said Akiko. "How is my father? I must come down and see him a little later."

"I left him having a post-lunch nap. Locked up safely, of course! I'm going for eggs from the Resort lot."

"If you are going to Waltonby, I should be very glad of a lift," Akiko said. "My feet are hurting a little. It would be nice, wouldn't it, Jamie?"

They climbed into Mrs. T-J's comfortable old car, and Akiko smiled happily. "Where are you going? I hope we are not taking you out of your way," she said.

"No, no. Only as far as the community. I buy eggs from them. They are much the best eggs for miles around. Free range of course. Perhaps you would like to take some to Mrs. M?"

"Oh yes, that would be a really good idea," Akiko answered enthusiastically. Jamie said nothing. He was uneasy, but he thought the plan could be quite useful in keeping eyes open for Diana.

"Oh good," said Mrs. T-J. "Now, here we are. Would you jump out and press the bell? It's on the left, there. Next to the gate."

As they waited to go through, Jamie's eye was caught by a figure approaching along the footpath. "Hey! Wait a minute, that's Mum! She might like to come in with us."

Lois came up to the car, carrying Jemima. "She's got a thorn in her paw," she said. "I'd better take her home and get it out."

"Don't go, Mum," said Jamie. "Let me carry her, and then you can come in and get some eggs."

"I get my eggs from Josie," she replied. "But I'd like to come in and have a snoop. We still haven't seen Diana."

The gates swung open, and Mrs. T-J drove in slowly. They made their way up the long drive, and Akiko looked back nervously to see the big gates slowly shutting behind them. "Are they good people here?" she said.

"Bit of a mystery, my dear, this lot. But they mind their own business and, as far as I know, have caused no harm. So we let them get on with it. And they do supply extremely good eggs! We don't go to the main house. They have their eggs for sale in an old bothy behind in the stable yard. There is always someone keeping watch for customers. The man in charge of Resort House is a very experienced businessman, apparently."

"Among other things," muttered Jamie.

"Have you met him?" Akiko asked.

Mrs. T-J nodded. "Once or twice. Grundy is his name. Solomon Grundy. Born on a Monday!" she added with a laugh.

"Perhaps it is not his real name," Akiko suggested.

"Possibly," Mrs. T-J said. "Now, here we are. I'll park over there and then we can fetch the eggs. Oh yes, look, there's someone in the bothy already."

They walked over and found a pleasant-faced woman waiting for them with a smile. "Good afternoon, Mrs. Tollervey-Jones. And welcome to your friends."

"Good afternoon. Now, I'll have two dozen of the lovely brown eggs, and a dozen white-shelled ones. I propose a session of baking for my special guest, and your golden yolks are spectacular in cakes. And is that butter over there? Is that your own?"

The woman walked over to the packs of fresh butter, and added one to Mrs. T-J's purchases. "Is that all now? We have some lovely apples here. This lot are eaters, and those are cookers."

While Mrs. T-J was deciding which to have, Akiko, Lois and Jamie walked out of the bothy and into the yard. They looked around curiously and saw the big house looming up behind the outbuildings. All the bedroom windows had blinds drawn, and Lois was thinking how unfriendly it looked, when one of the blinds was swiftly lifted and a face appeared.

"Diana!" Akiko said aloud, and waved vigorously.

"Christ! That's her!" said Jamie, waving vigorously. Lois stared hard, and thought she could see a moving shadow behind her.

Mrs. T-J emerged and joined them.

"It's Diana, Mrs. T-J!" said Akiko, pointing at the window. "She does not look happy!"

"Where, Akiko? I can't see anyone."

When Akiko turned back to the window, she saw the blind had been drawn down, and Diana had gone. Jemima, barking furiously, jumped out of Jamie's grasp and disappeared.

FIFTY

❧

Mrs. Tollervey-Jones had been all for marching round to the front door in search of Jemima, and demanding to see Diana, but Akiko pleaded with her to wait. Lois said she was sure Jeems was heading for the New Brooms van and home, and so walked off, refusing Jamie's offer of going with her. "Just be careful!" she called over her shoulder as she went.

"Are you sure you don't want to ask about Diana?" Mrs. T-J asked Akiko.

"Very sure," she replied. "We might cause something bad to happen to her, but now we know that she is there, I think it would be best to go back to Farnden and tell the others. Mrs. M will know what to do." She was not at all anxious to be around while Mrs. Tollervey-Jones set up a rumpus in the tightly controlled community Diana had described.

"Oh, very well, if you are sure," Mrs. T-J reluctantly agreed. "But I promise you I have no qualms about tackling

Solomon Grundy. In all my days on the bench, I found him a most cooperative person when occasionally some unfortunate from his house indulged in minor shoplifting in Farnden."

"So they are allowed out into the world?"

"Yes, I think so. Some of them seem a bit odd, but their previous lives have been appalling in some cases. Naturally some of them have difficulty in adjusting, and I believe some are difficult to handle. There have been one or two cases of unruly violence."

Akiko and Jamie were silent as they drove back to Farnden, and when they reached Meade House she asked if Mrs. T-J would like to come in for a cup of tea. Mrs. T-J smiled kindly. "Thank you, my dear, but I must be getting back to make tea for your father, dear man! Besides, I did not actually see Diana myself. If you remember, the blind had come down by the time you drew my attention to the window. So you were quite right to stop me bursting in! But I am sure Mrs. Meade will deal with it. I shall await a progress report."

It was now dark outside, and Ezekiel had come silently and unseen to Last Resort House to find Grundy. He needed money, and had no intention of risking capture attempting to retrieve the cello without being paid. Once he had cash in his pocket and a means of transport—Grundy would provide—he could be away for good. He felt once more in his pocket and was reassured by the cool feel of Nakamasa's gun. We're equally matched, he said to himself. He had seen a gun in Grundy's desk drawer. It was there, so Grundy had told him, only as a threat in rare cases of violent disturbances.

Grundy was waiting for him at the door. "Well, if it isn't

Mr. Parsons! Just the person I was hoping to see. But where is the cello? Ah, I see you haven't got it. Dear me, that is not good, Ezekiel."

"Never mind about the cello," Ezekiel said confidently. "You'll find it at Meade House. Your precious Diana lent it to the Jap woman staying there, her whose cello was stolen out of Meade House drive. Remember? Got rid of that one, have you, Grundy?"

"You know perfectly well I have. And I am quite confident of retrieving the replacement once the circumstances of Diana's theft has been explained to the Meades. You are making life difficult for yourself, Ez. And for me. I cannot now get it aged by Bert and restored to the Nakamasa woman as her original. She is sure to recognise it as a new one she has so recently been playing. So what do you suggest we do with it?"

"You could try it on somebody else. Bert makes a good job of them, doesn't he? You could offer it on the dodgy deals market as a genuine eighteenth-century one, you know, the thingummy model. Forget about the Japanese girl. Her papa will buy her another one. You can take that from me."

"Mm. Maybe. Now, I have a number of questions to ask you, Parsons, but not tonight. There is a bed made up for you, and we will talk tomorrow."

"Not if I can help it. You owe me a favour, mate, but a bargain will do. And don't forget I know enough about your scams to put you away for years! You are going to lend me that new Jeep you've got out in the backyard, and I swear I won't cough up the recent history and whereabouts of the Jap girl's instrument you stole. The Jeep is just the job for the bit of off-roading I need to do. And no squealing to the police. Wherever I end up, I can always put a cop on your tail.

Expenses and car keys now, please. Then I'll be out of your hair for good. Give my love to Foster, ho ho."

"I'll get you one day, Parsons, if old Lucifer doesn't get you first! Here, take the keys and bugger off, out of my sight, and good riddance. You can have the cash in my pocket, and that's the lot." He held out a wad of notes, and Parsons took them.

Grundy waited until he heard Parsons out in the yard, cursing because there was no light. He had deliberately given him the wrong keys, and now followed. He had put up with more than enough from Ezekiel Parsons. His patience was at an end, and in the darkness of the yard he approached the Jeep quietly. Then he spoke.

"Parsons! Wait! I gave you the wrong keys. Here's the right ones!"

Ezekiel turned from the Jeep and began to walk towards him. Before he could see what was happening, Grundy's hand came out of his pocket. There was a dull thud, and with a look of terror on his face, Ezekiel slowly crumpled to the ground and was still.

FIFTY-ONE

❧

DIANA HAD HEARD A VOICE IN THE YARD, DRAWN BACK HER curtains and looked down. There was no lighting, and she had seen only shadows. Two dark figures and the new Jeep. Then one of the figures had seemed to fold up, and the other bent over him. She waited to see what would happen next.

Now a security light came on, and another person ran out into the yard. It was Foster! And the bending person was Grundy, straightening up. But who was it on the ground, motionless? As she watched with mounting anxiety, Foster and Grundy turned the prostrate man over and began to carry him towards the garden door. It was the little man from the summerhouse! Perhaps he was ill? But why the garden?

Then Grundy tripped, and from the way his end of the little man fell from his arms she knew that he was dead. Her heart thudded and she felt faint. She was frozen with fear. They picked him up again and this time disappeared through into the garden. She must do something, she told herself, and rushed to her door, where she banged as loudly as she could, yelling for help at the same time. There was no reply. Nobody came. It was after curfew, and the house was silent.

"Good morning, Diana," said Solomon Grundy, coming unannounced into her room.

"It is certainly better than last night," she replied. "Why was I locked in last night? And why is my room in such a mess?" A moment's caution stopped her from asking about the night scene in the yard.

"Oh, sorry about that, my dear. We'll get it cleared up for you. Now, about the locked door. Rules, I'm afraid. Of course there may have been no need for you to be secured. But we worried about your strange behaviour, you know. People suffering from grief sometimes do foolish things. You were allowed up to your room to collect your things, and then, as it was really quite late, we locked you in for your own safety last night. When you have been here a couple of days longer, there will be no need for lock and key."

Diana glared at him. "Mr. Grundy! I am going back at once to my friends in Farnden. I shall send for my things. I will see that Bert's cello is returned immediately, and I hope to hear nothing more of your activities here. If I do, and it is as worrying as my short stay has proved, I shall go straight to the police."

Solomon Grundy's head went back, and he roared with laughter. "Wonderful, Diana! You are destined for great things on the stage, if you should choose that unreliable profession.

Now, I have work to do. Do pop your lovely head into my office and say goodbye before you go."

Fuming, Diana stormed down the stairs and out of the front door and began to walk up the drive to the gates. Half-way along, a figure emerged from the tall laurel bushes. "Hi, Di," he said. "Where are you off to so early?"

"Let me pass, Foster," she said. "I've had enough of you and your shady friends. I'm leaving, and don't try to stop me. And don't try to find me again, either! You deceived me rotten, with your slimy charm!"

"Ah, shame!" he replied. "I don't remember you putting up much of a struggle. But don't worry, Sol's told me to open the gates for you so you can make a dramatic exit." He laughed, then turned and marched ahead of her. At the end of the drive, he saw her safely outside and then said, "Bye, Di! I'm on rough gardening duty this morning, so I'll see you around. Cheerio!"

"Where did you get to, Diana?" said Lois, as the girl came into the kitchen. "We were worried about you."

"Oh, it's a long story," she said. "But I'm not sure I can talk about it at the moment."

"Never mind, then. Just relax. Gran will be back in a minute, and Jamie and Akiko have gone down to see Mr. Nakamasa."

"That is Akiko's father? The old boy who's staying at Stone House with Mrs. Tollervey-Jones? I need to ask you about her. At the moment I am homeless! And I remember you suggested she might have room for me to be a lodger for a while."

Lois nodded. "Absolutely right. I think she's really enjoying having someone in the house with her, and Akiko says her father already wants to go back to Japan. Going to retire, permanently, apparently."

Diana was silent for a few minutes. Then she said, "Has Akiko heard from Mr. Grundy at that Last Resort place? It seems that cello I borrowed was ready for delivery to a client, and he wants it back right away."

Lois sniffed. "The charming Mr. Grundy," she said, "has already collected it. Or rather, one of his minions has collected it. But thanks anyway, Diana. It was a nice thought."

"I was more or less given permission, you know. One of the residents, I think. Scruffy-looking fellow with black eyes. A bit sinister, I suppose. I should have known better. He showed it to me, and said he was sure Akiko could borrow it for a while. I think he may have done it to annoy Grundy. Anyway, I'll apologise to Akiko when she comes back."

"The black-eyed scruff? Did you know his name?" Lois held her breath. She had had no word from Cowgill, and assumed Parsons had not yet been caught.

"No," Diana said. "No idea. I saw him once or twice, and he was pally with a so-called friend of mine. Foster. The one I stayed with when he was briefly gamekeeper at the hall. That was a mistake, I'm afraid. Not functioning properly at the moment," she added, and fumbled for a tissue.

"You poor old thing, Diana," said Lois. "Come on, cheer up. It might never happen. That's what Gran always says."

"It already has happened. My mum and dad are gone, and I'm so lonely."

"What's the matter with you, my girl?" said Gran, coming in like the north wind through the kitchen door. "And why the tears? What have you been saying to her, Lois? I don't know, I'm sure. I go out for ten minutes, and when I get back my kitchen's full of weeping women."

"One weeping woman," said Diana, sniffing. "Hello, Mrs. Weedon."

"Coffee on yet, Lois? Or have you given up lifting the kettle?"

Lois sighed. "I'll do it now, Mum," she said. "Diana's back, and she's had a rough time. Not ready to tell us yet, though. Why don't we all relax and give the girl a break?"

Gran took off her cardigan and rolled up her sleeves. "Right. But first, let's sort this out. Diana's back from where? Your bed was all ready for you last night, gel. What kept you?"

"I was detained, as the police say. But not by the police. I went back to collect my things from Last Resort House, and got locked into my room. Grundy had a good explanation when I saw him this morning. But I never want to see him again. Or Foster the gamekeeper, for that matter."

"Was Grundy nasty to you? Is that what's upset you?" asked Lois.

"He's never nasty to your face," said Gran. "But stories get around about Solomon Grundy. And if that's his real name, I'm a banana."

"Which, as we often say, you are clearly not," said Lois. "But was he unpleasant, Diana?"

"No, he wasn't. Slimy and sarcastic, but nothing actionable."

"Then why—"

At that moment, Jamie and Akiko came bursting in, and seeing Diana sitting at the kitchen table, they were full of questions and relief at seeing her safely back. When she had explained about the cello to Akiko, she said she had a splitting headache, and thought she would take a painkiller and have a sleep.

"Didn't get much sleep last night," she said, "what with one thing and another."

Lois looked at her closely. "You've told us one thing, about being locked in, but what was the other?"

"Um, I need to get that straight in my head before I tell you," Diana said. "Can we talk about it later?"

FIFTY-TWO

⁓

THE KITCHEN GARDEN AT LAST RESORT HOUSE WAS A
model of productivity. Every kind of vegetable and fruit
grew there in rows so straight and orderly that they might
have been licked into shape by Solomon Grundy himself.
Narrow grass paths ran between each bed, and at the far
end, a small orchard of apple, pear and cherry trees acted as a
screen, shielding the community from anyone in the field
beyond. In one corner, sheltered by a high hedge of evergreen
shrubs, there was a neat fruit cage, where raspberries and
currants grew in abundance, and where any marauding
sparrow unlucky enough to become trapped was dealt with
summarily.

It was towards this fruit cage that Foster walked slowly in
the sun, carrying a half-filled sack. He turned, looked back
to the house, and saw Grundy watching him. He waved, and
walked on. When he came to the cage, he carefully opened
the framed netting door and, bending slightly, went in. In

the far corner, glaringly obvious to any intruder, was a patch of bare earth. He opened the sack and drew out a bunch of strawberry plants, which he set out covering the earth and then neatly planted them. Then he tipped up the sack, and shook out the contents. It was clean straw, enough to pack around the plants and cover the remaining soil. Then he muttered something, gave a mock salute, and returned slowly back to the house.

Grundy was at the door as he approached. "Mission accomplished?" he asked.

"Mission accomplished. Sir." His face set, Foster walked past him, through the group of residents shelling peas at a big table, on into the echoing, quarry-tiled hall and out through the front door. Grundy watched him go with a strangely regretful expression on his face.

"Mr. Foster leaving us, sir?" said Bert, appearing with a handful of green peas.

"He'll be back, Bert," replied Grundy. "Nothing surer."

DEREK RETURNED HOME AT LUNCHTIME TO FIND A CONFERENCE going on in his kitchen. Akiko, Jamie, Gran and Lois sat around the table, and when he entered they scarcely looked up.

"Hello, there!" he shouted. "Anyone at home?"

Lois looked up. "Oh, it's you," she said, and then, looking across at Akiko, asked what she thought about it.

"About what?" said Derek crossly. "What's going on here, Lois? Might I ask if there's any lunch to be had?"

"Sorry, Dad," said Jamie. "We've just been having a talk about Diana. She's back, and gone upstairs with a headache. She was at Last Resort House last night, locked in, and something very nasty happened while she was there."

"What nasty something?" Derek was losing patience.

"We don't know yet. She was too upset to talk about it."

Derek exploded. "If I hear one more word about that place in Waltonby, or missing cellos, or missing Dianas, then you can all clear out and leave me to get my own lunch!"

In the shocked silence that followed, Diana crept into the kitchen and sat down on an empty chair. "Sorry," she said. "I'm very sorry to have caused you so much trouble, Mr. Meade. It's like this. I think I witnessed a murder."

FIFTY-THREE

❧

COWGILL WAS JUST LEAVING FOR THE GOLF COURSE WHEN HE was called back by the sergeant on the desk.

"Phone for you, sir. Mrs. Lois Meade. Would you like me to say you're out?" The sergeant grinned knowingly.

"Cheeky devil," said Cowgill, starting back up to his office. "Put her through straightaway."

As he puffed up the last flight of steps, he reflected that perhaps he should have taken the sergeant's advice. A call from Lois always meant trouble. But her kind of trouble was always welcome. He had nursed a hopeless infatuation for her for years now, and sometimes wondered what he would do if Derek had a fatal accident. He suspected that faced with the big decision he would chicken out. Lovely as she was still, though her children were adult and she was a grandmother, he reckoned her feisty independence and seemingly inexhaustible energy would be the death of him!

"Cowgill? Is that you? You sound if as you've run the marathon."

"I'm fine. Just on my way out. You were lucky to catch me."

"Well, let's hope you're glad I did when you hear what I've got to tell you. I can come into Tresham, or you can drive over here on your way to the golf course."

"Is it very important? And you're right. I do have a four-some fixed up."

"It's important," Lois said.

WHEN COWGILL ARRIVED AT MEADE HOUSE, GRAN HAD AN unusually serious expression, and without any preliminaries ushered him into the sitting room, where, to his surprise, he found Lois, Derek, Akiko and Jamie, and an unfamiliar blonde girl who was introduced to him as Diana Smith.

"Good afternoon, everyone," he said. "Lois, are you going to tell me what this is all about?"

"Yes, I will. But Diana's got the really serious stuff, so I'll just explain what has happened since I last saw you, and then she can take over."

Lois then gave him a succinct account of how she had kept her promise and stopped the amateurish and dangerous plan cooked up by Jamie. She reminded him about Akiko seeing Parsons in a field just outside the village, and reported Diana's arrival with a cello, which turned out to have been stolen from Last Resort House. Diana had been encouraged to take it by a man sounding very like Parsons.

"I think it's your turn now, Diana," she said, and sat quietly next to Derek.

"I am Diana Smith. My parents recently died in a sailing accident, and I was befriended by a man named Foster. He invited me to stay with him in his gamekeeper's cottage in Long Farnden. Farnden Hall, it was. No sooner had I moved in than he got the sack! Then he said he knew where we could stay temporarily, and we went to this place with a strange name, over in Waltonby."

"Foster?" said Cowgill.

"Yes, that's right. Well, he was very charming at first, but then I heard him quarrelling with one of the other residents, and he was horrible! I think I came to my senses, and decided to leave. I didn't know it was like a prison, and you weren't allowed out beyond the boundaries. Anyway, I just went for a walk and ended up back at Farnden Hall, in the chapel shop there. Mrs. Norrington was always really nice, though we didn't much take to her husband!"

"And that's when you met me," said Akiko. "And said you could possibly borrow a cello for me. And you did!"

"Not realising I was stealing it," Diana continued. "The man who encouraged me was a scruffy type, but quite helpful. He found this newly made cello on a bench in the Resort workshops, and said I could borrow it for Akiko."

It was warm in the sitting room, and Lois felt Derek leaning on her. She prodded him, and he sat up with a snort. "What? Where?"

The tension was broken, and Lois laughed. "Go back to sleep, Derek. We'll wake you up when it's teatime."

"Carry on, Miss Smith," said Cowgill. "I imagine you are going to tell me who the scruffy type was and where he can be found. I am most anxious to talk to him."

There was a sudden silence, and then Diana said that she was afraid it was too late. "I think he's buried in a kitchen garden," she explained, and described what she had seen from her bedroom window.

AFTER THE WHOLE STORY HAD BEEN TOLD AND COWGILL MADE urgent phone calls, Lois asked Gran if she would kindly make tea. She was sure everybody, including the inspector, would be glad of a cup.

"Must be a serious moment if my daughter is polite to me," she said, as she went off to the kitchen.

She had just left the room when the front doorbell rang. An immediate silence fell.

"It's bad news," said Akiko. "It's my father! Something has happened to him. I can feel it!"

Jamie looked at her. "Don't be ridiculous, Akiko," he said. "Gran's opening the door, so we'll soon know."

Gran duly put her head around the door. "Lois, it's a Mr. Foster for you. I've told him you're in conference with the police, and he said that was just fine. He had something to add to your agenda. Whatever that means. Shall I send him away?"

Cowgill got to his feet. "No, Mrs. Weedon," he said. "I'll see him in Lois's office, if you will kindly show him in." The meeting broke up then, and Akiko asked Jamie if he would go with her to see her father. "I still have this feeling that something is wrong with him," she said.

"No escort needed now, Akiko," he said. "Parsons is dead, so you'll be perfectly safe on your own. I do have some work to do rescheduling our concerts. Give him my regards, won't you."

"I wonder if I might come with you, Akiko, to see if Mrs. Tollervey-Jones will have me as a lodger for a while?" Diana said.

"Of course. Are you ready? We can go straightaway, if Jamie does not want to come." Akiko had not missed the coolness in his voice. So was it all over? She sighed. He was the sort who liked to protect and look after girls. But not love them, apparently.

FIFTY-FOUR

~

FOSTER FILLED IN THE FINAL PIECES OF THE JIGSAW FOR Cowgill. He began by saying he had met Parsons years ago, and then lost touch with him.

"I suppose we were both petty thieves, Mr. Cowgill," he said. "You wouldn't have looked twice at us. Never stole anything really valuable. Just enough to keep body and soul together. Then Parsons got taken on by this Japanese businessman, who seemed a decent enough sort of chap. But Parsons discovered something about him. All to do with the Japs' ill treatment of prisoners in the death camps in Burma in the last world war."

"Do you know what it was, this dread secret?"

"Not exactly. But it was enough to keep a hold over his boss for years. Parsons claimed he'd talked to one of the survivors who remembered Nakky, as he called him. One of the most vicious, so *he* claimed, but there was no way of checking. Not much more than a boy, Nakky was. Parsons and I were still in touch at that time, and he told me about it. He was cock-a-hoop at the thought of a cushy billet for the rest of his life. Apparently the Jap was crazy about his daughter, and Parsons threatened to tell her what her father was really like, unless he stumped up a regular payment and a job. This was, you bet, at a good deal more than his salary as dogsbody assistant."

"I see. So what have you come here to tell me about the murder of Parsons?"

Foster gave him a shifty look. "Murder?" he said. "Don't you mean accident?"

"No. Murder, Mr. Foster. I understand you were a witness."

"Who told you that?"

"Never mind who told me. Now *you* tell me what you saw."

It was a well-prepared story. According to Foster, he had found Grundy returning from the kitchen garden in the middle of the night, with mud on his hands and boots. He'd then given him a cock-and-bull story about planting strawberries, and showed him the patch in the fruit cage.

"He wanted straw to be laid down to protect the plants, and asked me to do it early next morning. We'd got straw in one of the barns, and I did what he asked," he said.

"But you knew it was a grave, right? Had even had a hand in digging it?"

"Oh God, you've got it all, haven't you. Well, I'd heard Grundy and Parsons arguing and shouting last night. It sounded serious, and I listened. Parsons was plotting his escape, and Solomon Grundy wouldn't play ball. I think Grundy did him in. There was a sort of a smothered shot sound. Not very loud, but the place was quiet as the grave. Oops! Sorry, sir. Anyway, I could hear more or less everything, and I thought there'd been an accident. But now you're saying you know Grundy is a murderer? I expect you'll get him, then. I wouldn't waste any time, if I were you. He moves faster than a weasel, that Grundy."

"Thanks for the edited version, Foster, but you're wrong about one thing. I *would* look at you twice, and in order to do that, I'll ask you to come down to the station for official questioning. Possibly some revisions to your story. My sergeant's out in the car. He'll look after you."

"And Grundy?" said Foster urgently.

"Got him already. But thanks anyway."

THERE WAS REJOICING AT STONE HOUSE. WHEN MRS. TOLLERVEY-Jones was told about Parsons's demise, she showed no emotion exept delight.

"Thank goodness that dreadful man will be out of Mr. Nakamasa's life forever," she said. "He's told me all about him, you know, Akiko. I am sure he will tell you, too, when he is ready."

"I doubt if there's much more he can tell me," said Akiko grimly. "Papa was a different person before I was born, and I am concerned only with how he has been as a father to me. May I go to see him now? He has probably heard us talking and will be awake."

"Oh yes, I am sure he is waiting to see you. You know the way, my dear."

Akiko walked through to her father's room, knocked and went in.

"Papa?"

He stretched out his arms, and she went slowly over to

him. "It is all over, my daughter," he said gently. "And now we can start a new life together. Your Jamie is welcome to a share of you. I have quite decided on that."

"No need, Papa. It is all over with Jamie, too. In fact, I am not so sure that it was ever anything more than friendship on his side. I hope that we shall remain friends, but I have decided to pursue my solo performing career, which I can easily do in Japan. When you go back, I shall come with you. Then I can look after you and play my cello as much or as little as I choose."

"Are you sure of this, Akiko? I already have a promise from Mildred, er, Mrs. Tollervey-Jones, that she will visit."

"I am quite sure, Papa." Akiko nodded and bent her head as a token of respect.

There was a knock at the door, and Lois appeared. "All right for me to come in?" she said. "I just rushed down to tell you Jamie is going back to London. He is leaving in about half an hour, and there is just time for you to see him, Akiko, if you want to come back with me?"

Akiko flushed and hesitated. Then she said, "No, I think it is not a good idea. Please tell him I will write to him to explain why I must return to Japan with my father very soon. You have a very splendid son, Mrs. M, and I hope we will meet again someday. And give him my love."

"Lois, my duckie," said Derek, when she returned home. "Correct me if I'm wrong, but am I right in thinking this particular bout of ferretin' is over?"

"Mmm," answered Lois. "For the moment. By the way, is Cowgill still around? I've just remembered something I wanted to ask him."

FIFTY-FIVE

❧

"I SHOULD THINK WE CAN ALL GET BACK TO NORMAL NOW," Gran said. "Jamie's back in London, taking time off to get into practice again, Akiko Whatsit has gone to Japan with her precious father, and the FOR SALE notices are up outside Resort House."

"How do you know that, Mum? You've not been over to Waltonby, have you?"

"Josie told me. Apparently they did a moonlight flit after that Solomon Grundy, otherwise known as Alfred Black, was taken into custody. I expect the police will find out where they've all gone."

"What about all the pigs and chickens and the rest of the livestock?"

"Left them there, without food or water. A local farmer has taken them temporarily, until they get some contact with another branch of the community. If there is one. If you ask me, we shall hear no more of that lot."

"And a good job, too," Lois said, sitting down at the kitchen table. Gran put a plate of sandwiches in front her.

"Hey, what's this? Has the cook gone on strike?"

"Yes," said Gran. "I'm having a week off. If you want a hot meal, you can cook it yourself. And if you take my advice, you'll do what Derek says and book a holiday for the two of you. I reckon we're all exhausted with all the Nakamasa goings-on."

"Mrs. T-J doesn't seem exhausted. Mind you, word has got round that she's planning an autumn break in Japan."

"Ye gods," said Gran. "Whatever next? You'll be telling me soon there'll be wedding bells in the spring. Well, if she can catch a millionaire, so can I. So watch out! Oh good, here comes Derek. We can all sit down together."

"Have your spies told you how Diana's doing being Mrs. T-J's new lodger? I saw them out together, going for a walk with what looked like a new Labrador puppy. Stone House is full of surprises these days!"

Derek came into the kitchen smiling. "Guess what I've been doing," he said, bending down to kiss Lois on the cheek.

"Booking a holiday for two in sunny Spain," Lois said.

His face fell. "Trust you to ferret out where I've been," he said.

"Not difficult," she said. "There's a ruddy great brochure advertising the Costa Brava sticking out of your jacket pocket."

"Have you gone and done it, Derek?" said Gran. "I hope you have, boy. If not, this daughter of mine will have you changing your mind as soon as look at you."

Derek nodded, and like an amateur magician, he produced an envelope and placed it in front of Lois. "There we are, gel," he said. "Tickets for two weeks on the Costa Brava."

"I suppose you know what Costa Brava means?" said Lois.

"Yeah, of course. It means it costa lot to go there, and only a brava man would even think of it." Derek sat hack in his chair, sandwich in hand, looking smug.

"My, you're full of fun today, Derek Meade," Lois said. "It actually means wild coast, so should be just your thing. And I suppose you think two weeks in the Costa Brava will put all thoughts of ferretin' out of my mind? Well, I can only say it's a really nice idea, but there is a small matter of ferretin' not yet cleared up."

"We'll see about that, when we get back. Meanwhile, you'd better go to the shops and splash out on a bikini or two."

"Oh my God," groaned Lois. "Not beachwear! I'll take my jeans and a few tops and that'll be quite enough for me. Now, I shall have a lot to do reorganising New Brooms while I'm away, so I'll go and make a start."

"LOIS? DID YOU CALL ME EARLIER?" IT WAS COWGILL. Lois looked at her watch. She had been working in her office for two hours and felt like a diver coming up for air.

"No, not me," she said. "One of your other girlfriends, I expect."

"Other? Meaning you are one of them?"

"Ever hopeful, Hunter. But no, sorry. I've just been told I am having a second honeymoon with my dear husband on the Costa Brava. A little village called Cadaques. Two and a half hours from Barcelona, and chiefly known for being an artist's paradise. There's a gallery there full of Dali paintings. Whoever he is. We can give it the once-over."

"I see you've been consulting Wikipedia, my dear. Well, I must say I envy you. Don't forget to send me a postcard, and keep your eyes open for ferretin' opportunities."

"Well, since you mention it, I'm glad you rang. Even if it was a pretty feeble excuse. There is one thing left over from the Nakamasa case. Remember the theft of Akiko's cello? Well, I've had a letter from Japan. You know she's gone back there with her father. Well, it's from him. Apparently Akiko is still moaning about the loss of her original, and he's promised to do all he can to find it."

"I don't think that need concern us, my dear. Nakamasa can afford to search every avenue, straight and bent."

"Well, they've done the straight bit, so he says. Ads in all the media outlets all over the world, et cetera, et cetera."

"So he wants you to do the crooked bit? Is that it?" asked Cowgill.

"That's it, more or less. I was going to give you a ring to see if you've got any bright ideas. Needless to say he's offering a small fortune if I find it."

"You already won a small fortune on the lottery, didn't you, you and Derek! How much more do you need? I see this could be a very dangerous and foolish mission, and might land you in extremely murky waters."

"It's not the money. Well, not altogether. The cello was stolen from our drive, remember? And Akiko was a guest in our house and a colleague of our son Jamie. Derek doesn't agree with me, but I feel we should make some effort to find it. Get us off the hook, if you know what I mean."

"You're being ridiculous, Lois. But if you're adamant, then of course I will give it some thought."

By the time Lois had told Josie the news and Mrs. T-J had subsequently been in the shop for her supply of soup, most of the village knew that Lois and Derek Meade were off to Spain for a jolly.

"Such good news!" enthused Mrs. T-J, calling into Meade House to deliver the Women's Institute magazine for Gran. "I went to Cadaques once with my husband. He was a keen Dali fan. You know, those droopy clock faces in lunar landscapes! Wonderful little place. Do hope it's not spoilt now, like the rest of the Spanish coast. When are you going, Lois? I'm sure I've got some old photographs, if you'd be interested. Oh, and by the way, Diana has had a postcard from Jamie. He's in Guernsey for the weekend, giving a recital. She was thrilled to bits to hear from him, you know. Um, well, I must be off. Things to do. Goodbye, my dear. Let me know when you're off."

"That woman's finally lost it," Lois said, as Gran came in with a cup of tea. "Droopy clock faces? I ask you, Mum."

"What I'd like to know, Lois, is who's going to be in charge of the team while you're away. And not Dot Nimmo, I hope!" Gran frowned and banged the cup and saucer down so hard that the spoon rattled.

"Funny you should mention Dot," said Lois blandly. "Just the person I was thinking of. I am sure you'll give her any assistance she needs?"

"I'd give 'er her cards if it was me," answered Gran. "But if you must, you must. Why don't you just ask Hazel Thornbull? She's got all the paperwork at her fingertips in the office in Tresham. Much better idea."

"Or maybe Mrs. Tollervey-Jones? I'll think about it."

FIFTY-SIX

Mrs. Tollervey-Jones sat bolt upright in Lois's office chair, spectacles on the end of her nose and a beautiful old-fashioned fountain pen in hand.

The assembled team was silent, waiting for her to begin. Dot Nimmo was staring out of the window, deliberately taking no notice, and the others stared at the new deputy, willing her to get it wrong.

"Good morning, girls—and boy," she said, with a big smile at Andrew Young. "I am glad that all went well last week, and am sure we shall be equally successful during the week to come. Mrs. Meade will, of course, be back next Monday, but meantime I will hand out the work schedules which she prepared for you."

"Same as last week, aren't they?" said Dot. "There weren't no problems with my lot. What about you others? We usually go round one by one and see if anything comes up."

"Thank you, Mrs. Nimmo. So shall we move on to Mrs. Thornbull."

They all made great play of looking from one to the other to locate the mysterious Mrs. Thornbull.

"Oh, you mean me?" said Hazel. "Well, I usually come last, as I'm in charge of the Tresham office. But still, there is nothing to report out of the ordinary, so that's me done."

Each of the others had much the same report, until it came to Andrew's turn. "I should probably leave this until Mrs. M comes back," he said. "But it might be a bit urgent."

"I can always reach her by telephone," said Mrs. T-J. "What's the trouble?"

"It's about that cello that went missing. I've had a card from a mate who's on holiday in Spain, and he's been in Barcelona. Apparently he's interested in old musical instruments, and they have a world-famous collection in a museum near there. It was only a postcard, so I can't be specific. The card was a museum one, and it had a photo of a cello on the front, part of the collection. The name Montagnana caught my eye, because I remember Mrs. M mentioning it when she asked us to keep our ears and eyes open for the Japanese girl's stolen one."

"And Mrs. Meade is only a couple of hours away from Barcelona!" said Mrs. Tollervey-Jones excitedly. "Thank you, Andrew. I am sure she will want to hear about this straightaway. Have you got the card with you?"

"Sorry, no. Came out in a hurry, I'm afraid. But I could give her a ring when I get home. Mind you, I looked up sites on the internet and there's a fair few Montagnanas about in private hands."

"Worth a look! Thank you for your perspicacity, Andrew. Perhaps you will let us know how you get on?"

*   *   *

"WE USUALLY HAVE COFFEE AND A CHAT AFTER THE MEETING," said Dot.

"I'm very sorry, Mrs. Nimmo, but Mrs. Weedon, Gran, has gone on strike. If you would care to put on the kettle, I'm sure we could manage for ourselves?"

"Watch me," said Dot, and disappeared. A few seconds later there was the sound of raised voices, and she returned, followed by Gran bearing a large tray loaded with coffee and biscuits.

"Thought you were on strike, Mrs. Weedon?" Mrs. Tollervey-Jones managed an insecure smile.

"If you think I'm letting strange women into my kitchen, meddling with my things, you've got another think coming," Gran replied. "When you've finished, you can leave the tray on the desk. I'll collect it later, thank you, Dot Nimmo."

ANDREW FINALLY GOT THROUGH TO LOIS, WHO ASKED AT ONCE if anything was wrong with the family. Reassuring her, he told her about the postcard, and she was immediately interested. "Give me the details of the museum," she said. "We'll take a day trip to Barcelona. We meant to do that anyway. Thank you, Andrew. Well done."

"Are you having a good time?" said Andrew.

"Marvellous," Lois replied. "Sunburn, trippers, greasy food and boredom. Great!"

Andrew laughed and said he was sure it was doing them the world of good. "We miss you both," he said, as he ended the call.

Derek had just joined Lois on the small balcony outside

their room. "Who was that?" he asked, stretching his arms out to the sun, sea and sand in front of them. "Lovely day again, me duck. What do you plan for us today?"

"Same as yesterday, I'm afraid. But tomorrow we are taking a trip to Barcelona."

"Fine. But what's the hurry? We could do it on the way home. Who *was* that on the phone, anyway?"

"Andrew Young. He says there's a wonderful museum of rare musical instruments somewhere near Barcelona. His friend's been there and sent him a card. Must not miss it, he said."

"So which of us is the fan of rare musical instruments? Come on, Lois, out with it."

"And, if you'd let me finish, he spotted an old cello on the front of the postcard that he thought might interest us."

Derek groaned. "Oh no, not an old cello. Did it have a label saying 'property of Akiko Nakamasa' on it?"

"Don't be ridiculous! No, but the name Montagnana caught his eye."

"Same as Akiko's cello?"

"That's right. So we'll take a look, shall we?"

FIFTY-SEVEN

❧

DEREK HAD DECIDED THAT AS THEY HAD ALL DAY FREE FOR their trip, he would hire a car. "We can take turns driving," he said, "so both of us can have time looking at the scenery. Are you okay for driving on the wrong side of the road?"

"Why not? Are you?"

"I can drive anything anywhere," said Derek. "Just one of my many talents."

Lois looked at him, eyes shining and attractively sun browned. "You're really enjoying this holiday, aren't you, my love? I'm so glad we came." She made sure Derek could not see her crossed fingers under the table.

"It's a great place, isn't it. We must make it an annual event, like other people do."

"Do you think we could persuade Gran to come with us?"

"When she sees our photos, the problem will be to persuade her *not* to come with us."

Lois laughed. "Poor old Mum," she said. "Right, now, drink up your coffee and we'll get going."

THE MUSEUM WAS SITUATED IN A LARGE AND BEAUTIFUL HOUSE surrounded by trees. A discreet sign directed them to a car park at the back.

"Do you think we have to pay?" Derek's command of the Spanish language was minimal. Still, most people spoke English, he reckoned. He was lucky in this case. An elegant old lady greeted them in his mother tongue, and he relaxed. They paid a token entrance fee and were told to look around at their own pace.

"If you require any information other than that in the brochure, please do not hesitate to ask," she said. "Many of our instruments are extremely valuable, and so they are necessarily locked and alarmed inside the display cabinets. But I think you will find them well set out. Enjoy your visit. I shall be in the entrance hall if you need to locate me."

Contrary to his expectations, Derek was fascinated. Violin-shaped instruments were familiar, but many were not. "Look at this, Lois! Wonderful names! Bladder pipe— don't need that yet!—rackett—couldn't play tennis with that, could you? Oh, and here's a jolly one—hurdy-gurdy. All you need is a monkey on your shoulder. This is really interesting, isn't it, me duck?"

"Mm. Oh, Derek, here it is. Come and look! It looks just like—"

"Sshh! You never know who's listening," he whispered, walking over to join her at a tall glass case. Derek was silent as Lois read the information in a whisper: "Recent acquisition.

Montagnana Cello 1739. On loan for limited period from private collection."

"Hey, Lois! Do you reckon it could be Akiko's? Can you remember anything about it that we might recognise?"

Lois didn't answer, but stared at the instrument as if willing it to jump out of its cabinet. Then she walked all round, peering in as closely as she could through the glass. "Yep," she said after several minutes. "There it is. Look, Derek."

He looked, but could see nothing but the beautiful smooth surface of the ancient instrument. "Looks like a conker to me, the really good, shiny ones," he said, hoping to lighten the atmosphere, which had suddenly become oppressive.

"But look," whispered Lois. "See there on the back of it? A dark mark in the surface, shaped like a teardrop? It's very small. Look, there it is." She pointed with her finger to the glass, and at that moment they heard light footsteps approaching.

"It is a beautiful instrument, is it not?" said the elegant lady, advancing on them. You are lucky to see it. We have it for only a short time."

"I suppose it's worth a lot," said Derek. "These old things fetch quite a bit at auction, so I'm told."

"Beyond most people's wildest dreams," said the lady.

"Is it ever played?" Lois asked. "It seems a shame if it is silenced for ever."

"A romantic notion, madam. It belongs to someone who plays it frequently. But she has recently had an accident, and we are told may not be able to play again. Very sad. So we decided to offer it a temporary home, until it is sold. Our museum is well known among collectors, you see, even though we live very quietly."

"So how long is it here for? I do hope the owner gets better soon," said Lois casually. "Now, Derek, we must get on."

When they returned to the entrance hall, Lois looked about for postcards. There seemed to be none of the cello, and when she asked, she was told they had sold out, and it was not worth printing more, as it would soon be returned to its owner.

"Do come again, Mr. and Mrs., er . . . And please, do sign the visitors' book."

"Buggins," said Lois firmly, as Derek started to write. "Mr. and Mrs. Buggins from Birmingham, England."

"LOOK OUT, LOIS! YOU'RE GOING THE WRONG WAY ROUND THE roundabout! Phew! That was a near thing. You'd better let me drive."

"I'm fine, Derek, don't panic. There was plenty of room for the lorry as well as me. It'll keep them on their toes!"

They reached a relatively safe stretch of road, and Derek closed his eyes. "Think I'll have a snooze, Mrs. Buggins," he muttered.

"No, you won't. We need to talk about the cello," she said. "If it is Akiko's, we need to move fast."

"You know what I'm going to say, don't you. Get on the phone to Cowgill right now, and put the whole thing in his hands. He'll know what to do. I'm not having you mixed up with international crime, Lois. Ferretin' in Farnden is all very well, but this is too big. And by the way, what's the Spanish for ferretin'?"

FIFTY-EIGHT

❧

"Good morning, Lois! How are you, my dear, and have you had a good holiday?"

"Morning, Cowgill. Yes and no, if you want the truth. It was great to see how much Derek was enjoying himself, swimming and sunning himself half the day, and the other half eating and drinking. Fine for those that like it, but I'm not one of them. My fault, I know. Can't relax and think of nothing. But why am I telling you all this? Are you ringing me to tell me it was Akiko's cello, and you have retrieved it?"

"Yes and no, I'm afraid. With help from experts, they established it was indeed the missing Montagnana, the real one. But when the Spanish police got there, it had gone. Back to the rightful owner, said the woman at the museum. Not at liberty to give the name, she told our colleagues."

"You mean to tell me—? Oh, never mind. What are you going to do about it?"

"It depends how much you want the reward. Unless we

hear to contrary, we shall assume the rightful owner is bona
fide and leave it at that. If you want to pursue it further, then
I can give you a contact. But I suggest you leave it there. After
all, Akiko's broken heart will soon mend. It's probably more
to do with being dropped by Jamie than actually demanding
the return of the original Montagnana."

"Thanks for nothing. You obviously know nothing about
women in love. Anyway, I'll get in touch with her and ask a
few questions. How's the golf?"

There was a short pause, and then Cowill coughed.
"Ahem, in case you really want to know, I won the Captain's
Cup at the weekend. Went round in six under par."

"Wow! That sounds really serious! I hope you'll feel better soon. Bye. Keep in touch."

"AKIKO? IS THAT YOU? IT'S MRS. M HERE. YES, LOIS MEADE.
Some news for you, unless you know it already."

"Oh, is there a message from Jamie?"

"No, sorry, love. No, it's to do with the cello. Me and
Derek have just had a holiday in Spain. In Cadaques, on the
Costa Brava. Yep, very hot! Now, have you got a pen handy?
I'm going to give you the address of a musical instrument
museum near Barcelona."

"But we have a good one here in Japan, Mrs. M."

"Ah, but this one had your cello on display."

"What! How do you know it was mine?"

"The teardrop on the back. Remember you had it in your
description for the police? Well, it was there, in exactly the
right place. The instrument has since been checked and veri-
fied as a Montagnana of the right date . . . Yes, the police have
been there already, but by the time they got there it had been

moved on. The museum is saying that it was returned to its rightful owner. All fair and square and aboveboard, apparently."

"Right! Papa will know exactly what to do. I must go now at once and tell him. I am forever grateful, Mrs. M! Please give Jamie my love. Goodbye."

As soon as Lois had signed off, the phone rang again. It was Jamie, and he sounded very cheerful. "Hi, Mum. How's it going? Did you have a good holiday?"

"Yes, thanks. It was a great success in more ways than one."

"Like what?"

"Well, first of all, your father had a marvellous time and looks like a new man, with his summer tan and cheeky face. Your mother, on the other hand, looks like a boiled lobster and is peeling."

"Anything else?"

"Yes. We found Akiko's cello."

"What!?"

"We found the missing Montagnana, and then lost it again." She explained fully what had happened, and ended by saying that Akiko was going to tell her father, who would no doubt by now have parted with millions to get it back. "End of story," she added.

"Not quite," said Jamie. "I wonder if I could possibly come down to Farnden again for a couple of days?"

"As long as you don't bring any more Japanese cellists, we'll be pleased to see you."

"No, not that. I've been keeping in touch with Diana at Mrs. T-J's, and she thought it would be nice for me to have a country weekend, without any pressures."

"Hand in hand through the woods, that kind of thing?"

"Got it in one, Mum. I'll be with you next Friday, then. I'll drive down, so there'll be no meeting trains. Thanks a lot."

"How did the recital go?"

"Wonderful! Several encores, and a booking for a couple more in the autumn. It's a lovely place, Mum. You and Dad should go there for your next holiday."

"Jamie! Don't even suggest it. Goodbye, love, see you Friday."

"Who was that?" said Gran, coming in with a large mug of coffee. "No, don't tell me. It was Jamie, bringing a trumpet player from Timbuktu for the weekend? Or was it Inspector Hunter Cowgill with a new ferretin' job?"

"Almost right, Mother. No, Jamie has chummed up with Diana, and Cowgill has drawn a line under the cello case."

"Until the next time, then. Right, now I'm going down to the shop to see if Josie's got any white bread left. I'm sick of that rough brown stuff. You and Derek can have that, and I'll have some nice white toast for breakfast."

"And what've we got for lunch?"

"Steak and kidney pie, peas and carrots. That should make a nice change from that paella stuff. Fish and chicken and bits of sausage all mixed up together! Ugh!"

"Not sure you got that right, Mother. But steak and kidney pie is my kind of food."

Gran hunted for her purse, which was usually missing, finally found it in Jeems's basket and went off to the shop whistling, an unladylike skill of which she was very proud.

FIFTY-NINE

THE TEAM WAS ASSEMBLED, ALL EXCEPT HAZEL, WHO WAS late coming from Tresham, and burst in clutching a handful of post.

"Did you meet the postie?" said Lois. "Looks like a load of junk. Thanks, anyway." She put it to one side on her desk, and began to go through the schedules for the week ahead.

"All settled now, Mrs. M?" Dot Nimmo grinned. "Can I ask a question?"

"You don't usually ask permission, Dot. What is it?"

"Are we expecting your new deputy to join us?"

"Mrs. Tollervey-Jones? No, don't worry, Dot. She's gone up to London to buy some clothes for her trip to Japan. Anyway, there'll be no point in her coming to our New Brooms meetings. She wouldn't know one end of a broom from another!"

"Well," replied Dot, "I reckon she's got plenty of bottle, the old thing. You wouldn't catch me going to Japan."

"Let's get on now, then. Any problems?"

The meeting continued as usual, and after the girls and Andrew had all gone, Lois took up the pile of post. As she looked through, she saw one classy-looking envelope had a Japanese postmark. She threw the junk letters in the bin, put two bills to one side, and opened the last one. Seeing its enclosure, she went straight through to the kitchen, where Derek had arrived home for lunch.

"Listen to this!" she said. "And you, Mum, just sit down and listen for a moment. It's a letter from Nakamasa, Akiko's father."

She sat down at the table, and began to read.

"Dear Mrs. Meade, I hope that you are well. I am writing to tell you that Akiko and I are filled with gratitude for your detective work on our behalf. We traced the cello immediately, and on payment of what for me is a trifling sum, it was duly restored to Akiko. She is a completely different girl! And all thanks to you. I enclose a small fee for your work, and hope that we may meet again some day soon."

Lois peered into the envelope and looked at the enclosure. She drew her breath in sharply, but carried on reading.

"And now I must thank you, too, for introducing me to Mildred! We became very fond of each other so quickly, and I am looking forward to her visit in the autumn. She is a very fine lady. With very best wishes to you and your family, yours, et cetera."

"How much?" said Gran, coming straight to the point.

"Five noughts," said Lois.

"Good God!" said Derek.

There was a short silence, while Gran took off her spectacles and cleaned the lenses vigorously. Then she turned to the stove and said, "Never mind about noughts. I don't want this steak and kidney pie spoiled, so can we please get on with it?"

Derek put his arm around Lois's shoulders. "Well done, love. Now there'll be no more need for ferretin', will there?"

"No chance," said Gran, and put a steaming plate in front of Lois. "Get that down you, gel," she added. "Then you can go and tell Cowgill the good news."